ALL YOU

Knead

IS Love

Also by Tanya Guerrero

How to Make Friends with the Sea

ALL YOU Knead IS Love

TANYA GUERRERO

FARRAR STRAUS GIROUX
New York

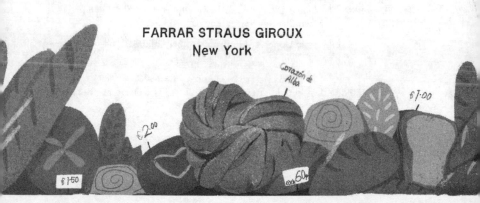

Farrar Straus Giroux Books for Young Readers
An imprint of Macmillan Publishing Group, LLC
120 Broadway, New York, NY 10271
mackids.com

Library of Congress Control Number: 2020910184

First edition, 2021
Book design by Cassie Gonzales
Printed in the United States of America by LSC Communications,
Harrisonburg, Virginia

ISBN 978-0-374-31423-1 (hardcover)

1 3 5 7 9 10 8 6 4 2

For Violet
Keep on marching to the beat
of your own drum

Love doesn't just sit there, like a
stone; it has to be made, like bread;
remade all the time, made new.

—Ursula K. Le Guin, *The Lathe of Heaven*

ALL YOU
Knead
IS Love

One

I wore my last remaining girlie shirt to the airport. It was pastel purple with a tiny frill at the sleeve and collar, and two heart-shaped silver buttons. It was exactly the kind of shirt Mom used to buy me. And the kind of shirt I swore I would never wear. Not anymore. Especially since it was already two sizes too small, but it didn't matter. I stood as straight as I could, angling my shoulders and neck the same way a ballet dancer would. I knew how because my parents had season tickets to the New York City Ballet at Lincoln Center.

The shirt. The stance. The touch of Vaseline I'd dabbed on my lips. It was my last-ditch effort to stay in New York City, where I belonged. Maybe Mom would take one look at me and change her mind.

"Qatar Airways flight 5179 to Barcelona will begin boarding first class, business class, and families with young children at gate C7 in ten minutes," a woman's voice announced.

Okay. This is it.

I fluttered my eyelashes.

Mom smoothed her silk Hermès scarf with her delicate fingers. She glanced at me. But it was like she wasn't really seeing me. Like she was skimming the newspaper with her tortoiseshell eyes.

"Well . . ." Mom stepped closer, into the light. Her skin was flawless, her lips a matte burgundy, her eyebrows perfectly arched. "I hope you take this time to reflect, Alba. To make some changes . . . I think Spain will be good for you."

I exhaled. My ballet posture deflated. "Okay," I mumbled.

Suddenly there was a mass of people crowding around us, bumping me with their carry-on bags as they lined up. A lady in a uniform the same shade as Mom's lipstick approached us. She had this ridiculous hat tilted on her head with a small gold pin of a deer or impala or whatever.

"Hello, Mrs. Green. I'm Sofia, and I'll be taking care of Alba on the flight." The lady smiled and bowed her head, and then she placed one of those sticky-label thingies on the side of my chest. I glanced at it and read it from upside down.

Alba Green
QR 5179
Unaccompanied Minor

The label made me feel like a dumb kid.

"Thank you, Sofia. May I have a moment with my daughter?" said Mom.

"Of course." The flight attendant stayed put. She half turned, focusing her gaze on the glass window with the big white airplane on the other side.

I stared at my black Converse and wondered what would happen if I dropped my backpack and ran. How far would I get before someone caught me?

"Alba."

I looked up.

"*Please*. Try not to hate me. This will be good for you. You'll see," said Mom, placing her hand on my cheek.

I stood there, speechless. No matter how Mom framed it, the bottom line was, I was being cast out. Banished. Mom had finally made good on her threats.

"We should go," said the flight attendant over her shoulder.

I stepped away, but Mom pulled me back. "Wait." She had tears in her eyes. Tears that dribbled down her cheeks, leaving grayish mascara tracks on her pale skin.

I was shocked.

I had never seen her cry.

"*Crying is undignified.*" Those were her words. Not mine.

"*Mahal kita*," she said, so softly I could barely hear her. *I love you*, in Tagalog. She only ever spoke it when Dad was around.

Out of habit, I scanned the terminal. But he was nowhere in sight.

Maybe she was just being sentimental.

Whatever.

I moved backward, slowly. I watched her wipe her face with the tips of her fingers. The tears were gone and so was her makeup. Under her right eye, the skin was a yellowish green—the color of a nearly faded bruise.

"Bye, Mom."

I turned my back on her, like she'd turned her back on me. I walked off and followed the clicking of the flight attendant's high heels.

Click-clack. Click-clack.

She gave my ticket and passport to another lady with the same uniform on. And then we turned into a corridor. The flight attendant started talking. *Blah. Blah. Blah.* "I like your short hair. It's so cute. *Perfect* for summer in Spain."

I nodded and kept on walking with heavy feet.

For once, I just wanted to stay home with Mom. Even if it meant being around Dad. Not that Dad was around much. When he was, it seemed like he could barely stand being in the same room as me.

He didn't want me.

And of course Mom did whatever *he* wanted.

So I guess she didn't want me, either.

I paused at the crack between the walkway and the entrance to the plane. My breath halted for a second and then heaved, as if there was only a bit of oxygen left on earth.

"Alba?" The flight attendant touched my arm.

I flinched.

This was it. My last chance to run.

My heart pounded against my chest, creeping up my throat until it felt like I was choking. I coughed, then swallowed. But the lump of fear, of anger, of sadness, of regret, stayed put.

They *really* didn't want me.

I was alone.

I stepped over the threshold.

Because what did I have left to lose?

Nothing.

Two

I'd forgotten how small airplane bathrooms were. As long as I stood in the same spot, there was just enough room to place my backpack on the lid of the toilet, pull out my extra clothes, and change. I stuffed the purple shirt deep into the bottom of my bag.

Breathe.

I stared back at myself from the mirror.

It was me.

The *real* me. Not the me I'd fabricated for Mom's sake.

I had on my favorite T-shirt, which I'd found in a thrift store. It was faded and gray, featuring a glam-rock David Bowie with a red bolt of lightning striking through his face. Mom hated it and Dad hated it even more. It was kind of ironic, since Mom was the one who'd introduced me to David Bowie's music. I remembered it like it was yesterday, because it was the first time I'd gotten suspended from school—I'd hurled an open carton of chocolate milk at

Alexis, the sixth-grade mean girl who insisted on making my school life a living hell. We were in a cab, on the way home. Mom's lips were sealed tight. She had nothing left to say to me. All she did was sit stiffly on the other side of the seat, as far away from me as possible. Once in a while, I'd steal a glance at her as she glared through the window, unmoving. But then a song came on the radio. The cab driver turned the volume up.

> *But I try, I try . . .*
> *Never gonna fall for (modern love) . . .*

All of a sudden, I noticed Mom's fingers tapping to the beat. Seconds later, the tip of her high-heel shoe joined in. Then she began mouthing the lyrics.

I was surprised. More shocked, really.

I couldn't remember having ever seen her bopping to a song before. *Huh.* I scooched a bit closer and then mustered the courage to speak. "This song . . . It's cool," I mumbled.

Mom jumped, as if I'd spooked her out of a daydream. But then her lips unsealed themselves, curling into a slight smile. "It's David Bowie . . . an icon. I used to listen to him when I was your age."

As soon as we got home, I looked up David Bowie online, and I've been obsessed ever since. Somehow, his music made me feel closer to Mom, even though in reality she was far away—distant and cold.

And now she *literally* was far away. Pretty soon, an entire ocean would come between us.

Just forget about her, Alba.

I grabbed a tissue and wiped the gloss off my lips. Then I splashed cold water on my face and ran my wet fingers through my hair. "Boy hair," Mom liked to call it. She always put on a judgy voice whenever she said it, as if short hair wasn't a girl thing. As if short hairstyles were exclusive to lesbians. I'd heard Dad say that once when he thought I wasn't listening. Except he'd used a different term for it, spitting it out like a curse word.

Whatever.

I went back to my seat in economy. Mom and Dad always flew business class. But I guess I wasn't good enough for that, either. Other passengers were milling along the aisle. They looked like happy, fresh-faced tourists—families with kids on summer vacation, couples going on their honeymoons, backpackers excited to explore the world. And then there was me—poor, pathetic me. I was probably the only twelve-year-old kid onboard being sent off against her will to live with her estranged grandmother. Any second someone would whip out the world's tiniest violin.

"Honey, please fasten your seat belt. We'll be taking off shortly."

I glanced at the flight attendant. "Okay," I said, making a big show of snapping my seat belt together.

She went away. I was alone again. Not completely alone,

but sort of. The seat next to me was empty, but in the seat next to that, there was an old guy with *really* thick glasses reading a *really* thick book. Every once in a while, he'd glance at me. I knew the look. It was the same one I got every time someone was trying to figure out if I was a boy or a girl.

I was *so* over it.

I just ignored him and stared at the tray table in front of me. The flight attendants were doing their safety demonstration. *Blah. Blah. Blah.* I wasn't paying attention.

Finally, the engine rumbled. I closed my eyes and waited for the surge.

A minute, maybe two, maybe five passed.

Then . . .

Whoosh!

The airplane thrust forward. For some reason I coughed. I choked. My heartbeat *thump-thump, thump-thumped*. It felt like I was running. Farther and farther. From Dad's angry gaze. Mom's screaming. Faster and faster. My arm hurt. Someone was squeezing it.

"Let go!" I thought it was just a voice in my head, but then I heard a gasp. My eyes snapped open. The old man with the book. His hand was touching my arm.

"I'm sorry," he said. "I didn't mean to scare you . . . Are you all right?"

I nodded, but I wasn't all right. Far from it.

The man took his hand away with this bewildered look. He went back to his reading.

Now that the plane had leveled off, the passengers around me were relaxing. Some flipped through magazines; others watched movies on the screens in front of them.

But I was too tense for any of that. My shoulders were stiff, my chest tight, as if there was a giant rubber band stretched across my rib cage. I tried closing my eyes. Maybe I could just sleep the entire way there.

Right.

If only.

Wishful thinking.

Instead, I peered out the window. We were already high up in the air, flying above the trees and buildings and roads and people. They became smaller and smaller, turning into little Lego trees and little Lego buildings and little Lego people.

We flew into the clouds. They made me feel kind of better.

Like *maybe* this wasn't the end of the world.

Whatever was up ahead, wherever I was going, couldn't possibly be as bad as what I was leaving behind.

Right?

Three

Sofia the flight attendant was hovering behind me.
Her minty breath wafted past my neck into my nostrils.

"Do you see your grandmother?" she asked.

Good question.

The last time I'd seen Abuela Lola, I was three or four years old. A time I referred to as the good old days. Before Dad started drinking too much. Before he became a controlling, abusive jerk. Before he forbade Mom from seeing any of her family or friends, or anyone who defied him. It felt like eons ago. Now Abuela Lola was merely a distant memory, a faded photo, someone I sort of, kind of remembered. Her name was actually Magdalena, but we'd always referred to her as Abuela Lola—Grandma Grandma. *Abuela* was Spanish, and *lola* was Tagalog. Apparently, I always mixed up the languages when I was little. Hence, Abuela Lola.

I scanned the crowd on the other side of the cordoned-off area. There were families with kids hopping, uniformed dudes holding WELCOME TO BARCELONA placards, random people craning their necks at the arriving passengers. And then there was this older lady with silver-streaked hair, gold hoop earrings, and a bright orange blouse with embroidered flowers. Her gaze drifted, landing on me for a second before moving on. I wasn't the person she was looking for. But something about her seemed familiar. The shape of her face, her cheekbones, high and angular just like Mom's.

"I think . . . that's her," I said in a hushed voice.

Sofia led the way.

Click-clack. Click-clack.

"Mrs. Rodriguez?" she said.

The older lady glanced at Sofia and then at me. She squinted. "Alba?" Before I could react, her mouth opened wide and she wiggle-danced in place. "Alba! It's you! You're here! You're really here!"

For a moment I stood there, not knowing what to do or say. Abuela Lola's excitement was confusing. When she reached over the metal barrier and pulled me toward her, it confused me even more. My instinct was to pull away. But her hands were soft and warm, and something about the way she smelled, like warm caramel, made me lean into her embrace.

"Well, I'll be going now. Enjoy your visit, Alba," Sofia said before leaving.

Abuela Lola finally let go, nudging me down the barricade. "Go on to the end of the barrier. I'll meet you there."

14

"All right."

I should have been walking faster. My feet were dragging. Thank god for my rollaway suitcase—otherwise I might have wobbled. I gripped its handle and steadied myself.

The barricade ended. Abuela Lola watched me, tilting her head as if she was studying a painting in a museum. I smiled; it felt unnatural. My lips and cheeks stretched awkwardly. It had been a while since I'd used those muscles.

"I should have recognized you. Your eyes are just like your mother's," she said.

I knew that. When I was younger, I used to watch Mom sitting in front of her vanity, sweeping her long lashes with mascara. *"You have my eyes, Alba. When you're older, I'll teach you how to make them even more beautiful."*

"Yeah," I replied.

Abuela Lola opened her arms. "Come here and give me a proper hug."

I held my breath and wandered into her embrace. I knew she could feel how stiff I was. But it didn't stop her from smothering me. She even made an *mmmm* sound.

"So," she said, letting go of me. "I've got an Uber waiting for us outside. Why don't we get out of here?"

I didn't say anything. I just followed her through the crowd, past the automated doors, and into a shiny black sedan. The car cruised and swerved and turned. Abuela Lola was quiet. I think she knew I was overwhelmed. I mean, I was. How could I not be? I'd just left my life behind, flown across the Atlantic Ocean on a plane by myself, landed in another country, and met up with a grandmother I hadn't seen in ages. She was practically a stranger, and there she was hugging me like no biggie, like she'd just seen me last Thanksgiving or Christmas or something.

I peeked at Abuela Lola's profile, trying to remember anything about her, perhaps a memory that might somehow comfort me. But there wasn't much to remember. Except maybe her scent. I had this vague recollection of a kitchen, the smell of vanilla beans and orange peels wafting in the air.

She turned, and her gaze found mine. I blinked and looked down at my lap, at my fingers twisting and turning into one another. My skin prickled. It was my nerves. They were on edge. Everything was just too much, especially Abuela Lola. Her eyes, her smile, her presence. I wanted to slide farther away from her. But I didn't want to hurt her feelings. So I stayed put.

That's when she reached out and cupped my hand in hers. I tried hard not to react. But my palm twitched, and I sucked my breath fast. As obvious as it was, she acted as if she hadn't noticed. Maybe she had, and she was just pretending she didn't.

Either way, she smiled and pointed at the passing scenery. "Look . . . You probably don't remember much of it, do you?"

She was right. Barcelona was as distant to me as Abuela Lola was.

I glanced out the window. Ultramodern glass structures

stood by old buildings that looked like giant sculptures, monuments and palm trees dotted the spaces in between, and cruise ships, all sorts of ships, rested on the sea beyond. It was a weird city, sort of like a collage—pieces of it didn't seem to match, but when you looked at it as a whole, it kind of made sense.

I had no memory of this place. None whatsoever.

After fifteen or twenty minutes, we veered to the left into a large rotary. At the center was a tall metal pillar with a statue on top. Abuela Lola let go of my hand and gestured at the statue. "That's the Christopher Columbus monument. We're almost home."

Home.

I attempted to swallow, except there was this lump in my throat.

That word—*home*—seemingly so harmless.

So why did it feel like my heart had been ripped out?

It was only then that it sank in. New York City was somewhere across the ocean, thousands of miles away.

Barcelona was home now.

For how long, I wasn't sure.

Suddenly, the car pulled over next to a building with colorful fans and parasols decorating the facade. A fancy green dragon jutting from the corner held a bamboo lantern in its grasp.

"You live *here*?" I didn't mean to say it out loud, but the words just slipped out.

Abuela Lola laughed. "I wish! No . . . This building is called Casa Bruno Cuadros. The original owner had an umbrella shop on the ground floor over a hundred years ago. Now it's a bank, and a destination for tourists interested in architecture." She paid the driver and we got out of the car. "My apartment is a few blocks away, but vehicles aren't allowed on the side streets—they're strictly for pedestrians and bicycles."

I looked down the alley where she was heading. It really was an alley. But it wasn't filled with trash cans. The pavement was made of weathered slabs of rock, and the buildings were old, not regular kind of old, but the kind that made you feel like you'd stepped out of a time machine. Like at any moment some medieval soldiers on horseback would come galloping toward us. Except there were tourists. Lots of them.

It was sort of a shock. *Nothing* was familiar to me. Well, maybe the tourists. New York City had a lot of those, too. Still, even with the somewhat-familiar tourists swarming around me, I stood there transfixed.

I wasn't like them. I wasn't here to sightsee, to sample the local cuisine, to buy souvenirs and then go back home.

This wasn't just a vacation.

This was my life now.

"Come, Alba," said Abuela Lola from up ahead.

I yanked my rolling suitcase and tried to catch up. "You really live . . . *here*?" I repeated.

She nodded. "Since 1968. I was eight years old when we

18

moved to Spain from the Philippines. Back then, the Barrio Gótico, this neighborhood, was even more amazing. It was always a tourist attraction, but nothing like it is today."

We kept on walking for another block or so. I ogled at everything and everyone with my mouth hanging open like a big dope. I coughed. My throat. My tongue. Even my teeth were dry, as if all the saliva had evaporated from the heat.

Abuela Lola placed her hand on my arm. "You know what, Alba? I think we're in need of some refreshments." She pulled me into a shop, suitcase and all.

"Oye, ¿qué tal, Magda?" said the blue-aproned lady behind the counter.

"Muy bien, Nuria. Tengo mi nieta, Alba, conmigo . . . ¡desde los Estados Unidos!" said Abuela Lola.

The blue-aproned lady smiled, clapped her hands together, and winked. "Así, te daré los mejores, entonces."

Oh crap.

Spanish.

I'd almost forgotten that people here didn't speak English. I mean, I guess some of them did. Maybe? Hopefully?

God, I'm screwed.

Abuela Lola led me to a small table for two. "Nuria's churros are the best in the neighborhood. Don't let anyone tell you otherwise."

I sat. Not even a minute went by, and Nuria appeared with a tray. She placed a plate of sugary fried dough sticks and two cups of thick hot chocolate on the table.

"Buen provecho," she said before going away.

Mmmm. It was the same sound Abuela Lola had made when she'd hugged me at the airport. Except she was dunking one of the dough sticks into the chocolate. She bit into it and made a face like she was eating the best thing ever.

"So, Alba. I'm just going to ask you, because I'm a believer in being straightforward . . . Do you identify as a girl? A boy? Somewhere in between?"

I gulped.

That *so* wasn't what I was expecting.

Four

Nobody had ever asked me that. I mean, *really* asked me. The kids at school, my teachers, complete strangers, even my parents—people just made assumptions.

Abuela Lola took another bite of her churro. "Well, don't look so shocked, Alba. I'm a modern woman. I know about these things. Whatever it is, just speak up and tell me, so I don't hurt your feelings."

I glanced at the churros. At the little cup of hot chocolate. At my sneakers. At the door.

Should I run?

My feet twitched. I stayed put, though. Where would I go, anyway?

I looked up and met Abuela Lola's gaze. I had expected someone colder, more distant. Someone more like . . . Mom. But my grandmother wasn't like that. At least I didn't think so. Unless she was putting on an act, like trying to be that cool, hip grandma that was chill with everything but in reality, deep down, was just doing it to earn brownie points.

Hmm . . .

I couldn't figure it out. Not yet, anyway.

I squinted at her.

Even if she was faking it, at least she cared enough to make an effort.

I cleared my throat. "Um, I'm . . . a girl. I mean, you can call me 'she,' 'her.' I'm just more comfortable this way . . ." I ran my hand through my short, messy hair. "I can't do the dresses, the makeup, all that girlie stuff. It feels like I'm in a costume. Like I can't breathe. You know?"

I stopped talking and waited for her to react. Abuela Lola took another bite of her churro. And then she smiled—the kind of smile that made all the wrinkles on her face stand out. "I appreciate your honesty, Alba. It's rare for a girl your age to know who she is, you know. To be so confident. So true to herself. I admire that."

Tears started stinging my eyes. But I held my breath and pushed them back. I didn't want her to see how much I was hurting. It was too soon for that.

"Thank you," I said.

She nudged the plate toward me. "Now, go on and eat your churros. They're not any good once they get cold."

To be honest, I was kind of queasy. But I took one anyway, dunking it in the thick hot chocolate. I bit into it. The dough was warm. The chocolate sweet but not too sweet.

Mmmm.

It *was* pretty good. Kind of great, actually.

When we arrived at Abuela Lola's apartment building, the first thing I noticed was the Chinese restaurant on the ground floor. There was a mustard-yellow awning with Chinese characters, and underneath it a sign that said RESTAURANTE CHINO. To make it even more cliché, a row of red fabric lanterns hung across the entire facade.

"*Everyone* wanted Chinese food in the 1960s. It was all the rage. So when we moved here, my father and mother opened this restaurant." Abuela Lola pointed at the windows on the second floor. "I live up there. Most days, it smells like fried rice. But you get used to it."

"But why not Filipino food? You're not even Chinese," I said.

Abuela Lola shrugged. "Nobody even knew what Filipino food was back then. But don't worry, the food is good. Our cook, Su, has been with us for fifteen years, and his wife, Ting, manages the place. I just sign the checks, that's all."

"Oh."

"Well, come on. Let's get you settled in."

We climbed a small set of stairs that led inside to a narrow foyer with a black-and-white tile floor, a curved staircase, and an elevator inside an ornate wrought-iron cage. It was what I would call a contraption. Something ancient, and probably not all that safe.

"Does that thing actually work?" I asked.

Abuela Lola opened the cage door. "Of course it works. Just because it's old doesn't mean it's broken."

I pulled my suitcase into the closet-sized elevator. It was so small that our shoulders were pressed together. After a second, the door creaked shut and we ascended very, very slowly.

"We're here!" Abuela Lola announced.

We exited the elevator. The hallway was jam-packed with potted plants, and there were two doors on opposite sides.

"Eduardo and Manny live over there. They own an antique shop a couple of blocks away . . . And this is us," she said, leading me to the indigo-blue door. The keys jangled as she unlocked it.

As soon as we walked in, I smelled it. Fried rice.

The expression on my face must have been a dead giveaway, because Abuela Lola winked and said, "I told you."

For a minute I lingered in the entryway, taking it all in. Every nook and cranny was filled with strange little figurines, framed photographs, and shelves of old books. Covering the wooden floors were throw rugs in a jumble of patterns. And the furniture was a mix of old and new—the centerpiece being the raspberry-colored velvet sofa.

It was so different from our apartment in New York. Not just the way it was decorated, but the feel of it, warm, cozy, lived-in. That was it. Abuela Lola's place was filled with memories and stories, layers and layers of them compiled over the years.

I held my breath for a couple of seconds.

Overwhelmed.

Abuela Lola wandered from one room to another. "I should call your mother . . . Hmm, now, where did I leave it? Aha!" She emerged from the kitchen with a cordless phone in her grasp.

Her finger poked at the numbers, and then she held it against her ear. She focused her eyes on one of the nearby rugs as her bare feet shuffled from side to side.

Thump-thump. Thump-thump.

My heart was beating in my ear.

"Hola, Isabel. Yes, she's here . . . No. No, she's fine. We had some churros, and now we're at home. Uh-huh. Okay . . ." Abuela Lola glanced at me.

I stuck my hand out.

Thump-thump.

"C-can I—"

"All right, goodbye, Isabel." She hung up.

It was silent.

Except it seemed that inside my stomach, my heart, my head, everything shattered, crashed, crumbled. My entire world had finally fallen apart.

And I was done. Done pretending that everything was okay.

I gasped for breath. And then seven words drifted out of my mouth. "She . . . didn't . . . want to talk . . . to me?"

"Oh, sweetie." Abuela came closer, hand outstretched.

I let go of my suitcase. My knees wobbled. I crumpled to the floor, tears streaming down my cheeks. All I could hear was Mom's voice. As if she was right there.

"Crying is undignified, Alba."

I squeezed my eyelids together. Hard. Instead of the blackness, I kept on visualizing my mom seated across from me. Except she was at home on her favorite chaise, not here in Abuela Lola's apartment. At first, she was peering at me, but then she looked down at her beige Ferragamo flats and cleared her throat.

"I think it's time, Alba," she had said so softly it came out sounding like a whisper.

Time?

For what?

Lunch? Yoga? A walk in the park?

Or maybe she wants to talk. Or, god forbid, send me to a therapist.

I snapped my back straighter and frowned, focusing my gaze on anything but Mom's eyes. The blue upholstery behind her. The hardwood floors gleaming beneath her feet. The tassels of the Turkish rug by the dining table. The huge waxy green leaves of the fiddle-leaf fig tree by the window.

26

Finally, I glanced back at Mom. The silence was deafening.

"Time?" I repeated out loud.

Mom adjusted herself on the chaise as if she was uncomfortable. The way she was looking at me, it seemed—I don't know—kind of weird. Impersonal. Like she was interviewing a new housekeeper or something.

"For a change. I've been thinking about it for a long time now . . ." Her voice trailed off.

"Thinking about what?"

Thump-thump. Thump-thump.

I could feel my heartbeat all over.

Mom cleared her throat again. *"I've been thinking it might do you some good to go live with Abuela Lola for a while . . ."*

"What?" I stood, my hands curling into fists.

She'd made such threats before, but I never believed she would make good on them.

"I've made up my mind, Alba," she said.

I took a step toward her. *"You mean, Dad's made up his mind. Right?"*

She shook her head. A wisp of her carefully coiffed hair escaped, caressing her cheek. *"No. This was my decision. Your father has . . . I mean, we have some things to sort out. It'll be better if you're away for a while."*

"NO!" I shouted. *"You can't make me!"*

"Yes. I can," she said calmly.

I could feel the anger, the heat of it, burning inside of me, burning so furiously that within seconds it was outside of me, making my skin flushed, knuckles white. There was so much I wanted to say, to scream at the top of my lungs.

But I couldn't.

My throat was clenched.

My tongue went limp.

I did the only thing I could.

I ran.

"*Alba!*" she shouted.

I ran as fast and as far away as I could.

A lot of good that did.

Mom was right.

She could make me go away. And she did.

Five

Abuela Lola's kitchen was a real kitchen. It was the kind with well-worn appliances, chopping boards with tons of knife marks, jars filled with herbs and spices, tomato-stained towels, and a collection of pots and pans hanging from the ceiling. Back in New York, our kitchen was like something out of a showroom, chrome and granite, spotless because it wasn't a place where meals were ever cooked. Breakfasts and lunches were purchased from the corner deli on my way to school, and dinners came from one of the delivery menus in the drawer next to the phone.

Nobody ever bothered to cook for me.

"Here you go. This will get some color back into your cheeks." Abuela Lola put a plate in front of me with what looked like toast with something gooey and creamy on top. "It's a Spanish tuna melt. What makes it Spanish is the crusty bread and the Manchego cheese. You won't be eating bottled mayo or sliced supermarket bread in *this* household," she said with her hands on her hips.

I stared at the white enameled plate with painted red roses, at the green fabric napkin beside it, at the fork and knife, at the perfectly caramelized Spanish tuna melt. It was too much all at once.

If Abuela Lola *was* putting on an act, she deserved an Oscar, an Emmy, a Tony, *all* the awards.

As I sat there in shock, the only word that popped into my head was *why*.

Why would she make such an effort? She barely had a relationship with Mom. I mean, she almost didn't recognize me at the airport. I might have been her granddaughter, but I felt more like some random kid she'd picked out of a crowd.

I unfolded the napkin and dabbed my eyes.

"Thank you" was all I could say. Any more, and I might have broken down all over again.

Abuela Lola sat down with a plate for herself. At first, we just ate. The food was delicious and comforting. Every bite was like a warm hug. Not that I was an expert on warm hugs or anything.

Huh.

So this was what it was like being taken care of.

I didn't even mind that my grandmother was most likely pretending for my sake.

It felt good. And I hadn't felt good in a long time.

I sat up straighter. "I—I wanted to say that I appreciate you letting me come here . . . To live with you. I'll do my best—"

"There's no need for that, Alba . . . You're my granddaughter. You're finally here. That's all that matters."

I inhaled deep, and then exhaled.

Maybe everything *would* work out.

Maybe.

Phew.

For the first time since arriving, I was relieved.

I was unpacking in my new room. It was tiny. The twin bed was up against the wall on one side; it was neatly made with periwinkle-blue sheets and a floral quilt. There was a white teddy bear leaning on the pillow. On one side was a table with a bouquet of dried lavender in a vase and an old-fashioned alarm clock. On the other side was a closet and a narrow chest of drawers. The best thing about the room, though, was the huge window with a built-in seat, loads of pillows, and a set of sheer curtains to filter the sunlight. It gave the room a soft glow. I could see myself sitting there for hours watching the street, all the people and everything I'd never seen before.

"You doing okay in here?" Abuela Lola's head popped into the room.

"Yeah. Pretty much done. Clothes in the closet. In the drawers. That's about it," I replied.

Abuela Lola studied the room. "You can change it . . . I won't be offended. I just didn't know what you'd like."

"No. It's fine. Much cozier than I'm used to." I plopped on the bed and picked up the teddy bear.

"That's Blanquito. He was your mother's."

I gazed at its brown plastic eyes and black threaded nose. It seemed impossible that it had belonged to Mom. For some reason I couldn't imagine her as a child.

Abuela Lola came into the room and sat beside me. "I know it feels like you're being punished, Alba. But that's not the case. Your mother just needs some time to figure things out . . . And meanwhile, you and me, we can get to know each other better. All these years have passed, and I've missed out on so much."

From the corner of my eye, I could tell she was frowning. Like she wanted to say something more, but the right words wouldn't come to her. For me, it was the opposite. I knew precisely what I wanted to say. I just wasn't ready.

"I know." Those words felt safe.

Abuela Lola smiled. It seemed like she was wearing a mask, though. Behind it, she was just as sad as I was. For a moment I thought about reaching out with my arms and hugging her. Like maybe her sadness and my sadness could bring us together.

But it was still too soon to let my guard down.

And besides, hugging was completely foreign to me, like the Spanish language—I didn't speak it, I could barely understand it, and just the thought of it made me feel super awkward.

So instead, I scooched a couple of inches closer. "Umm . . . I guess Mom liked bears, huh?" I said, holding Blanquito over my lap.

She chuckled. "Actually, your mother was terrified of bears."

"Terrified?" I stared at Blanquito, then at Abuela Lola. "Like *terrified* terrified?"

"Well, maybe not quite terrified, but definitely scared . . . You see, she couldn't have been more than two or three years old when she happened to see one of those nature programs on TV about Alaskan bears. There was this one scene where the bears were fighting over salmon. It got pretty vicious and bloody. She had nightmares for weeks. And then one day, I saw Blanquito in the window display of a toy store, and I thought he might help her forget about the scary bears—"

"Did he?" I asked.

Abuela Lola reached out and poked the teddy bear's belly. "He did. In fact, Blanquito hardly left your mother's side after that . . . Even when she was a teenager, she made me promise never to get rid of him. So here he still is."

Huh.

I didn't know what to say. It was weird. I mean, Mom

never struck me as a sentimental kind of person. More like the complete opposite—cold, indifferent, pragmatic. Yet here was Abuela Lola telling a completely different story.

Had Mom changed that much?

I had so many questions, but my brain was fried.

I yawned.

"Ah, you must be tired. Why don't you get some rest? We'll talk more later." Abuela Lola stood, and then she bent over as if she was going to kiss me on the forehead.

I leaned back and sort of flopped onto the pillows with half-closed eyes. "Okay. Thanks."

She tiptoed out of the room and closed the door gently.

It was just me and Blanquito.

I hugged him and couldn't help wondering if Mom had hugged him the same way, too.

Six

I must have conked out. When my eyes blinked open, it was dark outside my window, and the apartment seemed pretty quiet.

My stomach grumbled.

How could I be hungry after that tuna melt? How long had I been asleep?

I rolled out of bed and slipped my shoes on. Then I opened my door slowly and poked my head out.

Silence.

Weird.

I tiptoed down the hallway. It was kind of ridiculous. I mean, this was my grandmother's house, my home away from home. Yet I felt like I didn't belong, like I was an intruder or something. The air, the smells, the creaks and hums were unfamiliar to me, disorienting.

There was a glow coming from the kitchen. Maybe Abuela

Lola was still awake, drinking tea or something. But when I got closer, like several feet away, I heard her talking.

Is someone with her?

I snuck even closer and paused by the wall next to the doorway. At first, I didn't hear anything. But after a couple of seconds, Abuela Lola's voice broke the silence.

"She's *your* daughter, Isabel. It's not fair to shut her out."

I gasped and covered my mouth with my hand.

Abuela Lola sighed. "So you dump her on me and then forget about her? Just like that?"

Shut her out.

Dump her.

Forget about her.

Those words cut me.

Nobody wanted me. Not even Abuela Lola.

"What am I supposed to tell her? That her mother would rather salvage her relationship with her abusive husband than take care of her child? Is that it, Isabel? Is that what I should say to her?"

I stepped away from the wall. Tears filled my eyes, ran down my cheeks, and dripped onto the floor. So many tears that everything around me was hazy. I didn't even realize that I was standing in the doorway.

I couldn't see her clearly, but I heard Abuela Lola suck her breath in and drop the phone on the table. "Alba . . ."

I shook my head and backed away.

"Alba, I'm sorry."

But it was too late for apologies. I turned around and ran out the door. Not wanting to wait for the slow elevator, I found the staircase, then ran down the stairs, across the foyer, and onto the street.

"Alba! Wait!" Abuela Lola's shouts came from the window above.

But I didn't bother.

I wiped my eyes with the backs of my hands and ran, somewhere, anywhere, I wasn't sure where. The streets were confusing, zigzagging in different directions. I stumbled, running into people and buildings and signs and mailboxes and fountains. My legs, my feet just kept on going, even as my brain was trying to tell me I was lost.

So what?

Who cares?

Nobody.

Eventually, though, my lungs gave up and my side cramped. I found a quiet alley and collapsed behind a dumpster, hyperventilating. It took a while for me to catch my breath. But when I finally felt somewhat normal again, the thoughts returned.

No wonder Mom doesn't want to talk to me.

I knew it.

Abuela Lola was just pretending she wanted me here.

What now?

What do I do?

Where do I go?

The weight of it all—the stress, the pressure, made the tears come out again.

I'm such a crybaby.

But I couldn't stop. I wailed and coughed and choked. There was nothing I could do to console myself. I just went on and on and on and on, until I heard something—the crunch of broken glass under a shoe. My eyes scanned the cobblestones in front of me, stopping only when I saw a pair of black shoes that looked like a cross between clogs and Birkenstocks. I gazed up into a man's eyes. Even in the shadows, the blue of them caught the light and sparkled.

"Hola . . . ¿Estás bien?" the man asked gently.

I kind of shrank back and pressed my lips together. This man was a stranger, and I wasn't used to taking kindness from strangers. I was a naturally suspicious person, *and* I'd been brought up a New Yorker. Besides, he could have been a weirdo, a pervert, a serial killer for all I knew.

I looked down and hugged my knees, avoiding his gaze but keeping him within my peripheral vision. My back was touching the dumpster, and even though it reeked, I stayed put. I didn't know what else to do. For a good minute, the man just stood there, as if trying to assess the situation. Then he rubbed his salt-and-pepper beard and sat down on the concrete step nearby. Without being too obvious, I studied him from head to toe. Besides his weird choice in footwear, he seemed normal enough, middle-aged, taller than average, with crinkles around his piercing blue eyes.

Over his gray T-shirt and jeans, he had an apron that had seen better days.

I wasn't sure what he was doing.

Why is he just sitting there?

Truth be told, he made me kind of nervous.

But then I got to thinking about Ramona, the lady who worked at the Eighty-First Street subway station, where I used to hide out sometimes. The first time I saw her, I was huddled in a corner near her booth. Even though she was inside the glass enclosure, I could smell the sandalwood and cocoa butter wafting from the opening where people bought their MetroCards. From where I was seated, the only parts of her I could see were her neatly twisted braids styled in a bun on top of her head. It wasn't until about ten, fifteen minutes later that I saw the rest of her as she stood in front of me, pursing her cranberry-colored lips.

"*Are you in trouble or something? Do you need me to call someone?*" she asked with furrowed brows.

I shook my head and hugged my knees tighter.

"*Well, all right, then. Why don't you move over there so I can at least keep an eye on you.*" She pointed at the wall directly across from her booth. "*I know what it's like to need a place away from home . . . I'm Ramona. If you need anything, just holler.*"

I nodded, and she went back inside her booth.

Ramona and I might not have talked much. But during the last year or so, that subway station, that booth of hers, became one of my safe places. I knew I was okay as long as she was there watching me.

Maybe this man with the weird shoes and messy apron was just doing the same thing. Like Ramona, he wanted to make sure that nothing bad would happen to me.

Minutes passed and I loosened up. My breathing was calmer, my heart stopped beating so fast, my cramps dissipated. It was relatively quiet, except for occasional footsteps and laughter echoing around us. And my stomach was still grumbling from hunger. But I ignored it. I didn't have any money on me, and I wasn't quite ready to find my way back to Abuela Lola's yet.

After what must have been a good half hour, the man finally stood. He took one more look at me and then disappeared through the door behind him.

Later, dude.

Thanks for hangin'.

I was starting to wonder how long I could stay away before Abuela Lola called the police on me. Maybe she already had?

Creak.

The door opened again, and the man appeared, holding something wrapped in white parchment paper. He approached me slowly and then stopped at arm's length.

"Aquí, tomaló," he said, handing me the thing he was holding.

I stared at it. There was something poking out of the parchment—the tip of a small baguette. And I could smell cheese and tomatoes and olive oil.

My stomach grumbled again.

I reached out and took it, cautiously.

The man smiled one of those toothy kinds of smiles. "Te sentirás major despues de comer algo. ¿Bien?"

I nodded even though I had no idea what he had said to me. All I knew was that his tone was kind, his smile was genuine, and his sandwich smelled delicious.

He wiped his hands on his apron and grinned at me one more time before disappearing again through the door. I waited until I was sure he wasn't coming back before I started to devour the sandwich he'd given me. It had thin slices of cheese and juicy tomatoes and arugula, drizzled with strong-tasting olive oil. And the bread was chewy and crusty. Yet I was so hungry I could barely appreciate how delicious it was.

When I was done, I immediately felt better. Like the food had nourished not only my body but my soul, too. I stood and wiped the flurry of breadcrumbs off my T-shirt.

I better go back.

I took a deep, deep breath.

Everything is going to be fine, Alba.

I tried to convince myself it was true. Maybe if I kept chanting those words to myself, it would happen. Everything *would* fix itself.

So that's what I did as I wandered through the alleys.

I more or less remembered which direction I'd come from. Just to make sure, though, I stopped some random lady and mumbled, "¿Restaurante Chino?" to her, hoping she would understand what I was asking. She pointed at a street parallel to where I was walking.

Phew.

After ten minutes of strolling through the lamplit streets, I spotted the bright yellow awning and the stairs in front of Abuela Lola's building. Not just the stairs, but Abuela Lola herself, in the flesh. She was seated on the top step wearing a white cotton nightgown, a robe, and a frown.

I could feel my face getting hotter as I approached her.

"Your mother said you'd be back . . . But I was this close to organizing a search party," said Abuela Lola, holding her index finger and thumb an inch apart.

"I'm sorry," I mumbled.

Abuela Lola's expression was stiff. Yet somehow, I could tell there was pity lurking behind the hardness of her face.

"Come, sit," she said, patting the space next to her.

I hesitated but went anyway, dragging my feet as if I was wearing concrete blocks for shoes. As soon as I was seated, she squeezed my knee. "I'm the one who's sorry . . . You shouldn't have heard any of that."

I stared at my lap, at her hand resting on my leg.

"Sometimes I get carried away with my words. Especially when I'm talking to your mother. I don't really feel that she 'dumped' you on me. I just needed to make a point," she explained.

Bit by bit, I lifted my gaze and peered at her. "So you don't mind that I'm here?"

Abuela Lola squeezed my knee again. "Of course not! If there's any silver lining to this whole situation, it's that I finally get to be with my granddaughter. I am so, so happy you're here, Alba."

For a second, my shoulders tensed. I wasn't sure if I should believe her. But I wanted to. I desperately wanted to believe that, for once, someone wanted me, the real me, in their life. I exhaled and dropped my shoulders.

"Okay," I whispered.

"Good." Abuela Lola smiled and leaned in closer. "We need to set some ground rules, though. No more running off like that, all right? If you're upset, I want you to talk to me. Whatever it is, we can sort it out . . . Everything else, we can figure out along the way. How does that sound?"

I nodded.

She squeezed my knee one more time, then pushed herself up off the step. "Come. You want some tea? Cookies? A sandwich?"

I gazed up at her bright eyes and smile.

I wasn't all that hungry anymore.

But I also didn't feel like being alone.

Not at the moment.

So I smiled back and said, "Sure, tea and cookies sounds good."

Seven

The next morning, after tossing and turning through the night, I woke up with knots in my stomach.

A new day.

A second chance not to screw everything up all over again.

I would get out of bed, have breakfast, and then, maybe, something amazing would happen. Something life-changing.

Think positive, Alba.

But it was hard, you know. Thinking positive didn't come naturally to me. Gloom and doom was more my thing. It hurt less that way. If you expected bad stuff to happen all the time, then life was liable to be less disappointing, right?

Right.

Finally, I shuffled into the kitchen in my pajamas. The knots in my stomach had multiplied; it felt like my intestines had tangled around the rest of my organs.

"Good morning!" I said, trying my best to sound cheery.

Abuela Lola was at the stove, eyeing one of those stovetop

coffee makers. She glanced at me and smiled. "Buenos días. You're up early."

"Yeah, well, I didn't sleep much."

"Ah, jet lag. You'll feel better in a couple of days." Abuela Lola gestured at the kitchen table with her chin. "Sit. I'll fix you up some coffee. It'll help."

Coffee?

I watched her pour a generous amount of steaming milk from a small pot into a mug, and then top it off with some freshly brewed coffee. She placed it on the table in front of me, and then she poured herself a cup before sitting.

I reached for the sugar container, and dumped a heaping teaspoon into my mug, all the while eyeing Abuela Lola from across the table. She was wearing a tunic-type dress that was casual yet sophisticated. Her hair was pulled back in a single braid, and her face was devoid of makeup but fresh-looking, as if she'd already cleansed and moisturized it.

And she thought *I* was up early.

Geez.

Abuela Lola must be one of those old ladies who are up at the crack of dawn.

"So, after breakfast, I have an errand for you to run," she said casually.

"An errand?"

She raised her eyebrows. "Don't act so surprised, Alba. You're almost thirteen. I think I can trust you to walk a couple of blocks to buy some bread . . . Besides, it will be good for

45

you to explore the neighborhood a bit. You need to start brushing up on your Spanish."

I gulped air. Little did she know how horrible my Spanish was. Atrocious. Virtually nonexistent.

"Okay. Bread. Yeah. I guess I can do that."

"Good," she said with a nod. "El Rincón del Pan is four blocks to the right, on the corner. You can't miss it . . . And ask for Toni, the owner. He's an old friend of the family, so he knows what I like."

Great. Buying bread was easy enough. But schmoozing with some dude, a supposed family friend, was going to be more challenging. I wasn't much of a schmoozer, and besides, I wasn't all that ready to meet people. I mean, it still felt like my head was in New York City, one foot on the plane and the other in Barcelona. I was all over the place.

Humph.

Groan.

Sigh.

The street was quiet and chaotic at the same time. It sounds weird, but that's how it was. There were no cars or buses or motorcycles, yet there was traffic. Throngs of people meandered from one alley to the other holding shopping bags. Bicycles swerved among the crowds, avoiding the sidewalk cafés and trees and benches and flocks of pigeons eating scattered breadcrumbs from the ground. Voices echoed, bouncing off the narrow corridors, interrupted only by the occasional church bell and guitarist playing on the sidewalk. I was transfixed. I stood in front of Abuela Lola's apartment with my mouth hanging open. You'd think that, having grown up in New York City, I would have seen it all.

But this was . . . different.

Okay. El Rincón del Pan. Four blocks to the right. On the corner. You can't miss it. I started walking, trying my best to blend in. Back home I was *the* expert at blending in. It was easy. But Barcelona was new to me. Going down its streets felt like I was playing a brand-new video game—I had no idea where to go, what was up ahead, what I was doing, what would happen to me.

El Rincón del Pan.

El Rincón del Pan.

El Rincón del Pan.

Apparently, it meant "The Corner of Bread" or "The Bread Corner" or something like that. I kept on repeating it in case I forgot. Four blocks shouldn't have taken me that long, but there was so much to see—street performers, artists drawing chalk masterpieces on the concrete, little shops with all sorts of unusual trinkets.

I halted in front of a store window where something caught my attention. Rows and rows of silk scarves. My eyes hopscotched from the bright orange one with purple stripes, to the emerald-green one with pink diamonds, to the

47

tie-dyed one in various shades of blue. Those were the ones I knew Mom would like. The more I stared at them, the more my throat hurt.

Because *those* silk scarves were the kind that Mom used to cover up her bruises. Bruises that *my* father—gave her. Sometimes they were subtle, a couple of purplish-green spots near her collarbone; sometimes they were more obvious, finger marks around her neck; and sometimes they were so bad, even the scarves couldn't cover them up. On those days, only a turtleneck would do.

I spun around. All those thoughts, all those emotions— maybe I could blow them out of my body.

That's when I saw it on the corner. El Rincón del Pan. It was a teensy bread bakery in a strange-looking building. The structure was only three stories high, but the design was straight out of a Dr. Seuss book, curved and curly and wavy, with hardly any straight edges. Around the windows were concrete petals with wrought-iron leaves and stems. The bakery itself had a worn wooden front, arched doors, and a stained-glass window above the sign. I approached it, eyeing the display of breads, which were arranged in baskets, on trays, and on platters, with bouquets of herbs and dried flowers in between. Even from several feet away, I could smell the yeasty aroma.

At the door, I placed my hand on the knob and pushed.

Ding. Ding. Ding.

There was a tiny brass bell above me.

"Hola, nena. ¿Qué tal?" said a man by the display case.

I stiffened, pretending to browse the breads and pastries to buy myself some time. The entire walk there, all I'd memorized was the name of the place. I hadn't even considered what I was going to say in Spanish. "Um, quiero, uh, bread. I mean, pan. To eat," I blurted out.

That's when the man's gaze found mine. His eyes were sparkly blue and . . . familiar.

"Oh, hello again," he said.

It was him, the man from the back alley with the apron and the weird footwear.

My cheeks were blazing hot all of a sudden. "Um, hi."

Ugh.

Why?

Of all the people in the entire world?

"You are American?" he asked, raising his eyebrow as if he was confused or something.

I stepped back a tiny bit and squinted at him. "Why?"

"Nothing, really. It's just that last night I assumed you were a runaway. It's not the first time someone has turned up at the back. In this neighborhood, there are always people in need of a good sandwich and some kindness," he said with a smile.

At first, I didn't reply. I studied him from head to toe. In the dark, he'd looked older, more worn out. But under the bright lights of the bakery and with a clean apron on, he seemed more youthful, even with his graying hair and beard.

His Spanish accent was pretty thick, but his English was good—great, actually.

Is this guy for real?

"You speak English?" I asked, stating the obvious.

"I apprenticed in New York and San Francisco. That's where I learned to bake *and* to speak English." He reached for some baguettes from a nearby baking sheet and then stuck them into a tall basket before wiping his hands on his apron. "What can I help you with?"

I glanced at the wooden shelves and counters, at the baskets of round breads, oval breads, long breads, square breads, and buns and croissants and other sweet, sticky-type breads. I had no idea what I was supposed to buy. "My grandma, Magdalena, um, she told me to come here to get some bread."

"Magda? You are Magda's granddaughter? Of course! She told me last week. So Isabel is your mother. Fantastic!" He took my hand as if to bring me closer.

I pulled away.

That's when I spotted the name tag on his shirt: TONI.

"Oh, so you're Toni . . . My grandma mentioned you."

The man stepped back, but his smile stayed put. "Yes, that's me. Isabel, your mother, was my childhood friend. My *best* friend."

Best friend?

How come I've never heard of him before?

I stared at his salt-and-pepper hair and beard, at his eyes, blue as the sky on a clear summer day. This man. This place. Abuela Lola. The scarves, all those scarves in the window display reminding me of Mom. Suddenly I was overwhelmed again. My knees, my stomach, my heart went weak. I wobbled.

Ding. Ding. Ding.

A customer walked in, an old lady with a cane. Her penciled-in eyebrows arched when she saw me. Toni put his arm around my shoulders, and then he spoke to a woman by the register, who I guessed was the cashier. "Estel, voy un ratito a la trastienda."

Estel glanced at me and nodded. Toni guided me to the back of the shop, through a swinging door, down a short corridor. We entered a spacious room. I just stood there, taking it all in. There was plenty of sunlight streaming through the windows, illuminating the stainless-steel counters, ovens, mixers, racks, bowls piled on top of one another, all sorts of whisks and spatulas, and jars—jars everywhere filled with different-colored liquids and pastes. Up above were hanging bundles of dried herbs and flowers, as if a garden was growing from the ceiling.

"Sit."

Toni pulled out some stools. I plopped onto one of them. Slowly, very slowly, the numbness began to leave my body. I watched him turn an electric kettle on, and then he arranged a glass teapot and two cups on the table. He snipped a handful of white flowers from a nearby upside-down bouquet, dropped them into the teapot, and poured the boiling water over them. Within a few seconds, the water turned golden yellow.

"Manzanilla tea. You probably know it as chamomile. It's good for relaxing the nerves," he said, pouring some into both cups.

I took a sip. The tea was almost too hot, but the temperature of it jolted me. Its taste made me feel like I was standing in a field of flowers on a hot summer day.

"Thank you for this. And for the sandwich last night. And for—I don't know, for being nice to me." My voice came out sounding somewhere between a whisper and a croak.

"De nada. Don't even mention it." He stuck his hand out. "Why don't we give ourselves a fresh start, huh? I'm Antoni, but my friends and family call me Toni."

I shook his hand. "Alba."

"It's wonderful to meet you, Alba."

I took another sip, sneaking peeks at all the unusual things around us; it was sort of like a weird mash-up of a bakery and a mad scientist's laboratory. The glass jars were particularly interesting. Inside them, the colored liquids fizzed and bubbled, and there were blobby, leafy objects floating on the surface.

"What's in all those jars?" I finally asked.

Toni hopped off his stool with a gleam in his eye. "*These* are my yeast-water and sourdough children. It's what I use to leaven bread instead of commercial yeast. It's how people used to bake bread in the Middle Ages." He grabbed a couple of jars and put them in front of me. "In these jars, I've got dried fig and rosemary, fresh cherry, and tomato-basil yeast waters. And in this one, I've got a basic flour-and-water sourdough starter, which makes the most amazing-tasting crumb."

I frowned. He might as well have been speaking Japanese or Swedish or some other language I couldn't understand.

"I don't get it. How does *that* stuff end up as bread?"

Toni unscrewed the jars. "Go on, take a whiff."

I bent over and smelled each jar. Some smelled like fruity, fizzy beer, and others were more subtly sour, like banana mixed with yogurt.

"There is naturally existing wild yeast in everything organic. By mixing different fruits, vegetables, herbs, and even flour with water and sometimes sugar, you can harness the wild yeast through the fermentation process. Once that's done, then you can mix in different kinds of flours, more water, and salt to make bread." Toni set the jars aside, and then he brought out a large stainless-steel bowl with a kitchen towel over it. He took the towel off and pointed at the white goop inside it. "This dough has been fermenting for approximately eight hours. You see those bubbles? Those make all the holes in the bread when you slice it open," he said excitedly.

"Wow." It sounded stupid, but I couldn't find anything better to say.

To me, bread was just bread. I'd never considered that there was an entire science, or art, that went into making it. But Toni seemed much more than just an ordinary, everyday kind of baker. He was like a bread baker and scientist and artist rolled into one. It was overwhelming, but it also amazed me that someone could dedicate his entire life to making something as simple as bread.

"Anyway, I won't bore you with any more," said Toni with a chuckle. He took a baguette and a round loaf from a nearby tray and slid them into paper bags. "Tell that grandmother of yours that these are on the house. I insist."

I took the bags. "This smells good," I said with a smile.

"Well, I hope you think it tastes good, too. If you want, come back some other time. The shop closes in the afternoons for lunch and siesta, but I usually spend those hours experimenting back here."

He gave me this look. I'd seen a look like that before, one day when I was in Central Park. There was a little kid and her dad getting ice cream cones from the Mister Softee truck. As soon as the kid got her cone, she jumped up and down. In all her excitement, she loosened her grip and the cone dropped to the ground, splattering vanilla ice cream and rainbow sprinkles by her feet. She was about to burst into tears, but then her dad bent down and gave her this look of tenderness before handing her his own cone.

For whatever reason that memory had stuck in my head as if it was permanently attached with Krazy Glue. Maybe it was because I wasn't used to people looking at me that way—with tenderness and generosity.

My throat tightened, but I managed to say, "Okay."

"Let's go through the VIP exit," Toni said, leading me to a scratched-up metal door. It squeaked open, and I caught sight of the back alley and the dumpster from last night. "I look forward to seeing more of you, Alba."

I nodded. "Goodbye."

Toni closed the door. For a moment I didn't move. I thought about his kind eyes. I thought about the delicious sandwich he'd given me even though I was a total stranger. I thought about his bread and how amazing it smelled. I thought about all the weird and wonderful stuff he'd told me. Most of it didn't make any sense. But even then, for a couple of minutes, I'd found myself forgetting about Mom and Dad, and why they'd sent me away. Forgetting about all my problems. All that mumbo jumbo about wild yeast and bubbles and dough distracted me somehow.

I brought the bags of bread up to my nose and sniffed.

That smell.

There was something about that smell.

Eight

Back at Abuela Lola's, I spent almost the rest of that entire day passed out from jet lag and emotional overload.

But in the evening, Abuela Lola nudged me awake and said, "Wake up, sleepyhead. It's time to help me make dinner."

So there I was in the kitchen, helping my long-lost grandmother prepare our meal.

Huh.

Weird.

I was standing by the table, the loaf of bread glaring at me from the wooden chopping board. My knife was poised in midair. Abuela Lola had asked me to cut some nice, even slices, but I was too embarrassed to admit I'd never sliced bread before. I was sure it was going to be a massacre.

Abuela Lola stopped her tomato grating long enough to frown at me. "You do realize the bread isn't going to slice itself, right?"

"I know." I put the knife down. "It's just, well, I've never actually done this before."

"What?" she said, almost dropping the grater. "How is that possible?"

I shrugged. "We only ever had the supermarket kind that came in plastic bags. For toast and sandwiches. Besides, I was the only one in the house who ate any bread. Mom doesn't do carbs."

Abuela Lola gasped. "Nonsense," she said, shaking her head. "*Absolute* nonsense . . . Your mother practically *lived* on bread. I wouldn't have been surprised if she had gluten running through her veins," she said with a chuckle.

I furrowed my brows. "Like *bread* bread?"

"Yes!"

For a second, I pictured Mom seated at our kitchen table back in New York, picking at the keto bread roll from Whole Foods while mumbling something or other about being allergic to carbs and gluten and every food that was delicious.

Maybe Abuela Lola was confused? I mean, she was old— maybe her memory was slipping.

But what if she *was* right?

My insides felt all funny and fluttery.

Thump-thump. Thump-thump.

For some reason my heart was beating faster. It ached. Because all of a sudden, I missed her. Not the mom I'd left behind, but the mom I'd never gotten to know, the mom I might *never* get to know. The real her that everyone seemed to remember but me.

I gulped, trying to swallow the ache away. "So, um, like, how am I supposed to do this?" I asked, trying to distract myself with the task at hand.

Abuela Lola wiped her hands on her apron and sidled up to me. "Always grip the knife like you mean business," she explained, and showed me how she curled her fingers around the handle. "With your other hand, hold the loaf so it's steady. Then, when you're ready, start slicing with even pressure. Keep your eye on what you're doing, keep your fingers away from the blade, and never, ever hesitate. If you second-guess yourself, the end result will be a jagged, lopsided mess."

Crrruuunch.

The blade penetrated the hard crust. I watched her do the first few slices.

"Here," she said, handing me the knife.

I took it and did what she did.

Don't hesitate.

Not bad. The first slice was slightly uneven, but at least it wasn't the massacre I'd anticipated. I went ahead and sliced a couple more, and each time they were better and better.

"Perfect," Abuela Lola said after eyeing my handiwork. "That should be enough for the pan con tomate."

She took the bread slices one by one and toasted them on the flames of one of the stove's burners. Then she scraped a raw garlic clove on the browned surfaces and smeared them with some of the grated tomato before drizzling olive oil on top. "Here," she said, handing me a white paper package. "Put a slice of jamón over the bread while I make the omelets."

I opened the package. Jamón was a type of ham with dark meat and lines of creamy fat marbled throughout. It was kind of gross, but I went ahead and plucked some pieces, draping them over the pan con tomate as artfully as I could.

"¡A comer!" Abuela Lola flipped an omelet big enough for two on a platter.

We sat at the kitchen table, which was covered with an embroidered white tablecloth. Apparently, we were having breakfast for dinner—Spanish style. Abuela Lola seemed thrilled with the idea. But I was already used to eating cereal for dinner back home, so I didn't see the novelty in it. I helped myself to half of the omelet and a slice of pan con tomate, even though I was a little suspicious of the jamón. It was the bread I was interested in—Toni's bread. I tore off a corner of the toasted slice and put it into my mouth. It was crunchy and slightly chewy, a tad sour, and kind of earthy, almost nutty. It was so complex that I couldn't quite distinguish the other flavors.

"This bread is amazing," I said after swallowing.

Abuela Lola nodded. "Isn't it? Toni's bakery is one of Barcelona's best-kept secrets!"

For a moment I only sat, allowing Abuela Lola to do all the talking. It felt awkward eating and having a conversation. I couldn't get the timing right—the cutting and chewing and sipping while thinking of what to say every time a question was thrown my way. I was used to eating alone. On rare occasions, Mom would order sushi from the nearby Japanese place. But by the time the food arrived, she had usually lost her appetite. She would sit by the kitchen counter with the wooden chopsticks hovering over her sashimi, staring off at the wall—present, but not really there.

Having someone there, and present, was disorienting.

"Don't you like the food, Alba?"

I flinched. "I do. I'm sorry. I was just thinking . . ."

"There's nothing wrong with thinking. But you've got to eat, too," said Abuela Lola.

I tasted a forkful of omelet; it was light and fluffy, proba-bly the best omelet I'd ever had. Then I bit into the pan con tomate. It was good, too. Kind of salty, but good. And the bread! I couldn't get enough of the bread.

When Abuela Lola was done with her food, she got up and put her plate, her cutlery, and her glass in the sink. She turned the faucet on and took hold of the sponge.

"I can do the dishes!" I blurted out.

She turned the faucet off and dried her hands with a kitchen towel. "Well, I could get used to this," she said with a smile. "Oh. And before I forget . . ." I watched her disappear into the hallway and reappear with a set of keys dangling from her hand. "These are yours now. Welcome home, Alba."

I took the keys. They were warm, as if they'd been curled

up in Abuela Lola's purse. The key chain had a metal sun-flower pendant, and a second little pendant beside it with a letter *A* on it.

"Sunflowers are my favorite flower. There are fields as far as the eye can see in Carmona. It's a small town outside of Seville—or, as we say here in Spain, Sevilla—a city about a ten-hour drive southwest of Barcelona. One day I'll take you there." Abuela Lola kissed my forehead. "This old lady is off to bed now. See you in the morning."

"Good night," I replied.

When she was gone, I opened my palm and traced the metal flower petals with my finger. Sunflower fields as far as the eye could see. It sounded like something out of a dream.

A bright, sunny, happy place I couldn't quite imagine.

I lay wide awake in bed, because when you sleep all day, obviously you're going to be up all night.

Ugh.

Beads of sweat trickled from my head to my neck, across my stomach, down my legs. I wrestled with the sheets. Nobody had warned me that summer in Spain would be so hot. The decrepit-looking ceiling fan was useless. All it managed to do was make an annoying *whir, whir, whir* sound.

It was weird being in my new bedroom. Even though it was dark, the shadows on the walls were unfamiliar. The random creaks, the sounds from the street, the smell of the laundry detergent, the faint aroma of cooking oil combined with dried lavender—all those things made it impossible to sleep.

Besides that, I couldn't stop thinking and wondering. I tried to remember what it was like lying on my bed back in New York City. My sheets were definitely softer. Our apartment smelled like Febreze and orange oil from the furniture polish. And Scotch whisky. Dad's minibar was in his study, but for some reason the smell of his whisky—the rare, expensive kind that he liked to drink—permeated through the walls, into the air and everything it touched.

Most nights I would sleep with my headphones on, blasting David Bowie—usually "Life on Mars?"—which somehow made me feel like I was less alone. Maybe I wasn't the only one trying to drown out the shouting, the arguing, the slamming doors. But sometimes, even with the music on, I could still hear them. That's when I started leaving home in the middle of the night. I would tiptoe down the stairway and slip out the back door, into the alley where all the garbage cans were kept. It was the only way to avoid the twenty-four-hour doorman. When it was warm enough, I would sneak into the Diana Ross Playground in Central Park, a block and a half away. There was a metal tube slide that I would curl up in; something about it made me feel like I was in a rocket ship—maybe I *could* go to the moon or Mars and find David Bowie there with the rest of the world's rebels.

On colder nights I would visit Ramona at the Eighty-First Street subway station, or sometimes I would hang out at the bodega and read magazines. The guy who worked there, Sandeep, usually pretended he didn't see me, like I was invisible. Some days, though, he would give me a hot chocolate or cold carton of milk without saying a word.

All the reminiscing about home made my insides tighten. I kicked off the sheets and bolted from the bed. The window was open, and the curtains fluttered like wispy ghosts. I peeked outside. The street wasn't as empty as I thought. A yellow glow from the streetlamps lit up the narrow alleyways. There were people strolling by, laughing and joking. Maybe they'd had one too many sangrias, or maybe they were just having a good time—enjoying life. I was kind of jealous. I couldn't remember the last time I'd laughed. Really, really laughed.

I turned away from the window. The keys gleamed from my bedside table. I had this sudden urge to run. My legs twitched. My toes pressed against the wooden floor.

This time was different, though. I wanted to run. But not away, like I usually did.

I wanted to run *to* something.

Nine

El Rincón del Pan was completely different at night.
The building stood in the shadows, and in the dim light, the
window display looked like a spooky version of its daytime
self. I walked around to the back—the VIP entrance, as Toni
had called it—which was just a back door leading to a dumpster. I could see movement through its window.

Maybe I should leave?

I knocked on the door and stepped back.

"Alba?" Toni said.

Too late.

"I couldn't sleep," I said, biting my lip.

Toni opened the door wider. "Ah. Well, join the club," he
said with a chuckle.

I entered. It was even hotter inside than it was outside.
A bunch of metal bowls were lined up on counters with
mounds of glistening dough in them.

"You're baking right *now*?" I asked.

Toni went to the counter and began folding and rolling and tightening the mounds. "These are baker's hours. I'm usually here at three or four every morning preparing the bread for when we open."

I sat on a nearby stool. "So when do you sleep?"

"Good question. Most days from eight in the morning to three in the afternoon, unless someone calls in sick. Then I do not sleep at all."

I watched him shape the dough into circles and ovals and long skinny baguettes. It was kind of freakish how he could do it so fast, without even thinking.

"You want to help?" he said, looking up at me like he was a hundred percent serious.

"Me?"

"I don't see anyone else in here."

I swiveled the stool around to make sure. "Uh, maybe. But I don't—I mean, cooking and baking aren't my thing."

Toni began flipping the shaped pieces of dough into rattan baskets. "So what *is* your thing?"

"I-I'm not sure," I stuttered.

"Well, then, how do you know that baking is not your thing?"

I glanced at all the bowls and spatulas and bags of flour, trying to find some sort of excuse. But I couldn't think of one, other than I'd probably suck at it. I slid off the stool and approached the counter. "I guess I'll give it a shot," I said under my breath.

"¡Fantástico!" Toni said, and handed me a clean apron.

I hadn't realized until then that I was still wearing my pajamas. Though, technically, my pajamas that night were a pair of gray gym shorts and a ratty old New York City T-shirt with a big apple on it.

"So what do I do?" I asked.

He slid a large plastic bin across the counter and opened the lid. "In here, I have some dough that's been fermenting for several hours. It has to be gently stretched and folded one more time, and then it gets dumped on the counter and divided into four equal pieces. Then we shape it."

I peeked into the bin. The dough was one massive, swollen, bubbly pile that smelled like a cross between apple cider and sauerkraut. I glanced at Toni and blinked.

"Rule number one: Don't be intimidated," he said with a grin. "Go wash your hands and I'll show you what to do."

I went over to the almost-bathtub-sized sink. For a second, it felt like I was having an out-of-body experience. My sneakers were steady on the rubber mat below my feet. Yet it was as if I was floating up above near the ceiling, watching as the water rushed from the faucet, rinsing the soap suds off my skin.

Is this really happening?

It was past three in the morning. I was in the back room of a bakery in Barcelona with my mom's childhood best friend, learning to make bread. I couldn't believe it. I dried my hands on a kitchen towel and turned around.

Breathe.

The air was so hot that it felt like breathing in a freshly opened can of lukewarm soda or beer, except the aroma was a swirl of sour and fruity and sweet mixed with herbs and spices and wood and stone. It was strange and intoxicating.

"Ready?"

"Ready."

I stood next to Toni. He dipped his hands in a bowl of water, then tucked his fingers into the edge of the dough, pulling gently until it was stretched taut. Finally, he folded it into itself, toward the center until it resembled a jiggly ball. "You have to know the limits of the dough, Alba. Stretch it just enough, but not so far that it tears," he said. "Your turn."

Toni stepped aside. I tried to do exactly what he did, except when I did it, the dough stuck to my hands like chewing gum. "What am I doing wrong?"

"You're pressing too hard. Pretend your fingers are like butterflies, fluttering from flower to flower just long enough to get a taste of nectar," Toni instructed, waving his fingers gracefully.

"*Ohhh*-kay."

I repeated every action and movement, except I tried my best to make my fingers butterfly-like. At first, I was skeptical, but after a minute or so, the monstrous white blob began to cooperate with me and the dough barely stuck. Just a bit here and there, but it worked. Toni was right.

"How?" I said, gawking at him.

"It has to do with the nuances of touch. It's a skill that bread bakers learn along the way. Sometimes we have to squeeze, knead, and pull with all our might, and other times, we must be gentle, barely touching the dough so we don't lose all those air bubbles." He patted me on the back. "Go on and finish the stretching and folding. When you're done, scrape all of the dough onto the counter and we'll go from there."

"Okay," I said with a louder voice, hoping I sounded more competent.

Toni went farther down the counter so he could continue with his lightning-fast dough shaping.

I dipped my fingers into the bowl of water.

Gently dip, grip, stretch, and fold.

Again.

Gently dip, grip, stretch, and fold.

The bin tapped the metal counter with every movement. The appliances hummed. The ovens creaked and crackled with heat. It was almost musical—our breaths, the stretching and slapping of dough like the lyrics and beats of a song.

I was starting to get the hang of it.

When I was done, I pushed the entire glob onto the counter with a plastic spatula thingy. It landed with a poof of flour—the flour lingering like a cloud of smoke after a magic trick. I had never seen anything as glorious as that shiny mountain of bread dough before me.

It was nothing. I mean, I'd hardly done anything to help,

but somehow it was as if I'd just climbed that mountain, as if that mountain had actually been Mount Everest.

I peeped at Toni, whirling and twirling his hands. His movements were mesmerizing. I found myself holding my breath. It was as if everything was in slow motion. It could have been a dream, but it wasn't. The bakery was real. I was there. Toni was there. He didn't even know me. Not really. Yet he'd trusted me with his work. His livelihood. Nobody had ever trusted me like that before.

My heart, my stomach warmed. Not because of the heat of the room. It was the warmth of feeling wanted, of belonging, of doing something that mattered.

"I'm done," I announced.

"Ah! Great," he said, placing another dough ball into a basket. He walked over to another counter and grabbed a rectangular appliance. "The scale is a baker's best friend, Alba. Accuracy is key."

I watched as he sliced the dough mountain into four with a metal scraper; the sound of metal on metal was somehow satisfying. With his hand, he plucked one of the pieces and placed it on top of the weighing scale.

The monitor flashed: 488 grams.

Toni pinched a tiny bit off one of the other pieces and added it to the scale.

The monitor flashed: 500 grams.

"¡Perfecto! Now you do the rest."

I did nothing for a brief moment. From the periphery, I

could see that Toni was back to his whirling and twirling. It felt even hotter. The entire room was like a furnace. My hands were sticky, my neck and face were sweaty, and my feet were getting tired of standing.

But I was happy.

I couldn't remember the last time I'd felt that way.

I smiled and went to work.

Ten

It was almost six by the time I got back to the apartment. I slid my key into the lock as quietly as I could, hoping
Abuela Lola was still asleep. The door swung open without
a sound.

Phew.

I tiptoed inside. The apartment hummed like it was vacant.
I continued tiptoeing down the hallway toward my bedroom. Then I heard a swish and a crinkle. Abuela Lola was
seated on the living room sofa with the newspaper in her
grasp. Her eyeglasses were perched on the tip of her nose.
She didn't look at me, but I knew she knew I was there.

"I hope you brought back some more bread," she said with
the calmest of voices.

I took the paper-wrapped loaf from under my armpit and
held it up. "Um, how did you know where I was?"

She put the newspaper down and finally met my gaze.

"'Toni texted me early this morning," she said, pulling her cell phone out of her pocket.

"Oh."

"It was *very* considerate of him."

"I'm sorry, Abuela Lola. I know I wasn't supposed to run away again. But—but I couldn't sleep. And I wasn't technically running *away*—I was running *to* Toni's. I promise I won't do it again," I said, staring down at my feet. I had been here only two days, and I had already gotten in trouble twice.

"I'm not mad at you, Alba."

I looked up. "You're not?"

"No, of course not. It's not like you snuck out to go to a party, or to do drugs, or to commit some sort of heinous crime. Although next time, I'd appreciate it if you just told me beforehand," she said with a nod.

Next time?

If Mom had been the one seated in front of me, she would have threatened to lock me in my bedroom for the rest of my life, ship me off to a nunnery in the Swiss Alps, take away everything I loved and burn it in a bonfire.

I exhaled. Relieved.

"All right."

Abuela Lola lifted her newspaper again. "You should go and rest now. I'll wake you up in a few hours, and we can go downstairs for some lunch. Su and Ting are dying to meet you."

I shuffled to my room and closed the door. The sight of

my bed was almost too much. My shoulders. My arms. My hands. My legs. My feet. They'd all turned to mush. I collapsed on the mattress with a bounce. It didn't even matter that the sunlight was streaming through the curtains, making it brighter than bright. I curled to the side, and it was only then that I realized I still had the loaf of bread in my arms. Its crust was hard, but I hugged it anyway.

When we entered Restaurante Chino, it was practically empty. The food couldn't be that good if nobody was there. As if she'd read my mind, Abuela Lola gestured at the two tables with customers. "This place was packed just a few hours ago. Tourists like eating early so they can go off and do all their sightseeing. But we locals eat lunch at two or three. It's *much* more civilized."

Suddenly there was a gasp from behind me. I turned around. A lady with wavy, dark chin-length hair and red lipstick started babbling with Abuela Lola. I couldn't tell if she was speaking Mandarin or Spanish or a bit of both; she was talking too fast. "Ahhh. Alba!" was all I understood.

"Ting, this is Alba. Alba, this is Ting," said Abuela Lola.

"Hello . . . Uh, hola," I said.

Ting took my hand in hers. She studied me from head to toe, which wasn't very hard because she was about my height. Then she babbled a couple of sentences, adding several clucks toward the end. Abuela Lola laughed. I looked at both of them, trying to figure out what was so funny.

"She said she's going to fatten you up like a juicy Peking duck," said a voice from one of the tables.

It was a girl about my age, with black hair held back in a ponytail and green cat-eye glasses.

Abuela Lola went over and kissed her on both cheeks. "Marie, I was hoping you'd be here. Alba, this is Ting and Su's daughter. She's going to be a ninth-grader at Colegio Americano de Barcelona—an American school that's a couple subway stops away—so you two should have a lot to talk about."

"Hi," I said with an awkward wave.

"Why don't you girls chitchat? I'll go see what Su's cooking in the kitchen." Abuela Lola nudged me toward a chair and disappeared down a hallway with gilded wallpaper and framed prints of cranes, peacocks, dragons, and all sorts of flowers.

I sat and fidgeted, and checked out the restaurant, all the while avoiding Marie's gaze. It was pretty much the same inside as it was outside—worn, painted in reds and golds, with so many hanging lanterns you could barely see the ceiling.

"So are you shy, snobby, jet-lagged, or all of the above?" asked Marie, while staring at me with a raised eyebrow.

I stiffened. "Uh, jet-lagged. And I guess a bit socially inept."

Marie's eyebrow relaxed. "Oh good. I mean, not about the jet-lagged part. What I mean is, I don't mind socially inept. I'm outgoing enough for two people."

I grinned even though I wasn't sure exactly why. There was something about Marie—something likable? But I couldn't quite put my finger on it.

"I'll admit I might have gotten a bit too excited when your abuela told me you were from New York City. I've never been there. Well, I've never been anywhere, actually. But I've seen loads of photos of all the beautiful buildings—the Chrysler, the Flatiron, the Dakota, the Guggenheim. Gosh. There are just too many . . ." She rested her chin on her hand and gazed into the air dreamily.

"I take it you like architecture, huh?" I said.

Marie sprang off her seat so fast that her ponytail swished and her glasses got all crooked. "*Like?* Uh. More like *looove!*" She pulled a sketchbook out of her bag and placed it on the table in front of me. "Take a look and give me your honest-to-goodness opinion."

I opened the sketchbook. Out of the corner of my eye, I could see Marie watching me with the most stoic face imaginable. I tried to ignore her, focusing on the pages instead. They were the color of brown cardboard, and on them were the most exquisitely detailed sketches I had ever seen—of buildings and tree-lined streets and people and cars and clouds and birds. The lines were drawn with an inky pen, but the splashes of blue, green, yellow, red, and purple were done in watercolor. Her style was modern, like futuristic modern, but there were classical details that somehow blended in.

"These are amazing! How long have you been doing this?" I asked.

Marie exhaled. "Like *forever*. When I was little, my parents used to buy me dolls and toy doctor kits hoping I would be a surgeon or a scientist one day. But all I ever wanted to do was draw houses and buildings, and build imaginary cities."

"Were your parents disappointed?"

"At first. I mean they *did* name me after Marie Curie. But after a while they just accepted it. Especially when they found out architects are in high demand in the Middle East," she explained.

"Hope you girls are hungry." Abuela Lola appeared with Ting and an older man with a stained apron and a black cap, whom I assumed to be Marie's father.

His face was shiny, and his eyes crinkled at the corners when he smiled and stuck his hand out. "Su, Marie's father," he said.

I shook his hand. "Nice to meet you," I replied.

"¡A comer!" Abuela Lola said loudly.

Clearly, telling people to sit and eat was Abuela Lola's favorite pastime. Everyone helped themselves to noodles with veggies and steamed ginger chicken and fried rice with sausage and fluffy bits of egg. I already had food on my plate, but Ting winked at me and then shoveled more of everything on top. It was chaotic—all the eating and talking and chopstick clicking.

Abuela Lola leaned over and said, "In the restaurant business, we call this *family meal.*"

I nodded and stared at my plate.

Family meal.

There was a stinging feeling behind my eyeballs. I gulped some water and blinked.

The last thing I wanted was to think about Mom and Dad. It was too painful.

"*Psst.* Alba, you want to go for ice cream after lunch?" Marie whispered.

"Um. Okay," I whispered back. "Wait. Why are we whispering?" I said in a normal voice.

She looked at me and I looked at her, and then we both laughed.

Eleven

The neighborhood was ridiculously crowded. There were too many tourists wandering around with ice cream cones and selfie sticks and foldable maps. Marie didn't seem at all fazed. She expertly dodged person after person, not a drop of sweat on her lemon-yellow sundress.

"Does it ever get quiet around here?" I asked.

"Yeah, it does. In the fall and winter. Summer is *the* worst. But you'll get used to it . . . Just steer clear of the drunkards. Especially at night. If you're not careful, you might trip on some guy passed out on the sidewalk."

I chuckled. "We have our fair share of those in New York."

"Well, you'll do just fine, then."

We stopped in front of a closet-sized ice cream shop. The sign, ICE CREAM, YOU SCREAM, was spelled out in a drippy font. Inside, there was a freezer case with fluffy heaps of ice creams and sorbets, some familiar, some strange.

TURRÓN

TUTTI-FRUTTI

FLAN

ARROZ CON LECHE

HIGO Y VAINILLA

All the Spanish words were blending into one another. It was dizzying *and* intimidating. An ice cream shop shouldn't be intimidating. But it was. I felt like I needed a Spanish-English dictionary just to order.

"Have you decided yet?" said Marie.

I hesitated. "Um, I guess, strawberry."

It was the safest flavor imaginable. I expected Marie to tell me I was *bo*-ring. But, surprisingly, she didn't.

"Dos helados de fresa, por favor," she said to the guy behind the counter.

As the guy scraped at the pastel-pink heap in front of us, Marie chatted with him in Spanish. I kind of zoned out, my eyes blurring at the motion of his hand scooping the ice cream into perfect little mounds. My eyes stung. I blinked and looked away, right into a pair of unfamiliar eyes, one of which had a black star drawn around it. A kid, a teenage boy, was gawking at me from the other side of the shop, which wasn't all that far, considering how small it was. He was tall and gangly, with a mess of long, dark hair.

Ugh.

Even in another country there were still *those* who couldn't help staring at me. For whatever reason, people—especially teenage boys—found me fascinating, as if I was some bizarro creature they were encountering at the zoo for the very first time.

What was so odd, anyway, about a girl with short hair choosing to wear clothes that just happened to be displayed in the boy's section? I mean, weren't pants just pants and T-shirts just T-shirts?

Humph.

I shot him my cold, hard, keep-on-staring-and-you're-going-to-regret-it glare, and his eyeballs retreated back into their sockets. He kind of slouched, trying to blend in with the crowd.

"Alba, here." Marie handed me a waffle cone with two giant scoops, and then she proceeded to lick her own ice cream cone all the way around. "Mmm. You can never go wrong with strawberry," she said with a smile. "Let's go."

As we left, I could sense that the gangly weirdo was eyeing me again. But I just ignored him.

Loser.

By the time we reached the corner, I'd forgotten all about him.

Marie led the way through the bustling alleyways, sure-footed in her ballet flats, as if she'd memorized every single cobblestone in our path.

"Here we are."

For a moment we paused under a stone archway. Beyond it, there was a quiet courtyard with a church and an octagonal fountain. In the middle, a tree jutted from the concrete, dappling the area with shady spots.

"What is this place?" I asked.

"It's the Plaça de Sant Felip Neri. Over there"—she pointed to the small edifice with a blue-gray wooden door under a circular window—"is a baroque-style church named after Saint Philip Neri. You see all those pockmarks on the walls? They're from the bombings of the Spanish Civil War. The church was a makeshift orphanage at the time. A lot of children were killed."

No wonder something about the courtyard was solemn. It was the kind of place where people spoke softly and stood still.

"Isn't it kind of sad? I mean, to hang out in?"

Marie pushed her glasses up her nose. "I suppose you could look at it that way. But for me it's peaceful. I can sit here and sketch for hours."

I felt a drip on my finger. My ice cream. I'd forgotten all about it. We went over to the fountain and sat on its ledge to finish our cones.

"So . . . you missing home yet?" Marie asked.

I glanced at my shoes, not because I was avoiding her gaze, but because I was trying to figure out what to say. Did I miss home?

"I don't know. Maybe."

"What about your friends?"

I wanted to keep on staring at my shoes. But instead, I

found Marie's gaze and held it. "Nah. I mean, I didn't have any *real* friends. There were the kids I ate lunch with. The kids I sat next to in class. The kids I'd say hi to in the hallways. But that's it. Calling them my friends is a bit of a stretch."

"I know what you mean."

"You do?"

Marie grinned. Her eyes, though, told a different story. They were blinking and glossy and kind of faraway. "Being the no-nonsense, talks-too-much, know-it-all type isn't easy. I guess it turns people off. Plus, it doesn't help that I'm the scholarship kid at school. But I'm used to it. Or as used to it as I *can* be."

I would never have guessed that she was sort of like me.

An outsider.

"That sucks," I said.

Marie bumped my shoulder with hers. "Yeah, it does. But my mom says it will help me develop a thicker skin. Prepare me for the future."

An image of my parents flashed in my mind. I closed my eyes, willing them to go away. I didn't want to think about the reasons why they were the way they were.

Why Mom wasn't tougher.

Why she didn't just walk away.

Why she'd turned her back on me.

Marie's mom was right. Life was filled with victims and bullies.

In my case, it was my mom and dad.

I blinked and glared at my shoes again. "Thanks for the ice cream."

"Anytime."

And then it was quiet. Except it wasn't, really. There was something about this place. It seemed to whisper. It seemed to be saying something to me. I looked around. The fountain. The cobblestones. The old buildings. The tree. The church, its wall riddled with scars. They still stood. They had survived a war, bombings, deaths.

You can survive this, too, Alba.

I peeked at Marie. She was studying the details of a nearby building, following its lines and curves as if she was memorizing them to draw later on.

"How are you so sure that being an architect is what you want to do, like, for the rest of your life?" I asked.

"Because it doesn't feel like work to me," she replied without hesitation.

I frowned. "But work *is* work. At some point it's not going to be fun anymore."

"Well, of course I expect it's not going to be fun all the time. I'm not *that* naive." Marie pulled her knees up and rested her chin on them. "Last summer, one of the restaurant's customers invited me to intern for a few days at his firm. He's kind of a big-shot Barcelona architect. When I got there, all I did was photocopy and file blueprints, greet clients, and just do whatever menial task they asked me to do.

It was kind of boring. But just *being* there, seeing everything that went into creating houses and buildings . . . It was magical. The next day he brought me to one of their work sites. And I tell you, the hours felt like minutes. I was there all day, but it went by in the blink of an eye. *That's* how I know."

"Huh. That's so cool," I said, trying to sound sincere.

I was jealous, though. Marie seemed to have everything.

Parents who loved her. Parents she loved back.

Real smarts. Not just street smarts.

A future.

"Don't worry, Alba. You'll figure it out. Sometimes it just takes a while." Marie looped her arm through mine. "Come on. I have *so* much more to show you."

I followed her, because I wanted to be her friend. But I also had an ulterior motive. One that I wouldn't have admitted to her in a million years.

I wanted just an itty-bitty slice of her life.

A taste of love, confidence, happiness, and success.

Maybe, if I hung out with her long enough, I would get to have it.

Twelve

Marie's passion was contagious. All of a sudden,
there was this fiery ball inside me. A hunger to learn. Something. *Anything.* Abuela Lola seemed to think so, too. She
arranged it with Toni so that whenever I wanted, I could
hang out with him at the bakery. A summer apprenticeship
of sorts.

Beep! Beep! Beep!

My alarm went off. It was four in the morning—baker's
hours. I hurried out of bed and changed into my favorite sweatpants, so worn at the knees they were almost see-
through, and another one of my thrift-store T-shirts, featuring
a cat wearing an astronaut helmet in outer space. It didn't
even matter that I had eye boogers, stank breath, and bed
head. I left the apartment as fast as I could. Outside, the street
was still dark. Kind of empty. The occasional footsteps and
voices echoed. It was calm for a change. Nothing like New
York, "the city that never sleeps." Even at all hours of the

morning, there were cabs and cars and buses zooming in all directions; people going home, going to work; delivery trucks unloading goods at restaurants, supermarkets, and magazine stands. It was always noisy and bustling no matter what.

I hopped the curb and skipped over the broken cobblestones. For some reason I was anxious to get to the bakery. Toni might be disappointed if I was late.

Hurry, Alba.

Snort!

I jumped to the side.

Snort! Snort! Wheeze. Hmm. Hmm.

There was a guy passed out beside a garbage can making all sorts of noises. He had drool leaking from his mouth onto his EAT, DRINK, LIVERPOOL FC T-shirt.

Yikes.

Marie was right about the drunkards. The rest of the way I was more cautious, watching out for random arms and legs and heads poking out from the shadows.

Finally, I got to the bakery's VIP entrance. I pulled the door open and peeked in. A wave of heat hit my face. And then Toni materialized behind the shiny steel counter. He was shaping dough with a scraper, back and forth, side to side, until each lump was tight and round. I stepped inside.

"Buenos días, Alba. There is coffee by the window. Help yourself," said Toni, looking up at me while his hands continued working.

"Morning, Toni." I waved, and then went over to where the aprons were hanging. Coffee sounded good. I could have used the caffeine, but I was too nervous to eat or drink anything. It felt like the first day at a new school, except I was the only student in class.

Gulp.

I wandered over to the bins of fermented dough. "Should I start with cutting and weighing?" I asked.

"Yes, please. I'm almost done shaping this batch of boules . . . Those, I'll make into batards."

Boules. Batards. So many terms were unfamiliar to me. Yet I was too embarrassed to admit that I had no clue what he was talking about. At least I knew what a baguette was. It was a start. I was going to have to do some research. Otherwise, Toni would soon discover what an ignoramus I was.

I dipped my hands in a bit of water and then scraped clumps of fluffy dough onto the counter. Slice. Weigh. Slice. Weigh. Every time, I made sure the weight was precisely 500 grams. Except for our breathing and the sounds our hands and utensils and bowls made, it was quiet. Too quiet. I started humming a song to give myself a rhythm, "Under Pressure," by Queen and David Bowie.

> *Pressure pushing down on me*
> *Pressing down on you, no man ask for*

Slice. Weigh. Slice. Weigh.

"You can play some music if you want."

I stopped humming. "Oh. Sorry."

Toni plopped some dough into a basket. And then he looked at me with his bluer-than-blue eyes. "I didn't mean for you to stop. It was nice. The way you were humming . . . It reminded me of your mother. She *loved* music when she was your age."

I nearly dropped a blob of dough onto the floor.

My mom?

What was he talking about?

The only time she ever showed any enthusiasm for music was that one instance, when "Modern Love" was playing on the radio in the cab—the day she introduced me to David Bowie. Other than that, her default reaction to anything music related was to cringe and touch her forehead as if she had a massive headache.

"She loved . . . music?"

He chuckled. "Well, yes. Isabel loved lots of things. But music was definitely one of them. She used to hum and sing all the time. Even when nobody was listening. And at concerts she would hold her arms up in the air and dance. I got tired just watching her."

"My mom. She—I mean, you and her—went to concerts?" I replied with a frown.

What he was describing—I just couldn't picture it. It was

like trying to imagine a *Tyrannosaurus rex* wearing lipstick and high heels.

Toni made this cringey sort of face. "You sound *just* like my son. He thinks I was born an old fart. I cannot possibly know anything cool or rad or hip, or whatever word you kids are using these days."

"*Rad?* I think I saw that on an old T-shirt once," I said, trying to hold in the giggles.

"Ha! That's pretty much what *he* would say . . . I rest my case," he said, shaking his head.

I grinned and watched him go back to work. So did I.

Slice. Weigh. Slice. Weigh.

"You have a kid, huh?" I blurted out.

There was this hush in the room. I glanced at Toni's back; the space between his shoulders tensed.

"Yes. Joaquim. He's thirteen."

I opened my mouth to ask where his son was, but my breath got in the way. The only sound that came out was something between a croak and a gasp.

"Joaquim lives with his mother. I see him on weekends, sometimes more during the summer. In fact, he'll be here tomorrow," said Toni.

"Ah. Okay."

Toni looked at me from over his shoulder. "Come, I'll show you how to fold and shape."

I went over and watched him. Toni folded the dough in

half, top to bottom, and then half again, side to side. Gently, he coaxed the lump into a round shape. With his scraper, he pushed and pulled the round a couple of times until the surface was taut. It was mesmerizing. *Almost* as mesmerizing as one of those slime-squeezing videos on YouTube.

"That's what we call surface tension. It helps the dough retain its shape and allows it to rise without collapsing on itself." Toni handed me the scraper. "Here, give it a shot."

For a moment I hesitated. But what the heck. It was only flour, water, and salt. The world wasn't going to end if I screwed it up. I took hold of the scraper and approached another blob. My fingers curled into the dough—folding once, twice, three times and four. With the scraper, I pushed the mound toward me until it rolled into a ball. I glanced at Toni.

"Push it gently from side to side and then forward again until the skin tightens," he said.

I did as he instructed. By the time the dough was in front of me again, it was indeed a tighter ball. Below its surface, different-sized air bubbles peeked through.

Toni hugged me from the side. "Well done, Alba."

"Thanks!"

My shoulder was warm and tingly where Toni had squeezed me. As if an entire web of deadened nerves had been reawakened. I couldn't remember the last time Mom had touched me like that. And Dad, well, he was never much of a hugger. In fact, the last five years or so it was like

I hardly even existed. Whenever we were in the same room, his eyes glazed, looking around me, over me, through me, but never *at* me. The day I left for Barcelona, I'd lingered near the open door of his study while Mom waited for the doorman to come pick up my suitcase. Dad was at his desk, his gaze on the computer screen, his hand caressing the glass of whisky by his side. I dragged the soles of my sneakers on the hardwood floor, hoping they would make an obnoxious sound. They did. *Eeeep!* For a second, he looked away from the screen and saw me. He pushed his chair back and stood. My heart raced. Was he actually going to say something? Do something? *Thump-thump, thump-thump.* He walked toward me. I was afraid, but also kind of hopeful—hopeful that maybe some teensy part of him, buried deep down inside, still cared. He was closer. My lips parted; I was ready to say something. But then, *boom*, he shut the door, firmly. Right in my face.

I blinked, still shocked by the memory of it.

How was it possible that someone like Toni, someone I barely knew, could care more about me than my own father?

It was so confusing.

So sad.

Just forget about him, Alba.

I blinked again.

Concentrate on the dough.

Okay.

In my head I repeated all the steps for shaping. I moved on

to the next blob on the counter. After a minute of folding and pushing and pulling, I had another tight ball ready to go into the proofing basket. It was satisfying having so much control. To know that if I did things in a precise way, the outcome would always be the same.

Predictable.

Unlike my life.

I had zero control.

Nothing I did mattered.

I blinked.

It was so, so clear to me now.

Mom didn't want me. And my father—the man who was supposed to love me no matter what—didn't want me, either.

Maybe he had never wanted me.

Maybe I shouldn't have been born in the first place.

The scraper fell from my grasp, bouncing to the floor. My hands had gone numb. I wobbled. I could hardly breathe.

"Alba, are you all right?" asked Toni.

I stared at the blobs of dough—they were fuzzy. Out of focus. I gripped the counter.

"I-I'm sorry. I got dizzy . . . from the heat. I—I think I need to lie down," I mumbled.

Toni held my shoulders. "It takes a while to get used to the heat. Come, I've got a sofa in my office."

He led me through the door into a small room with a cluttered desk, a tiny fridge, a shelf chock-full of cookbooks, and a brown sofa that had seen better days.

"Sit."

I collapsed onto the sofa. It groaned and sagged under my body. Toni opened the fridge and took out a bottle of water.

"Hydrate and rest. I'll finish the shaping and check on you in a bit," he said, handing me the bottle.

I nodded. He vanished through the door. I opened the bottle and gulped down the water. It didn't make me feel any better. I curled up and closed my eyes. Darkness. The hum of the fridge; I concentrated on that noise.

Hummm . . .

Just don't think about it. Don't think about them.

Hummm . . .

A fresh start. Move on. Forget.

Hummm . . .

Yup. That's what I'm going to do.

Hummm . . .

Hummm . . .

Hummm . . .

Thirteen

I was in a half-conscious state—the one where your eyes aren't quite open, but you're awake enough to know where you are more or less. My forehead was throbbing in that creepy way, when you're almost sure someone is staring at you.

Wait.

There *was* someone staring at me—a boy. For a second, I just took in his shaggy hair, his tanned skin, his freckles, and the black star drawn around his right eye.

I squinted at him.

It was the kid. The teenage boy from the ice cream shop. The one who was gawking at me.

"What are *you* doing here?" I asked.

"Mi papá . . ." He looked at the door as if he was contemplating an escape. "Toni. He is my father," he said with a thick Spanish accent.

"Oh."

Of course the weirdo is Toni's son.

Just my luck.

I squinted even harder, studying the crudely drawn star around his eye. "Is that, like, um, eyeliner or marker on your face?"

He frowned. "Eyeliner, of course."

"Hmm . . . Paul Stanley from KISS. Am I right?"

"How did you know?" he asked, widening his eyes.

I sat up and shrugged. "It's kind of obvious. I mean, if you know anything about *real* music."

The boy grinned, and then he sat down on the sofa beside me. It bounced and made a squeaky sound. "I am Joaquim," he said.

"Alba."

It was kind of noticeable that he was stealing glances through the messy clumps of hair covering his face. I tried to ignore him. I focused on the floor, my sneakers, his boots. *Whoa.* His feet were big—almost twice the length of mine. Long legs, too. Knees jutting out, as if the sofa was too low. I hadn't realized how tall he was at the ice cream shop. Tall, gangly, and awkward.

So was the silence.

Awkward seemed to sum up the past few minutes.

"Anyway," I finally said, "are you in a band or something?"

"Something, yes. I am not sure you can call us a band yet."

"What's that supposed to mean?"

Joaquim scrunched his lips to the side and searched the

air with his gaze. "We are kind of like puzzle pieces . . . All mixed up. You cannot see what the picture is supposed to be yet. You understand?"

I nodded. "Yeah. I get it. You haven't found your look and sound yet, huh?"

"We practice . . . But still, nothing," he said, falling to the backrest with a sigh.

"Well, if it's any consolation, I haven't found my beat yet, either."

He tilted his head and scrunched his lips to the side again. "What do you mean?"

"What I mean is, like, you know, I haven't found what I'm good at yet," I explained, sinking into the backrest near him.

"Ah. Sí, comprendo."

All of a sudden, the door opened and in walked Toni. "Oh good, you've met," he said with a smile.

It got all awkward again.

"Um, yeah," I said.

"Alba, your abuela just called. She said you should head home soon," said Toni, with this frowny look on his face. He went over to his desk and began shuffling some folders. "Estel called in sick. I'm going to have to work all weekend again."

I peeked at Joaquim. He sank into the sofa with his chin sticking out like a pouty kid. Toni tucked one of the folders under his arm, and then he stood straight, gazing at Joaquim with watery eyes.

"Lo siento, Joaquim . . . Maybe you can go with Alba this weekend. I'm sure she'd like to see El Tibidabo," he said, glancing at me.

I sat up. "El Tibidabo?"

"It is an amusement park, up on a mountain overlooking the city," Toni explained.

"Cool," I said.

"Okay," Joaquim mumbled.

Toni smiled, but it seemed kind of forced. "¡Perfecto! Anyway, I am sure you will have more fun without me." He waved and hurried out of the office.

I looked at Joaquim. He looked at me.

"Uh . . . can I, like, bring a friend?" I asked.

Joaquim shrugged. "Sí. Whatever."

At first, I thought nobody was home. But when I passed Abuela Lola's bedroom, I could hear the shower running and the echo of her voice as she sang an unrecognizable song. The creaky old pipes were rattling and banging like drums or maracas or some other percussion instrument.

I was about to open my bedroom door when the phone rang.

Cring. Cring. Cring.

My hand paused in the air in front of me. I didn't move a muscle.

Should I answer it?

Hmm, maybe? I guess . . . After all, it's my home, too.

I jogged down the hallway back toward the kitchen. I dived for the cordless phone. "Hello?"

Silence.

"Hello?" I repeated.

There was breathing on the other end. Maybe whoever it was couldn't understand.

"¿Hola?" I tried.

"Alba."

The phone started to slip from my grasp, but I caught it.

"Mom?"

"How are you?" she asked softly.

I breathed deep, hoping my voice wouldn't falter. "I'm fine. I mean, good. I—I met your friend Toni . . ."

More silence.

"Mom? Are you there?"

"Yes."

I held the phone closer to my ear. "So I'm learning to bake bread. *Real* bread."

"That's nice."

God. Is she even listening?

The space between the phone and my palm got all moist. *Ugh.* What could I possibly say to make the conversation more than just nice?

"How come you never told me about him?" I asked.

Sigh.

I could hear her breath seeping out of her mouth. I imagined her sitting there with her posture—always straight, always stiff, always elegant. Her hand was likely on her scarf, caressing its silkiness with the tips of her manicured fingers.

"People just outgrow one another," she said matter-of-factly.

I wasn't even Toni, yet for some reason my cheeks were stinging as if she'd slapped me.

I heaved.

Don't cry. Don't cry. Don't cry.

"But. Toni—"

"I have to go now."

She was shifting the phone, her ear, her hand, her breath, brushing up against the mouthpiece. It was muffled. Garbled.

"Goodbye," she said abruptly.

Then she was gone.

The dial tone—*beep, beep, beep, beep, beeeeeep.* And then nothing.

It flatlined.

I was numb.

All I could think was *Has she outgrown me, too?*

Fourteen

I was in no mood for lunch.

Obviously.

But Abuela Lola wouldn't have any of it. "Nonsense. Some chicken adobo will fix you right up."

I was sulking.

She thought I was tired.

I didn't see the point in telling her about the phone call with Mom.

Knock. Knock.

"That's them." Abuela Lola grabbed her purse. "¡Ya voy!"

She opened the door.

"¡Ay!"

"¡Hola!"

"¡Un beso! ¡Un beso!"

It was a whirlwind of pastel pink, madras, and white linen. Eduardo and Manny were the gay couple who lived across the hallway. Eduardo was the older one and, from the looks of it, Spanish, with wavy, mostly gray hair; a prominent nose; and eyes the same exact shade as green olives. Manny was Filipino. His brown eyes turned up at the corners like a cat's, framed by perfectly plucked eyebrows. In fact, everything about him was catlike—his long limbs, his posture, the way he moved gracefully.

"Ahh, just look at her," Manny said after pecking me on both cheeks. He glanced at Eduardo. "She's like the love child young Mia Farrow and circa-eighties David Bowie never had. With just a dash of Nora Aunor."

Eduardo squinted at me. "I see it. Her cheekbones, her chin, her neck. She has that smoldering Nora Aunor look."

I had no clue who Mia Farrow or Nora Aunor were, but the idea of having David Bowie as my dad made me grin like a dork.

Abuela Lola swatted them both with her hand. "Oh, stop confusing the poor child. ¡Vámonos! I'm hungry."

We left the apartment and crammed into the elevator. When we got outside, I followed them to the side of the building. Eduardo took his car keys from his pocket and pressed some sort of remote. A small automated door rolled up, revealing what was quite possibly the world's smallest garage, with the world's smallest car in it.

"This is my pride and joy, Sara Montiel," said Eduardo, gesturing at the car.

I gawked at the small green vehicle, which reminded me of a frog. "We're going in *that*?" I asked.

Eduardo opened the passenger-side door and folded the seat up. "Sara is a fully restored 1958 SEAT 600. Get in . . . You shall see. She purrs like a kitten."

Oh-kay.

I climbed into the back seat and scooched over. Abuela Lola was about to follow, but Manny touched her arm. "You can sit up front, Tita Mags." He slid into the back seat beside me and winked.

And then we were off. The car zoomed over the cobblestone streets.

I leaned close to Manny and whispered, "Who is Sara Montiel?"

He gasped and touched his heart. "Only the most *fabulous* Spanish actress of all time. Beautiful. Talented. A goddess."

"Okay. I get it," I said with a giggle.

The car slowed to a crawl, winding through the narrowing streets, dodging random pedestrians.

"I thought cars weren't allowed in the Barrio Gótico," I said.

Abuela Lola looked over her shoulder. "Well, they aren't. Unless you're a resident, and very few residents have cars."

All of a sudden Eduardo hit the brakes. Three metal pillars jutted out from the road, blocking the way. I craned my neck. There was no room for us to pass, even for a car as teensy-weensy as Sara. "What now?" I said.

Eduardo opened the glove compartment and pulled out another remote. He pointed it through the windshield and pressed a button. A second went by and then—*whoa*. The pillars slowly moved downward into the concrete, disappearing completely so we could pass. It was pretty much the coolest thing ever.

"How?" I gasped.

Eduardo grabbed a pair of sunglasses from his shirt pocket and put them on. "Bond. James Bond," he said with a gruff voice.

"Susmaryosep!" Manny cackled and rolled his eyes. "He says that every single time."

I laughed.

Abuela Lola gestured forward. "¡Date prisa!"

The car took off—one, and then two, and then three, and then four streets. I lost count. Finally, Eduardo pulled into a parking space. I peeped out the window. *Huh.* The neighborhood was a combination of old residential buildings crammed into alleyways and more modern ones lining the wider streets. Splashes of color showed where some artists had created murals and others had spray-painted graffiti masterpieces. Even though there were lots of stores and restaurants, there were hardly any tourists, as if only the people who lived in the area frequented the place. To be honest, it was sort of crummy and run-down.

"We're here," he announced.

"El Raval is home away from home," Manny said with a smile. "This is the neighborhood where the majority of Filipinos live."

We got out of the car, and almost immediately there were greetings right and left.

"Ate Mags! Musta na po?"

"Uy, Manny! Ang ganda naman ng kilay mo!"

"Tita! Matagal din tayo hindi nagkita!"

I could hardly believe how many people knew Abuela Lola and Manny, and even Eduardo. One lady pinched his belly and said, "Huy . . . Parang tumataba ka, ata!"

Manny chortled. "She thinks you've put on some weight."

Eduardo scowled.

We strolled down the alleyways. The buildings were so close together you could almost jump from one balcony to another. In the spaces between, there was a tangle of laundry lines with clothes drying on them; it almost looked festive, as if the clothes were party streamers.

Abuela Lola gazed at the balconies with twinkly eyes. "I love walking down these streets, listening to the sounds of chismisan as the laundry flutters in the breeze."

Chismisan—I knew that meant "gossiping."

When I was little, Mom would murmur it to me whenever she didn't want my dad to understand. Because if he did find out what the neighbors were saying, he'd get angry—and maybe even violent.

It wasn't until I was older that I finally figured out what they *were* saying.

That my father was an abuser. A wife-beater. An alcoholic.

That my mother was a victim.

That I was the poor, helpless child.

They weren't wrong.

"Hay naku!"

"Diba?"

"Grabe!"

I looked up at the men and women and children on those balconies, hanging wet shirts and pants and skirts and dresses, underwear and bras. They were chatting with one another. Hollering at one another. Their laughter echoed down the alleyways, casting a cheeriness on the entire neighborhood.

"And this here is the LBC. That's how Filipinos send balikbayan boxes to their families back in the Philippines." Abuela Lola waved at the people working inside.

"Balikbayan boxes?" I asked.

Manny opened his arms wide. "Care packages in *really* big boxes."

"¡Gigantisimos!" said Eduardo.

"Ah. Por fin." Abuela Lola stopped in front of an unassuming-looking restaurant called Los Hermanos.

"Best Pinoy food in town," said Manny.

Inside, there were round tables, square tables, a counter with stools. Almost every single chair had a person in it. A flat-screen TV in the corner blared some Filipino movie. That was it. There wasn't much decor. But nobody seemed to care. There was a whole lot of eating going on. I couldn't blame them. The food smelled *ah*-mazing.

We were ushered to a table in the corner. Abuela Lola

refused the menus. Instead, she recited our order as if she'd already decided ahead of time. None of the food sounded familiar to me.

Adobo.

Kare-kare.

Crispy pata.

Relyenong bangus.

Pancit palabok.

"And a round of calamansi juice," she said with a satisfied nod.

I must have been frowning or squinting or something, because as soon as the server went away, Abuela Lola shot a questioning look at me. "What's the matter, Alba?"

I shrugged. "Nothing. It's just that I don't know what any of that food is."

Manny gasped and placed his hand on Abuela Lola's forearm.

"Hays. This is a travesty. How you've been missing out, my poor child," she said with a sigh. Then she gestured at some of the dishes on the neighboring tables. "*Those* dishes are all Filipino classics! Adobo is chicken or pork marinated in vinegar and soy sauce, then cooked with lots of garlic, peppercorns, and bay leaves. It's practically the national dish! Kare-kare is an oxtail stew with a rich peanut sauce. Crispy pata is pretty self-explanatory—crispy fried pork knuckles. *Yum.* And relyenong bangus is a deboned milkfish stuffed with its own meat, seasoned ground pork, carrots, and raisins. Finally, there's the noodles, in this case, pancit palabok, which are rice noodles with a shrimp sauce, topped with shrimp, smoked fish flakes, pork cracklings, and boiled eggs."

I gawked at her. "That's a lot to remember."

"It's *all* good. You'll see," she said, elbowing me playfully.

I just sat there taking it in. The aroma. The laughter. The sound of Tagalog and Spanish and English bouncing off the walls. It affected me somehow. I had this weird sensation, like I was out of place but, at the same time, part of something I'd never been part of before. I was a quarter Filipino and a quarter Spanish, yet I'd never actually thought much about it until now. Sitting there with Abuela Lola and Manny and Eduardo and a roomful of Filipinos, I felt my insides becoming warm and cozy.

I was at ease. Like I was supposed to be there. Even though I was probably the most clueless Filipino person in the room, it was like I belonged somehow.

To a family.

To a community.

To something greater than myself.

Fifteen

That night I was supposed to sleep early so I could wake up for my morning excursion to the amusement park with Joaquim. But after hours of tossing and turning and listening to the creaks of the apartment, I gave up trying.

I got dressed.

I tiptoed outside.

I hopped, skipped, and jumped over the broken cobblestones and drunkards.

And found myself at the back door of El Rincón del Pan.

Knock. Knock.

Toni opened the door a crack; for a second, all I saw was one blue eyeball.

"Alba," he said, opening the door wider. "Why am I not surprised?"

"I couldn't sleep." I went inside and took a deep whiff. "Hmm. Do I smell cinnamon?"

He grinned. "You have a good nose. I'm making torrijas."

"What are torrijas?" I asked.

"I'll show you," he said, nudging me toward a tray on the counter. "Torrijas are a Spanish version of French toast. Traditionally they're eaten during Easter, but these days we enjoy them all year round. I make some whenever I have day-old bread."

I peeked into the tray and saw thick slices of bread drowning in fragrant milk. "What's in it?"

"Eggs, milk, sugar, cinnamon, and some orange zest. The slices need to suck up the milk and egg mixture for an hour or so. And then we'll panfry them with some olive oil. The finishing touch will be a coating of cinnamon-sugar."

"*We'll?*"

Toni shrugged. "¡Por supuesto! You *are* here to help, aren't you?"

I grinned and put on an apron. We went over to the stove, and Toni showed me how to fry up the torrijas until they were golden brown. Then we placed them on some paper towels to drain off the excess oil before dipping them into the cinnamon-sugar mixture.

"You got it under control?" he asked.

"Yup."

Toni went off to another counter to shape some dough while I finished the rest of the torrijas.

At first, we didn't talk much. He was busy concentrating, and so was I. But as I stared into the cast-iron frying pan, watching the pieces of bread caramelize, thoughts were cooking up in my head. And the questions—all sorts of questions nagged me.

"Toni?" I said, keeping my eye on the pan.

"¿Sí?"

"So, like, how come you and my mom lost touch? Did something happen?" I didn't dare look at Toni, but I could hear his dough scraper sweeping the counter.

He exhaled. "It's complicated."

With my spatula, I took out the cooked torrijas and slid them gently onto the paper towels. Then I turned around, glaring at Toni until he met my gaze. "I'm almost thirteen. My parents kicked me out and sent me to live with a grandmother I barely know, to a country I barely know . . . And here I am. It's four in the morning, and I'm standing here making Spanish-French toasts with some guy I barely know. I *think* I can handle complicated."

Toni plopped a dough ball into a basket. "I'm sorry. You're right." He went over to the other side of the counter and pulled out two stools. "Sit," he said.

I should have been eager for answers after that whole spiel. But suddenly, I wasn't so sure. *Did* I want to know? I hesitated and then sat next to him.

"Like I said . . . Your mom and I were the best of friends." He paused for a second, peeling bits of dough from his cuticles. "Actually, we were more than friends—"

My back snapped straighter. "Really?"

"No, no. Nothing like that. We were more like brother and

sister. Neither of us had siblings, and when we were growing up, a lot of the times it felt as if all we had was each other."

"Oh," I said.

"But things changed after high school. We went off in different directions. I took an apprenticeship at a bakery, working long shifts. I guess I wasn't around much. Your mom didn't know what she wanted in life. Then she met your father in Ibiza one summer. As they say, he swept her off her feet. She decided that what she wanted was to move away from everything she'd ever known. Away from your grandmother. Away from me . . ." His voice faded.

The blue in Toni's eyes softened; it was like watching a bright blue flower slowly wither.

"So you never saw her after that?" I asked.

"I did. Many years later, when I was working at a bakery in New York. I was arranging some bread, and she walked in. Just like that. I saw her before she saw me. But as soon as she did, as soon as she recognized who I was, she gasped. She put her hand on her heart. And then she ran off. I called out to her, but it was too late. She was gone."

I furrowed my brows. "But why?"

"I wish I knew, Alba. All these years, I've been so worried about her. I've written emails, letters. She's never replied. Your abuela said it's because . . . because your father doesn't want her speaking to anyone from her past. Not even her own mother." Toni stopped talking and fiddled with his apron.

111

My ears were burning, the heat spreading to my cheeks, my neck, my chest, my stomach.

I *knew*.

My father wanted to control *everything* Mom did. *Everyone* she spoke to.

I *knew*, because he'd tried to do the same to me.

Tried but failed.

To be honest, I didn't want to remember. But a memory just barged into my head. That first time I'd cut my own hair—I'd had to use the kitchen shears. For years I'd begged my mom and my dad to let me get a short haircut. "*No*," they said every single time I asked. After a while, Mom just ignored me. But my dad, he got angrier and angrier, his face and neck turning a deep crimson as he reached out and slammed whatever object was closest to him—a glass, a book, a vase. "*Not my daughter*," he'd shout loud and clear. That day, though, the day I'd finally dared to do it myself, it was *me* he'd slammed. Against a wall. "*I don't know who you are anymore, but you're not my daughter*," he spat out.

A single tear escaped from the corner of my eye. I wiped it away, embarrassed by my sudden burst of emotion.

"I'm sorry if this upsets you," said Toni.

"It's all right." I hopped off the stool. "I asked, you answered."

He stood. For a moment he turned one direction and then another and then another, as if finding his bearings. A few awkward seconds passed. Then he halted in front of a giant plastic bin of dough.

"You want to learn how to make ensaïmada?"

I stepped forward.

I tightened my apron.

I held my chin high.

"Yes. I do."

I was going to learn how to make ensaïmada.

And there was *nothing* anyone could do to stop me.

Sixteen

Need. More. Sleep.

Those were the words groaning in my head as I waited for Marie in front of Restaurante Chino. The plan was that we would all meet there, and then head to El Tibidabo.

"Hey," Marie called to me.

I blinked and purposely opened my eyes as wide as they would go. Maybe I would seem more awake. "Hey," I said back.

Marie was wearing a purple skirt the color of grape soda, the kind that twirled into a circle, and a yellow blouse with sleeves that flared like tulips. I must have had a funny look on my face, because she glanced down at her outfit and frowned.

"What?" she said.

"Um, aren't you a tad overdressed for an amusement park?"

"Overdressed?"

I pointed at her skirt. "How are you supposed to go on rides and stuff with a skirt on? I mean, unless you're okay with everyone seeing your underwear."

"Oh, I don't do rides," she said matter-of-factly.

"You don't *do* rides?"

"No. Why?"

"Well, uh, what are you going do while we're there?" I asked.

Marie whipped out her sketchbook from her tote bag. "I'll sketch."

"Suit yourself," I replied with a shrug.

"¡Buenos días!"

We turned around. Joaquim was moseying toward us with a big grin plastered on his face. His hair was even shaggier than I remembered, and the way he was dressed—with a cotton tunic, loose bell-bottom jeans, and a floppy hat— reminded me of Zoot, the Muppet house band's saxophone player. From the corner of my eye, I could see that Marie was . . . amused? Shocked? Horrified? I couldn't quite tell which one.

Joaquim bent down to kiss Marie on both cheeks. "Hola. I am Joaquim."

"You're tall," she said, raising her head to get a good look at him.

"Really?" he replied sarcastically.

I slapped my forehead with my hand. "Okay. Okay. Marie, this is Joaquim. Joaquim, this is Marie. Can we go now?"

He grinned again. "¡Por supuesto! Vámonos, chicas."

According to Joaquim, it was a leisurely stroll to Plaça de Catalunya, where we would catch the subway, which would take us to a tram, which would take us to a cable car, which would take us near enough to walk to El Tibidabo. Except his legs were way longer than mine and Marie's, so we straggled behind. When we weren't concentrating on dodging tourists and street performers and vendors, Marie would interrogate me with this squinty-eyed look on her face.

"Is that eyeliner he's wearing?"

"Are you sure he's only thirteen?"

"Can we trust him?"

"Has your abuela even met him?"

After a while, I just swatted her arm and said, "Do you really think Toni would send us off with an ax murderer?"

Marie raised an eyebrow. "Well, what if he doesn't know? He could be an ax murderer, a drug dealer, a kidnapper, a cult recruiter . . . The possibilities are endless."

"We are here. The L7 train." Joaquim finally halted, pointing at the L7 sign with a lopsided grin.

Marie and I glanced at each other, and we both giggled. Joaquim looked down at his feet, over his shoulder, and all around. "Did I make a joke or something?"

"Something like that," said Marie.

Joaquim frowned. "I do not get it . . ."

"We're just being silly, Joaquim. C'mon," I said, shaking my head.

We descended into the subway station. For a second, it reminded me of New York City. Only for a second, though, because the station was clean and it didn't smell like pee. I searched for graffiti, but there was none. When the sleek red-and-white train pulled in, it wasn't crammed with weirdos. Okay, maybe just a couple of weirdos. Marie sat down next to a half-asleep geezer, and Joaquim and I stood, gripping the metal poles so we wouldn't fall over when the train swerved.

"Your friend. I do not think she likes me," said Joaquim, hunching down so he was closer to my ear.

I peered up at him. He had this hurt look on his face, like a puppy that had been screamed at for pooping on the floor. It was adorable. "Don't worry about it. I'm sure you'll grow on her."

He furrowed his brows. "Grow? Like a plant?"

I had to keep myself from laughing. So I tried to make my face as stiff as possible. "It's just a saying, Joaquim. It means that eventually, she'll want to be your friend."

"Ah." Joaquim stood tall and pulled his shoulders back. "And you, Alba? Do you want to be my friend?"

I could feel the back of my neck get hot. All I could do was stare at my sneakers. "Yeah, sure."

Joaquim didn't reply. But he nudged me with his elbow.

"¡Avinguda Tibidabo!" announced the conductor.

When we exited the subway station, we were in an entirely different part of Barcelona. The wide avenue was lined with trees. There weren't any buildings crammed together. Instead, there were houses—mega-huge and fancy ones with turrets and balconies and painted tiles and arched windows and manicured gardens. The vibe felt somewhat like the Upper East Side of Manhattan, or Central Park West, or Greenwich Village—neighborhoods where rich people lived. In a way, it reminded me of home. Except these homes had something artsy about them, as if there were eccentric painters like Picasso and Dalí still living here.

Marie already had her nose tucked into her sketchbook. Every few seconds she would glance at one of the mansions while her hand drew lines and curves on the paper.

"We will miss the Tramvia Blau if you keep on sticking your head in that notebook," Joaquim said with a chuckle.

Marie rolled her eyes. "It's a sketchbook. Besides, I thought *you* were in charge of this outing."

"Claro que sí . . . Of course," said Joaquim, backing away from Marie.

I wanted to laugh. It was like watching a mouse intimidate a giraffe.

Ding! Ding! Ding!

Joaquim parted the curtain of hair in front of his eyes. "¡Allí! It is here, the tramvia," he said, pointing down the street.

I followed his finger. An old-fashioned blue tram with a bright red bumper was approaching us. After a minute it stopped. Marie tucked her sketchbook under her arm, but not for long. As soon as we got on board, she found a window seat and whipped it out again.

"You okay here by yourself?" I asked.

"Yeah. Don't worry. Go find a seat . . . I'll just be here sketching away," she said, waving me on.

I followed Joaquim to the back of the tram. It was crowded, but we managed to smoosh ourselves into a wooden seat meant for one. Joaquim's knees jutted out into the aisle, jabbing unsuspecting strangers

"Discúlpame," he said sheepishly every single time someone glared at him.

The tram took off. At first, it was quiet. All I did was peer out the window at the passing scenery. There were rows of trees with pale dappled trunks and vibrant green leaves. There were people, lots of them, enjoying the warm summer breeze. And the houses—each one seemed grander than the next the more uphill we went.

Joaquim poked his head next to mine. "One day, I would like to live here," he said wistfully.

For a second, I didn't reply. An image flashed in my mind of me and Abuela Lola and Mom inside one of those houses. Sunlight was streaming through the windows. Mom was in a white dress and red shoes, twirling round and round as David Bowie sang "Let's Dance." Abuela Lola gazed at her and smiled. And I watched them both, my skin tingling from happiness.

"Alba?" Joaquim said.

I blinked. And then blinked again, trying to erase the image from my consciousness. "Uh. So, Joaquim, where do you live, anyway?"

"Far. On the other side of town, in Poblenou. It is . . . an interesting neighborhood. Lots of factories and warehouses. But my mother is an artist. So she needs the big space for her paintings."

"Ah." I nodded. It was the first time he'd mentioned his mom. I was intrigued. And curious, but I had no idea how to pry without sounding nosy. "An artist, huh?" I finally said.

"Yes. A hungry artist," he replied with a cringe.

"You mean a starving artist."

"Sí."

Joaquim tucked his hair behind his ear, and I could see both his eyes. They were big and sort of multicolored, like marbles—filled with swirls of blue and gray and brown and green.

"My mother, she believes art has value just because it is art . . . She and my father, they used to fight a lot. She says he works too much, he only cares about money. And my father, he gets angry, because he says you cannot eat paintings. But you can eat bread, sell bread to pay the bills." He shrugged. "So, one day, she left and took me with her. That was five years ago."

I turned away from his gaze and stared at my lap. So his mom left Toni. I should have felt bad for him. But all I felt was envy. I wished my mom had had the guts to leave my father a long time ago.

"I'm sorry." I found his marble eyes again. "That must have been hard."

He shrugged. "Un poquito . . . But it is better now. They do not fight so much anymore."

I went back to the window. Except it wasn't the trees or the passersby or the mansions I was seeing. It was my own reflection on the glass. Just me. The sunlight was shining from behind like a bright, blinding spotlight, reminding me of how lonely I suddenly felt.

Seventeen

El Tibidabo wasn't at all what I was expecting. I thought we were going to an amusement park like Six Flags or Universal or even Disneyland. El Tibidabo was on top of a mountain overlooking the entire city of Barcelona and the sea and horizon beyond it. The amusement park itself was pretty small, with only a handful of dinky rides, well, maybe not dinky, but kind of old-timey. And behind it was a humongous cathedral with pointy turrets that reminded me of icicles. I thought it was kind of weird that there was a place of worship so close by—praying and roller coasters didn't seem to go together. But in Spain, I guess they did.

"First we will ride El Avió, and then we can eat. ¿Sí?" said Joaquim at the entrance.

My stomach grumbled. It was still kind of early for Spanish lunch, but the long journey had made me hungry. "Can't we just eat first?"

Joaquim shook his head. "No. It is tradition. El Avió always comes first."

"You don't *exactly* seem like the traditional type," said Marie, peeking from the top of her sketchbook.

"All right. Whatever. When in Rome, right?" I said.

"But we are in Barcelona." Joaquim had that dopey, puppy-dog look on his face again.

Marie slammed her sketchbook and stared at him, as if she was trying to figure out if he was for real or not. I mean, I guess it wasn't his fault that the occasional phrase was lost in translation. Joaquim's English was pretty good, *much* better than my Spanish. But since he didn't go to an American school like Marie did, surely there would be times when he'd get confused.

I nudged Marie with my elbow and smiled. "Of course. Barcelona. I mean, it's right there all around us!" I exclaimed with a sweep of my hand.

"Oh. Yeah . . . *Oh*-kay. I'm going to go study that view of, um, Barcelona, and draw it. Just come find me when it's time to eat." Marie waved and took off toward a walkway leading to the cathedral.

"¡Vámonos!"

Before I could even react, Joaquim tugged on my wrist and dragged me toward god knows where. Several seconds passed, and then we arrived at a small, boxy white structure with a crane on top. On the crane was an ancient red airplane from, like, a hundred years ago.

"We're going on *that*?"

Joaquim's eyeballs were all shiny. "It is amazing, no?"

I wanted to glare at him and say no, but I didn't want to rain all over his parade. So instead I imagined that my eyeballs were also super shiny, and then I said, "Totally!" as if this ridiculous ride was the coolest thing ever.

We went into the building. It was empty except for the dudes that worked there. They checked our tickets and then led us to a metal staircase that was more like a ladder. *Clang.* Our footsteps vibrated through the metal. I leaned closer to Joaquim and whispered, "How come we're the only ones here?"

He frowned. "Most people, they prefer the newer rides. But trust me. El Avió is a legend."

"Okay . . . ," I said, ducking my head so I could get into the plane.

The interior was mint green and black with touches of wood. There was a row of seats on either side. Since Joaquim was so tall, he had to bend over to get inside. He tucked himself into the front seat, and I plopped into the one next to it.

Whir. Whir. Whir. Whir.

The plane started moving, so slow I thought it was just the wind rocking it forward. But then I glanced at Joaquim and he gave me a thumbs-up. "Three . . . Two . . . One . . . Go!" he yelled.

Go we did. Except we still weren't going very fast.

"Is it supposed to speed up?" I asked.

"No, the plane only cruises."

"Cruises?" Last time I checked, *cruising* meant faster than a snail.

Joaquim poked my arm with his finger, and then he pointed outside my window. "You are missing it. Just relax and enjoy."

I slumped back in my seat and looked outside. The plane was creeping past the edge of a precipice, and suddenly, there was nothing below us. "Whoa," I mumbled under my breath.

"Yes, totally, whoa," Joaquim said with a big grin. "When I was small, I begged mi papá to take me again and again and again."

My heart tightened in my chest. I pretended to look out the window so Joaquim wouldn't see the slickness in my eyes. What he'd said reminded me of the one great memory I had of my father. Before everything fell apart.

I was maybe three or four. We were in Central Park. Just me and him. It was the first warm weekend of spring, so the park was full of families and tourists and joggers and dog-walkers and people lazing on blankets reading their books. I was sitting on his shoulders. My father gazed up at me with his deep blue eyes and said, *"You wanna give the carousel a whirl, Alba?"*

I bounced on his shoulders excitedly, because for the longest time I'd wanted to ride the Central Park Carousel, but Mom had always nixed the idea. Every single time she would say something like *"She's too small"* or *"She's not ready"* or *"Maybe next time."*

But this time *was* the next time, because Mom was at a charity luncheon and my father was in charge. As soon as we entered the circular brick building, my father carried me off his shoulders and placed me right in front of the carousel. *"Take your pick,"* he said.

I scanned the various horses. Almost immediately, I spotted a black stallion with a white mane and tail. It was the fastest one; I was sure of it. *"That one,"* I proclaimed.

"You sure you don't want the pink one?" he said, pointing at a pastel pink one with a rainbow striped saddle.

I shook my head adamantly.

"Okay, then." After he paid for the ticket, he led me to the black stallion and helped me get on it. *"You hold on tight. I'll be over there watching."*

The music started and my horse galloped up, down, up, down as the carousel revolved. It was dizzying. But it was also exhilarating. A few minutes passed and then it stopped. When my father came to get me, I clung to the horse and said, *"Again! Again!"*

My father chuckled. *"All right. This time I'll tell them to go even faster,"* he said with a wink.

I rode the carousel six more times after that.

"Alba. Look." I blinked. Joaquim was pointing at someone through the window.

It was Marie. She was standing on a concrete ledge, waving at us. I waved back, unsure if she could see us. But it didn't matter. I smiled at her and then I smiled at Joaquim. The plane went around over the precipice again.

Whoa.

And it was at that very moment that I realized something.

The long flight across the ocean—the one that I'd been so unsure about.

It had brought me to a better place. A better life.

Mom had been right all along.

"¿Qué quieres tomar?" asked the concession-stand guy.

I grabbed my sandwich from him, eyeing the row of bottled drinks. "Um, Coke . . . Coca-Cola?" I replied.

He was about to hand me an ice-cold can of Coke, when on either side of me Joaquim and Marie simultaneously shouted.

"¡Espera!"

"¡Un momento, por favor!"

I glared at them. "What?"

Marie placed her hand on my arm, shaking her head as if I'd just committed the most atrocious mistake known to man. "Fanta," she said.

Joaquim nodded in agreement. "Fanta."

I shrugged and looked back at the concession-stand guy, who by then had his head tilted, impatiently. "Fanta, please," I said.

"¿Límon o naranja?"

With my elementary-school-level Spanish, I figured he was asking me if I wanted lemon or orange flavor. "Naran-*ha*," I attempted to say, the *ha* part sounding like I was laughing. *Ha-ha-ha.* Not anywhere near the way the concession-stand guy had said it—hard, the *h* sounding as if he was clearing his throat.

The concession-stand guy shook his head back and forth, and mumbled, "Guiri," under his breath as he handed me the can of Fanta. I wasn't sure what *guiri* was supposed to mean, but I could tell it wasn't something nice.

All of a sudden, Joaquim stepped real close to the counter and, with an angry frown, said, "Oye, tío . . ."

"Lo siento, lo siento." The concession-stand guy held his hands up and backed off.

I had no idea what the disagreement was about. Instinctively, though, I knew it must have been about me. My face got hotter and hotter as I watched them.

An awkward moment passed.

Marie gestured at the seating area. "Come on, I'm hungry."

Joaquim glared at the concession-stand guy one more time before taking me by the wrist toward an empty table with a white umbrella. It was situated near the Ferris wheel, over-looking the entire vista of Barcelona.

Once we were seated, I looked back and forth between the two of them. "So what was *that* all about?"

"*Guiri* . . . is an insult," said Joaquim, crossing his arms like he was still pissed off.

An insult.

Figures.

"*Insult* might be a bit of an exaggeration. It's more of a pejorative term for tourists, usually Americans or Brits who stick out like sore thumbs. You know, the ones who don't even make an effort to learn the local customs and language," explained Marie. "But that's not you, Alba. Not at all. That guy doesn't know what he's talking about."

It was obvious that she was trying to make me feel better.

I couldn't help but wonder if he was right, though.

Was I just a clueless American tourist?

Marie fiddled with her sketchbook. "Let's just forget about that guy, okay?"

"Vale." Joaquim nodded and uncrossed his arms.

"All right," I said.

It was silent for a minute. Our eyes dodged one another's as we tried but failed to avoid the awkwardness. Marie kept on fiddling with her sketchbook, so much that Joaquim's gaze fell on it. He reached forward with his finger until he almost touched its cover. "Can I take a look?" he asked.

I expected her to roll her eyes and snatch it away. She didn't, though. It was almost as if the guiri thing had softened her somehow.

"Sure," she replied, pushing it toward him.

Joaquim wiped his hands on his pants. When he was sure they were clean, he opened the sketchbook, studying each and every page with his humongous eyes. Marie pretended to look out at the view, while I pretended to read the ingredients of my Fanta. It was weird how quiet it was again.

Finally, Joaquim closed the sketchbook. "Your drawings are beautiful, Marie. Like Vincent Mahé but with softer colors."

"*You* know Vincent Mahé's work?" said Marie, leaning so far forward that her chest was on the table.

"Sí. Mi mamá, she has a collection of his books in her studio."

"Huh."

It was silent. I curled the tip of my finger onto the tab of my Fanta.

Pfffftttttt! Pop!

The orange soda fizzed out of the opening, spilling onto the table. I quickly took a sip.

Joaquim grinned.

So did Marie. "We forgot napkins." She got up and headed back to the concession stand.

That's when Joaquim scooted his chair closer to mine and whispered, "Alba . . . You think I am growing on her yet?"

I gazed at the seriousness in his expression—wide eyes,

creased forehead, lips parted in anticipation. It was so . . .
sweet.

"I think so, Joaquim."

He beamed like the Empire State Building on the Fourth
of July. "Good." And then he unwrapped his ham sandwich
and took a big bite.

Eighteen

When we got back home, Marie dashed off to the restaurant. "I have to help set up for dinner. Later!"

And then it was just Joaquim and me loafing around out front. It was dusk, but the streetlamps weren't on yet, so everything was cloaked in a gray veil of light. All the colors were duller and darker. The shadows hadn't yet appeared. I glanced up at the apartment windows; it was glowing bright from within, like a beacon signaling me to come home.

But I didn't want to.

Not yet.

"Thanks for today. It was fun," I said, stepping back and forth, side to side, wishing there was some pole or something I could lean on.

"You are welcome." Joaquim's smile was lopsided, as if it couldn't decide which way to curve. "You want to walk to the bakery with me?" he asked.

"Sure. Okay."

We strolled. It was weird, because I wasn't used to strolling. In New York City, people speed-walked. Anyone who dared walk slow would get the stink eye. In Barcelona, though, people took their time to breathe, to see things, to stop and take a rest if needed. All the shops and bars and restaurants were pretty busy, but it wasn't the kind of busy that was frantic. Men and women were seated at sidewalk cafés, drinking glasses of wine accompanied by little plates of olives and cheeses. Kids still out and about were playing by the fountains, hopping on and off benches, while their parents window-shopped.

"So . . . ," I muttered under my breath.

It felt like I should say something, but I didn't know what.

Suddenly, though, I heard a song. It was faint at first. I stopped walking and listened.

Ch-ch-ch-ch-changes . . .

It was him. David Bowie. His voice was floating from an alleyway.

"Do you hear that?" I said to Joaquim.

He looked confused for a minute. But then he tucked his long hair behind his ear and tuned in to the sound. "Bowie . . . ¡Genial! Come on!"

We ran toward the singing. It got louder as we approached an unassuming bar. The exterior was black, adorned with red roses, and through the window I could see a chandelier, upside-down lamps, and weird-looking murals of masked people.

Ch-ch-changes . . .

It was quiet, except for the song and our breathing. Joaquim and I stood there listening to the lyrics about accepting change and getting older and youth and alienation and finding your identity in this crazy world we live in.

I'd always loved that song. But it had never taken hold of me like it did at that moment. It felt like a sign from the universe, a period at the end of a never-ending sentence, a deep breath after having held it for a very long time.

Everything I had inside—all the sadness, all the rage, all the frustration, all the pain, all the joy—came out all at once. My breath heaved. The tears rolled down my face, dropping from my chin to my shirt.

I should have been ashamed.

Crying is undignified.

It wasn't, though.

I *wasn't* ashamed. Not anymore.

I gazed at Joaquim through the wetness in my eyes. For some reason I expected him to look all embarrassed and uncomfortable, like most teenage boys would. But instead, he moved closer and waited for me, like a tree with a mossy trunk inviting you to sit down and lean on it. I crumpled against his chest and cried some more.

Eventually, the song ended.

I tilted my head up high, so I could see his face. "I'm sorry. It's just a lot has happened. You know? And David Bowie . . . This song . . . it . . . it . . ."

"You must not explain, Alba . . . I understand. This is why I *love* music so much."

"Thanks." I pulled away and wiped my cheeks with the back of my hand.

Joaquim stuck his arm out. "We should go. Because they might think we are trying to sneak into the bar, no?"

"Right." I giggled.

We looped arms and skipped down the street like a couple of clowns.

When we got to the bakery, we jostled past all the customers taking advantage of the end-of-day fifty-percent-off bread. Toni was behind the counter bagging loaves and handing out change. Despite the chaos, he managed to smile and greet each and every person by name. Without saying a word, Joaquim jumped into action, taking over the bagging as Toni manned the register.

Me, on the other hand, I did nothing. I watched them, father and son working together. Despite whatever strained relationship they had, at least they had one. There was a chemistry, a choreography, an invisible string that connected them.

Something I definitely didn't have with either of my parents.

I breathed in the intoxicating smell of bread. It calmed me. It made me feel like I was meant to be there.

The paper bags crinkled. The loaves slid in and hit the bottom with a thud. The register dinged.

The old ladies said, "Gracias," or "Buenas noches."

And Toni waved and replied, "Hasta luego, señora," adding each one's name.

Finally, the bakery was empty. Almost all the bread was gone.

"Gracias, mi hijo." Toni pulled Joaquim closer and hugged him from the side.

Joaquim didn't say anything. Not one word. He just grinned and fell into the embrace with a faint blush on his cheeks.

"Alba, would you like to join us for an early dinner? I have some cream of tomato soup in the back, and we can make some grilled cheese sandwiches with this leftover bread," said Toni, lifting the lone batard from the display case.

"Oh, um . . ."

It was tempting. But I'd already hijacked the excursion to El Tibidabo. I wasn't about to steal any more of their father-son bonding time. Joaquim shot me a pleading gaze from across the room. I shuffled my feet for a second or two.

"Nah. I should get back to Abuela Lola . . . I'm sure she's expecting me," I said.

"Of course. But you'll come back on Monday, ¿sí? I think it's time you learned how to make your own dough from scratch."

I stopped shuffling and looked right into Toni's smiling eyes. "Really?"

"Really."

I ran to the counter, hopped over, and hugged him. "Thank you, thank you! Yes. I'll be here. At the usual time."

"Good."

My shoes dropped back onto the floor. I glanced at Joaquim. He was stiff and awkward like a coat rack in the middle of an empty room. "You wanna walk me out?" I asked him.

"Sure." He came around to where I was standing.

"Adios, Toni," I said.

"Adéu . . . That's in Catalan. You're going to have to learn it one of these days," he said with a wink.

Great. As if having to learn Spanish wasn't bad enough.

I walked to the door and then outside, with Joaquim close behind. At the entrance I turned and faced him. "Thanks again. For everything."

His cheeks were blushing again. "Anytime."

"Okay, bye . . . Adéu." I trudged off, slowly. But I could still feel his eyes on the back of my skull, watching me.

"Alba!"

I paused and swiveled around. "Yeah?"

"Will you help? With my band?" Joaquim had that puppy-dog expression again.

I frowned. "But I don't know anything about starting a band."

"But you know music. And you feel it . . . here," he said, grasping his heart.

That much was true.

I didn't want to disappoint him.

And besides, it might be fun.

I inhaled and then mumbled, "I can try."

"Perfecto."

I ran off before he could utter another word, because the last thing I wanted to do was change my mind.

I was back in my room trying to decide if it was too early to get into my pajamas, and if Abuela Lola would care if I wore them for dinner, when I heard a sound through my open window.

"*Psssttt!* Alba!"

I stuck my head out and spotted Marie.

She was looking up. "Alba!" It was almost as if she was whispering and screaming at the same time.

"Yeah?" I shouted back.

She waved me down.

"Okay, okay. Give me a minute!" I tossed my pajamas on my bed and jogged along the hallway. "Just going to see Marie for a bit," I said to Abuela Lola, who was busy cooking something up in the kitchen.

"Bla-di-bla-di-bla," she mumbled back. Whatever she'd said didn't sound all that important. So I kept on going.

By the time I got outside, Marie was seated on a bench, tapping her fingers impatiently. "Finally," she said, exhaling as if she'd been waiting forever.

I plopped down next to her. "Finally, what?"

"Finally, I get to hear what happened after I left."

"What do you mean?" I asked.

"With you and Joaquim . . ."

"Me and Joaquim?" I raised my eyebrows.

Marie giggled and poked me with her elbow. "I think he likes you."

"Me?"

"Yeah, you. Is there another *you* on this bench?"

I scrunched my nose and leaned my back straight against the wooden bench. It was only then that I realized how crowded the alleyways were. The throngs almost seemed as if they were following one another, like a bunch of ants carrying breadcrumbs single-file.

"Where are all these people going?" I asked.

Marie followed my gaze. "Back to their hotels and bed-and-breakfasts and Airbnbs. They'll drop off all their shopping bags, shower, rest, and then come out again for dinner and drinks. It's like this every summer."

"Huh."

There was a moment, sort of quiet, but not. And then Marie exhaled again. "So?"

I glanced at her and squinted. "There's no *so*. Nothing. Nada. Joaquim and I just hung out for a bit and then went to El Rincón del Pan."

Even though everything I'd said was true, my cheeks felt warmer than usual. I mean, sure, I left out the part about the bar and the David Bowie song, and Joaquim comforting me right smack in the middle of the street. But that wasn't exactly a *so*, was it?

"Really?" She didn't look convinced.

"Well, he did ask me to help with his band."

"Aha!" Marie bounced off her seat with a grin on her face.

I scowled. "It's nothing. I swear."

"We'll see."

I racked my brain for something clever to say. A retort. The last snappy word. But I couldn't think of anything. So I went back to leaning on the bench and crossed my arms over my chest. All I could do was watch the ant people navigate the streets in front of me.

We'll see . . .

Marie's words echoed in my ears, over and over again.

Nineteen

It was way too early. I could tell, because the sunlight barely penetrated through the curtains. Maybe I should have closed my eyes and gone back to sleep. I'd stayed up late, playing "Changes" over and over again. I couldn't stop thinking about Marie and Joaquim and El Tibidabo and the bar in the alley where I'd cried with Joaquim's arms wrapped around me.

We'll see.

My cheeks got all warm and tingly.

There was no way I could go back to sleep.

Especially with the pigeons cooing outside. Like a billion of them.

I sat up. The mattress creaked under my butt.

Knock. Knock.

The door opened. Abuela Lola's eyeball peeked through. "Ah. You're awake," she said, stepping inside.

"Unfortunately."

She opened the curtains and then turned around, her face

brighter than the sun. "Well, if you're up for it, Eduardo and Manny have invited you to Els Encants."

"Els Encants?"

"It's Barcelona's biggest flea market. Not to be missed," she said, peeling the quilt off me.

As soon as I heard her say *flea market*, my muscles tensed like those of a cat about to pounce. I *loved* thrift stores and flea markets and junkyards—basically any place with lots of old stuff. Secondhand objects somehow felt alive to me. The little spots and cracks told stories, the faded patina from people's hands—I tried to imagine who they were.

Mom always said old stuff reeked of dust and mothballs and death.

And my dad, well, he preferred everything to be new, shiny, and expensive.

Maybe that's why they got rid of me.

I wasn't new anymore. I definitely wasn't shiny. And maybe I reeked, too.

I sighed and then hopped off my bed. "I'll get dressed."

Abuela Lola smiled. "Good. There's toast and coffee in the kitchen."

Sara Montiel, Eduardo and Manny's tiny frog car, zipped through the streets. I had no idea how Eduardo did it. He was like a Formula 1 race-car driver. At times he went so fast, Sara would glide over a bump, flying for a brief moment before landing gracefully on four wheels.

After driving through what seemed like miles and miles of historic architecture and glassy structures and fountains and statues jutting from stone plazas, we passed a weird-looking building—tall, with multicolored windows that reminded me of fish scales, and a shape that, well, um, was sort of elongated like a standing up cucumber.

"That's the Torre Glòries. Isn't it fabulous?" said Manny.

Fabulous wasn't really the word for a cucumber-shaped building. I stared at it through the car window. "It's . . . interesting," I finally replied.

Eduardo guffawed from the driver's seat. "You can say it. It looks like un pajarito. A *very* big one."

"A bird?" I said with a frown. I mean, my Spanish was atrocious, but I could have sworn that *pajarito* meant "bird."

Manny leaned over and whispered to me, "He means a penis."

"Oh."

I imagined I must have resembled one of those shocked cartoon characters with eyeballs popping out of their sockets. Manny covered his mouth with his hand and giggled.

All of a sudden, Sara Montiel lurched to a stop. Eduardo pulled into a teensy parking space, and we got out. Or, rather, I crawled from the back seat and inched my scrunched-up body through the door.

How on earth would Eduardo and Manny fit all the

vintage bargains they planned to buy into the Matchbox-car-sized trunk?

I stretched my limbs and then twisted myself in the direction where they were headed.

Whoa.

Els Encants wasn't what I expected. There was a modern three-floor, open-air structure with a roof that could have passed for a giant sheet of wavy tinfoil. Tons of people were milling around in all directions. I'd never seen anything like it.

"¡Vámonos!" Eduardo said as Manny gestured for me to catch up.

The closer I got, the more junk I could see—plain old junk, junk with potential, and good junk. The stalls held a variety of artfully displayed antiques, glass bottles, mirrors with age spots, piles of dusty books and toys, vintage clothing hanging from racks and old dress forms, and random crap like reclaimed wood planks.

I gawked at Manny, who was fanning himself with a lace fan.

"How are you supposed to look through everything?" I asked. "There's just so much stuff."

Manny shook his head. "You're not. That would be impossible."

I scanned all the stalls, confused.

Eduardo touched my shoulder and winked. "We know where the good stuff is."

"Correct. We're sukis with several of the sellers here . . . They know what we want."

"Sukis?"

Manny grinned. "It's Tagalog for 'regular customers,'" he explained. "But don't worry about us. You go wherever you want. We can meet back at the entrance in two hours."

I nodded. "Okay. Thanks."

Manny stretched his arm out like a dancer and waved. I watched his mint-green T-shirt and Eduardo's striped shorts and straw hat disappear through the crowd.

I had twenty-five euros to spend, thanks to Abuela Lola.

I wandered inside, following the tide of bodies. Stall after stall after stall. I was overwhelmed. There was so much of everything, it was hard to concentrate. Then a pile of cookbooks caught my eye. They were arranged on a table next to some enameled pots and pans. There was a book on how to cook tapas, with what looked like tomato smeared on the cover. Another book with ratty pages about paellas. And one on desserts, called *The Baking Bible*, which sounded too serious to me.

"Hola, nena. ¿Te interesan los libros de cocinar?" asked the old man minding the stall.

I glanced at him *and* his mustache. There was no avoiding it. He wore a bright yellow Hawaiian shirt with parrots on it, but all I could see was his perfectly waxed mustache, twisting on his cheeks like a pair of curly fries.

"Uh, no se . . . I—I don't . . ."

"American?" he asked with a smile.

My stomach lurched.

Was he going to call me a guiri?

Ugh.

Why did it feel like there was an American flag etched on my forehead?

I glanced back down at the books, hoping he would stop talking to me.

That's when I saw it, tucked underneath a cast-iron frying pan. Another cookbook, on its spine spelled out in bold letters *Tartine Bread.*

I suddenly didn't care about being called a guiri or having an imaginary red-white-and-blue flag on my forehead. "Excuse me. Can I look at that book?" I said, pointing at it.

Mustachio Man dusted the book off and handed it to me. "It is rebajas . . . sale. I give good price."

I flipped through the pages, glancing at the recipes and photos of bread bakers and sourdough loaves of all shapes and sizes. It was practically brand-new. The text was in English, too.

I met Mustachio Man's gaze, trying to look indifferent. "How much?"

"Sixteen euros," he said.

That was more than half my money.

I snapped the book shut. "Ten."

"Fifteen."

"Twelve."

"Sol."

I grinned, guessing he meant *sold.* I gave him the money,

and he wrapped the book in brown paper and twine and then handed it to me.

"Gracias, nena," he said.

"Gracias." I waved and jumped back into the crowd.

I passed a stall filled with knickknacks. Another stall with rows and rows of old dolls with different hairstyles and outfits. It was as if they were watching me. There was one in particular, with lifelike emerald-green eyes. The doll had coiled ringlets of golden hair, but her porcelain face was so badly cracked, I feared she would fall apart at any moment.

Creepy.

I hurried past.

Dolls—just the thought of them made my arm hairs stand on end. When I was really little, my father would bring me home a doll every time he went on a business trip. Baby dolls. Barbie dolls. Girl dolls with braided yarn hair. I hated all of them.

After a while, he stopped buying me dolls. In fact, he stopped buying me much of anything.

I paused in front of a stall overflowing with vintage clothes and accessories. Something caught my eye. Tucked into the corner was a female half-mannequin, an antique one made out of resin or some sort of plaster. She had a head of coiffed auburn hair and cornflower-blue eyes. Around her neck was a silk scarf in shades of red, orange, and blue that reminded me of flames, the kind that would flicker from an Olympic torch. A warm breeze blew past, and the scarf fluttered, making the mannequin look like a goddess.

It made me think of Mom.

The tears were trying to squirm out. I closed my eyes, pressing my lids down hard.

I'm not going to cry.

"¿Estás bien?"

I opened my eyes. A woman dressed as if she belonged in an old Hollywood movie was peering at me.

"Bien, bien," I mumbled.

Her wine-colored lips curved into a smile. "¿Te gusta algo?" she asked, sweeping her manicured hands over the display.

I pointed at the flame scarf.

She followed my gaze. "Ah. Sí, es precioso."

It was probably the most beautiful silk scarf I'd ever seen.

"Um. How much?"

"Para tí, diez euros," she replied with a wink.

Diez was ten. *Okay.* Doable. I didn't even want to haggle.

I nodded and reached for the back pocket of my jeans to grab my wallet. But my pocket was flat. Empty. My heart skipped a beat. I nervously patted all my other pockets. Nothing. Nada.

Where's my wallet?

Did I leave it somewhere?

I glanced at the lady and mumbled, "Be right back." And then I ran to the stall where I bought the bread book. But when I questioned Mustachio Man, he just shrugged like he hadn't seen it or like he hadn't understood or like he didn't have a care in the world.

Shoot.

What now?

I whirled around and around, trying to find Manny and Eduardo. A couple of minutes passed and, finally, I spotted a flash of mint green by a display of silver and glass trinkets. I hurried past the crowd, trying not to bump into anyone or anything.

"Manny!" I shouted as soon as he was within earshot.

When he saw me, his brow furrowed. "Alba, are you okay?"

"My wallet . . ." I stared at him blankly and touched my back pocket with my hand. "It's gone."

Manny tapped his forehead. "Oh, sweetie. It's my fault. I should have warned you."

"Warned me? About what?"

"The pickpockets. They're all over the place. You should always be aware and keep your wallet and valuables some-where safe," he said, gesturing at his zipped-up tote bag.

"Oh." I didn't know what else to say. My face was numb, and so were my fingers and feet. It was a weird feeling. I felt weak. Powerless. Like I'd been violated even though only thirteen euros, an old school ID, and an empty MetroCard had been taken from me.

God, I am such a guiri.

Even the pickpockets can tell.

"I'm so sorry, Alba. Here—" Manny unzipped his bag, took out his wallet, and handed me a twenty-euro bill.

I stared at it and shook my head. "I—I can't take that."

Manny shoved it into my palm. "Of course you can."

"But I can't pay you back."

"Oh, you will," he said with a wink. "From time to time, Eduardo and I go out of town, and you'll be in charge of watering our plants and whatnot."

"Thanks." I tried to smile even though I was still shaken up, embarrassed, humiliated, you name it. Then an image of Abuela Lola flashed in my mind. It was her money that had been stolen. Her money that she'd given me. "Manny, you won't tell Abuela Lola, will you? I wouldn't want her to worry . . ."

He winked again. "Tell her what?"

"Thanks." I sighed with relief.

"Now, go find yourself a treasure or two," he said, squeezing my shoulders.

A treasure.

The scarf.

Mom's scarf.

I held the money tight in one fist, tucked the cookbook under my arm, and marched back into the crowd, determined.

I may have been a tourist, a visitor, an outsider.

But I *wasn't* a guiri.

Twenty

I held on to my shopping bag as Sara Montiel halted in front of Abuela Lola's building.

Manny opened the door and hopped out. "Alba, sweetie, will you help me carry some things upstairs?"

"Sure." I hoisted myself out and followed him to the trunk.

"Okay. You take this and this," he said, passing me a canvas tote and a wooden crate filled with stuff. "And I'll take this, this, and this."

As soon as he slammed the trunk shut, Eduardo stuck his head out of his window and said, "Os veo en el restaurante." And then he drove off around the corner.

The restaurant. Lunch. My stomach grumbled.

We shuffled into the building, the packages teetering in our arms like wobbly Jenga blocks. It was even worse in the elevator, which jerked every time it started and stopped.

"I hope there's nothing breakable," I blurted out after

leaving the elevator and tripping on an uneven tile in the hallway.

"It's mostly jewelry. But there are a couple of art deco perfume bottles in that box you're holding," said Manny.

I gulped and tightened my grip. When we got to his and Eduardo's apartment door, Manny managed to unlock it without dropping a single item.

"Welcome to La Casa de Tesoros . . . The House of Treasures," he said, pushing the door open with his foot.

For a second, the sunlight blinded me. But then my vision adjusted and I saw it all. The treasures. Eduardo and Manny's apartment was like a mini-museum, except in between the antiques and artifacts and artwork, there were sofas and chairs and tables and a ton of houseplants. It was eclectic, modern, yet chock-full of personality. Unlike my parents' apartment back home in New York, which was so stark it looked as if nobody lived there. Except for my bedroom, of course, which might as well have been another planet—a messy one.

Meow. Purr. Purr. Purr.

There was an orange tabby cat at my feet.

"Oh, that's Rita Hayworth. She found us in an alley a couple of years ago and followed us all the way home," said Manny, picking the cat up and carrying her like a baby. "You can be her human when we're out of town. It's a tough job—she's *very* demanding."

Purr. Purr. Purr.

"She's cute."

Manny frowned. "She's not cute. She's *fabulous*."

I giggled. "Okay. You're right. She's *fabulous*."

"Come. I'll show you where you can put that." He gestured to the crate in my arms.

I followed him down a hallway with a black-and-white tile floor; it was like the one in the foyer, except the tiles had an intricate pattern, almost like the hearts and spades on playing cards. Covering the cobalt-blue walls were framed paintings and photos of faraway places I didn't recognize.

"Here we are." Manny opened a carved wooden door that looked sort of Indian or Moroccan.

"Whoa."

"I know. It's beautiful, isn't it?"

We lingered at the entrance. Manny cupped his face with his hands and stared at the room. I could practically see the heart emojis floating from his eyeballs.

"What is all this stuff?" I asked, gawking at the walls covered with metal trees and plants and flowers, at the ceiling with all sorts of winged creatures hanging as if they were flying through stars made of crystal, at the glass cabinets filled with priceless-looking collector's items.

"It's a lifetime of treasures. Hence, The House of Treasures," he said with a dramatic wave. "I used to work in theater and film, doing costumes and set design. And after I retired, Eduardo and I started traveling, collecting treasures from here and there . . . Some we sell at our antique shop.

And some we keep here—we call it our Sala de Curiosidades. Our Room of Curiosities."

"I've never seen anything like it."

Manny took the wooden crate from my arms and placed it on the floor. "Eduardo likes to joke that we're one step away from becoming hoarders, but there is a method, a beauty to this madness. Don't you think?"

"Yeah. Uh-huh." I didn't know what else to say. I was too enraptured by it all, studying every single thing I could lay my eyes on.

"You see this?" Manny tugged on my shirt.

In one of the cabinets, there was a huge glass jar filled with eyeballs and clear liquid. I gaped at them. "Tell me those aren't real," I said.

Manny chortled. "They are! I bought them from a science museum in Italy that was closing down. They were part of the set I did for a theater production of Mary Shelley's *Frankenstein*."

"That's just—"

"And over here," he said, gesturing to a narrow wall, "is my button collection. I currently have ten thousand. It was Eduardo's idea to hammer small nails into the wall and attach the buttons to the heads."

I didn't even know button collecting was a thing. My gaze skipped from button to button to button. They were almost like tiny pieces of art, or tiny jewels, suspended from the wall. It was kind of amazing, actually.

"You should seriously consider charging people tickets to come in here," I said half-jokingly.

"*Never!* This place is only for special people. Those who can appreciate its uniqueness. We even have a closet of costumes for loaning. Anytime a friend needs an outfit for a party, they come here."

Another door opened. Inside was a walk-in closet with racks and racks of costumes and shoes and hats, ranging from the traditional to the absurd. Manny caught me eyeing a pair of sparkly red platform boots.

He squealed. "Eeeeee! I had those specially made for a drag-queen musical production of *The Wizard of* Oz. It. Was. Outrageous!"

I tried to picture that in my head. A drag-queen version of Dorothy. God, I wish I could have seen it for real.

"Anyway. You're welcome to the costume closet anytime you want. Your abuela is like a mother to me . . . So I suppose that makes us family," he said.

For some reason my insides clenched, and the back of my throat pulsed like my heart was trying to escape from my chest.

"Thank you," I said softly.

Manny rubbed my back with his hand. "Come on. The smell of fried rice is making me hungry."

Restaurante Chino was bustling. It was that overlap between the tourist lunchtime and the Spaniard lunchtime, so there was a chaotic mix of locals and travelers from different countries. I could hear the twang of American accents; the speedy rhythm of Mandarin, or maybe Cantonese; and a couple of other languages I didn't recognize.

There weren't any tables available yet, so Eduardo and Manny stood outside enjoying the fresh air while I loitered inside by the entrance with Marie and Abuela Lola as they greeted customers. Marie was also helping out with seating, while her mom hurried in and out of the kitchen, making sure orders were expedited.

"Thank you for coming," said Abuela Lola, smiling, to a group who'd just finished their meal.

Busy babbling with one another, the customers ignored her and walked out.

"Well, *that* was rude," I said under my breath.

Abuela Lola sighed. "It's just part of the business, Alba . . . Customer service with a smile."

Humph.

I *was* used to people back home being rude, with the classic New York City attitude. But still, it seemed different when someone was doing it to your own grandmother. Whatever happened to respecting your elders? Even *I* knew about that.

Marie wandered back from the dining room without a drop of sweat on her forehead. "They're just cleaning up a table, so I'll seat you in a couple of minutes."

"How about you? Aren't you going to eat?" I asked her.

"No. I had the staff breakfast before service started. That will tide me over for a while."

"Oh."

Marie sidled over. "We could go for ice cream later . . . and continue our conversation. *Wink-wink.*"

I glared at her. She laughed like a hyena.

That's when the door opened, showering the entrance with blinding beams of sunlight.

Marie grabbed a pile of menus and smirked at me. "I'm going to seat these people, and then we'll see what else I can pry out of you."

We'll see.

Humph.

I was about to tell her to mind her own business, when I heard a gasp on the other side of me. I turned. Abuela Lola had her hand over her mouth, eyes blinking as if she was seeing a ghost. The rings on her fingers glimmered, the stones reflecting on the walls like some sort of disco-ball effect.

"Abuela Lola?" I whispered.

She didn't react. I followed her gaze. Slowly. For a second, I couldn't tell who she was staring at. But then the person stepped inside, just a little, and it hit me.

Mom.

No. It can't be.

But it was.

Mom's eyes were wide open—spooked almost. And for the first time in a long time, her hair was pulled back, away from her face and neck. She had bruises. Lots of them. And a fresh wound on her lip. Her body seemed thin, her white cotton blouse and jeans looking as though they were hanging from a clothesline.

I thought of that porcelain doll I'd seen at Els Encants, which, with one wrong move, might shatter.

I couldn't believe it.

She really *was* there, in front of me.

Yet she wasn't looking at me. Her gaze was stuck on Abuela Lola.

Suddenly, she murmured something—but I couldn't hear it. Again. A bit louder.

"I—I left."

That's when it happened. Her face crumpled. Her body drooped. She held on to the doorway as the tears gushed.

"I left . . . I left . . . I left," she repeated over and over.

Abuela Lola's skirt swished against her ankles as she walked toward Mom. When she was near, she stopped, tilted her head, and reached out with her hands. "You didn't leave, Isabel . . . You came home."

Mom let go of the doorway.

Abuela Lola scooped her into her arms. "You're home, Isabel. You're finally home."

I didn't know what to feel, what to do, what to say. I should have been happy. But I was numb. The longer I stood there watching them embrace, the worse I felt. Just when things were starting to look up for me—a new home, new friends, a newfound purpose in life—she showed up.

Mom was going to ruin *everything*.

Before anyone could say anything to me, before anything else could happen, I ran.

"Alba!" I ignored Marie.

"Alba!" I ignored Abuela Lola.

"Alba!" I ignored Eduardo and Manny.

I kept on running.

Because that's what I always did.

Twenty-One

I ended up at El Rincón del Pan. I wasn't thinking, but
my feet just led me there, as if they knew what I needed.

Toni.

At the back entrance, I paused to catch my breath.

Huuuuhhhh . . . Huuuuhhhh . . .

That's when I realized my face and neck were soaking wet
with tears. There was clear snot leaking from my nose.

I was a mess.

This whole thing was a mess.

I slid down onto the floor and curled up against my knees.
The tears wouldn't stop. So I sat there and kept at it, whimpering like some sort of stray, wounded animal.

"I left . . . I left . . . I left."

I kept on hearing Mom's voice.

But it wasn't until I was sitting there by myself next to the
dumpster that I realized what exactly those words meant.

She'd finally done it.

She'd left my father.

After all those years. All those fights. All those cuts and bruises.

"Alba, is that you?" A groggy-looking Toni peeked through the back window.

I sniffled and wiped the snot as best as I could. "Yeah."

The door opened, and out walked Toni with a frown as deep as the Grand Canyon. He didn't say anything. He bent down, pulled me up, and then half carried me to his office. I sank onto the sofa.

"You want to talk about it?" said Toni. His frown was still there, but the rest of him looked calm and soothing.

"My mom," I mumbled.

"Isabel?"

I nodded. "Yes. She—she's here."

"In Barcelona?"

I nodded again.

"Did something happen? Is she all right?" The calm and soothing part of him was gone. Toni leaned forward in his seat, muscles and limbs tensed.

I looked away and stared at my shoes. "She says that she left my father."

"Oh." It was Toni's turn to stare at his shoes. After a minute, calm once more, he glanced back up and said, "Are you okay?"

"I don't know. It's just . . . unexpected, I guess."

"Do you want to be alone? You can stay here as long as you need to," he said, moving as if he was about to stand.

"No." I scrambled to the edge of the sofa. "Maybe . . . Can you show me how to start the dough from scratch?"

"Are you sure?"

"Yeah. I need something to keep my mind from . . . I don't know. I just want to make some bread."

Toni breathed deep, then smiled. "Then let's go make some bread, Alba."

I followed him into the kitchen. Just being there already made me feel better.

"Bien. Why don't we start with a basic sourdough boule," said Toni.

"Okay."

He plucked a large jar with a bubbly white blob in it. "This is Jabba, my whole wheat starter."

"As in Jabba the Hutt?"

"The one and only."

I laughed.

Toni got the kitchen scale, placed a large measuring cup on top, and turned it on. "First, we weigh out the room-temperature water. For this loaf, we will use three hundred and fifty grams." He poured water from a pitcher until the number on the scale hit 350. "Then we will add fifty grams of Jabba." *Plonk. Plonk. Plonk.* Blobs of Jabba the starter dropped into the water. When the number hit 400, he took the measuring cup off the scale and whisked Jabba into the water. "You got it?" he asked.

"Yup."

Next, he placed a bowl on top of the scale and grabbed two different bags of flour. "You can measure out the flour." He handed me a metal scoop. "We need four hundred and fifty grams of bread flour, and fifty grams of whole wheat."

I took the scoop and carefully measured out both flours until the scale read 500 grams.

"Perfecto," said Toni, whisking the two flours together. "Now you have to pour the liquid into the flour and squish it all together until all the dried bits are gone."

I did as he said, carefully pouring the Jabba water into the bowl with the flour in it. Then he handed me a wooden stick.

I frowned. "A stick? Shouldn't I use my hands?"

"You can. But it is *very* sticky right now."

"Ah." I poked the stick into the bowl and mixed until it was a shaggy mess. "Is that what it's supposed to look like?"

Toni covered the bowl with a large kitchen towel. "Don't worry. It doesn't look like dough now, but after a one-hour autolyse, we'll add the salt, do several stretch-and-folds, and you'll see. It will be as smooth as a baby's bottom," he said with a chuckle.

All of a sudden, my stomach grumbled.

"You must be hungry," said Toni.

"Starving."

He went to a rack and grabbed a loaf of bread and a knife. "Well, why don't I make us some sandwiches?"

"Yes, please."

By the time my first-ever made-from-scratch sourdough boule was done, it was four in the morning. After the autolyse, which was the stage where the flour absorbs the water, there were a couple of hours of stretch-and-folds; several hours of bulk fermentation; the final proof, wherein the shaped dough is supposed to rise; and then finally the baking in a *very* hot oven.

It may have taken forever, but not once did I think about how upset I was with Mom for barging in on my fresh start. When we weren't busy making the bread, Toni would distract me with sandwiches and tea and funny stories from Joaquim's childhood. It was only when I was standing outside Abuela Lola's apartment door, holding the paper-wrapped bread boule, that my stomach-wrenching dread returned.

Mom was somewhere on the other side of the door.

What would I say to her?

I lingered in the shadows with my hand in my pocket, tracing the shapes and grooves of my sunflower key chain. There was no avoiding it. I had to go in there.

Clink. Clink.

I cringed at the noise my keys made. I cringed some more when the bolt snapped, the sound making it seem as if I'd used a hammer to unlock the door. I closed the door gently and tiptoed inside. The air smelled of stale coffee. It was quiet.

I guessed they were still asleep.

Phew.

Thank god.

I could avoid the awkwardness for a while longer.

I snuck down the hallway.

Shhh, Alba. Don't. Wake. Anyone. Up.

But then I heard something. Whimpering. It was muffled, like someone was crying against a pillow. It was coming from inside Abuela Lola's study/second guest bedroom. I staggered, leaning against the opposite wall. My breathing shallow. Fast.

Mom was in there crying her eyes out.

Why?

My father wasn't worth all those tears.

She was finally free of him.

I only wished she'd done it sooner.

But then again, if she had, maybe I would never have been sent away. And coming to Barcelona was the best thing that had ever happened to me. At least that much she'd gotten right.

Silence.

The whimpering stopped. There was a creak of a mattress. My heart seized in my chest. I wasn't ready. I scampered to my room. I could figure it all out later.

Rest first, Alba.

I fell on my bed. The loaf crunched in my grasp. I hugged it.

I was so proud of that loaf of bread.

I couldn't remember another time I'd ever been as proud. Well, maybe that one time in first grade. I'd come home from school with a clay bowl I'd made. I had painted a greenish-blue glaze on it, because my mom's favorite color was celadon. I was so proud of it—proud and excited to give it to her. The bus dropped me off. The doorman greeted me. The elevator dinged. *Up, up, up.* The apartment door swung open.

"Mom!"

But nobody answered. I heard voices. I shuffled past the entryway. The voices were coming from my father's study. I inched toward it. And then I saw them.

Mom was shoved against the bookcase with my father grasping her neck. The veins bulged on his arm. She was choking, grasping for air. Her eyes wandered. They found me.

Crash.

The bowl slipped from my fingers and shattered. So did my heart.

Twenty-Two

"Good morning." I waltzed into the kitchen like it was a same-old, same-old kind of day.

"Buenos días, Alba," said Abuela Lola, tight-lipped.

Mom was sitting there in a trance. She had on one of Abuela Lola's nightgowns—a billowy white cotton sleeping dress. Cupped in both hands was a mug of steaming coffee. Her gaze was fixed on the steam, like she was hypnotized.

I unwrapped my bread boule and placed it on a wooden cutting board, slicing it how Abuela Lola had taught me. I couldn't help smiling just a bit. The loaf was perfectly crusty, and the crumb's holes were uniform—open, but not so open that the butter and jam would fall through.

"Here, let me toast those for you," said Abuela Lola. She grabbed the slices and popped them into the toaster.

I sat and waited. If it had just been me and Abuela Lola, we would have been chatting about this and that by now.

But the awkwardness of Mom's presence had sucked all the chatter from the room.

The bread slices popped up. Abuela Lola arranged them on a plate, and then she poured me some coffee. "A comer," she said. And then she took a piece of toast, slathered some butter on it, and then drizzled honey on top. When she was done, she put it on a plate in front of Mom. "Come, Isabel . . . Es tu favorito."

Mom didn't react. Abuela Lola gingerly took the coffee cup from her grasp and replaced it with the toast. "Come, Isabel," she repeated as if she was talking to a child.

Finally, Mom blinked. She took a small bite of toast and chewed. After she swallowed, her vision seemed to focus, as if the jolt of honey had awakened her. "Mi favorito," she whispered.

I had no idea that toast with butter and honey was her favorite. It was basically carbs with fat and sugar. As far as I knew, she didn't eat any of those. But maybe she did. Maybe that bread-loving, concert-going version of my mom *had* existed after all. I'd heard the stories from Abuela Lola and Toni, but to me those stories might as well have been about Bigfoot and the Loch Ness monster.

I *so* wanted to believe.

I couldn't, though. Not unless I saw *her* for myself—the old version of *her*.

Ahhh . . . huhhh . . . I breathed deeply, trying to shove those thoughts, those feelings aside.

What's the point?

She's just going to disappoint me, like she always does.

Sigh.

Crunch.

I bit into my own bread, which I'd covered with slices of Tetilla—a delicious cheese that Abuela Lola had introduced me to.

"Alba."

I looked up from my coffee. Mom was gawking at me, like she was seeing me for the first time since arriving.

"Hi," I said softly.

"You—you look . . . h-happy," she said, stumbling on her words. She took another bite of her toast.

"I made that bread," I blurted out.

Mom stopped chewing. The bread—she studied it for a long moment. "I—I didn't know you liked to bake. It's good . . ."

Abuela Lola cleared her throat. I'd almost forgotten she was there. "It's wonderful, Isabel. Alba has been spending a lot of time with Toni at his bakery." Abuela Lola pulled a chair out, then sat down with an overly cheery smile.

"Toni?" Mom frowned.

For a second, I could have sworn that a spark lit up in her eyes.

For some reason it made me angry, frustrated. Why didn't she have *that* kind of spark in her eye when she looked at me?

I bolted off my seat. "Yes. Toni. Remember him? Your best friend? Maybe if you'd bothered to call me, you would have known what I was up to this whole time," I spat out.

I was expecting Abuela Lola to gasp, protest, whatever. But all she did was pucker her lips even tighter.

"You're right. I'm sorry." The hushed words slipped out of Mom's almost unmoving mouth.

My chest ached. I shouldn't have said what I'd said. But I had so much pent-up anger. I'd been holding it in for years, allowing it to fester, to grow.

Ring. Ring. Ring.

The kitchen phone. Abuela Lola started toward it.

"I'll get it," I said, practically diving across the room. I wanted a way out. No, I *needed* a way out of the conversation. "Hello. Hola," I said into the mouthpiece.

"Hola, buenos días. ¿Puedo hablar con Alba, por favor?"

There was only one person I knew with a deep yet dorky voice.

Joaquim.

"Um. Hi. It's me," I replied.

"Ah. ¡Hola!"

Even though I couldn't see him, I could tell he was grinning.

"Hope you do not mind that I am calling you."

"It's fine. But, um, how did you get this number?"

"My father. I told him you agreed to help with my band. You will help, no?" he said, all squeaky.

"No. I mean, yes. Of course I'll help."

"Good. Are you free today?"

From the corner of my eye, I glanced at Mom pecking at her toast like a little bird, and at Abuela Lola twirling her rings on her fingers.

The last thing I wanted was to be cooped up in the apartment with both of them.

"Yeah. I'm free."

"Where should we meet?"

Hmm. How am I supposed to help him with his band?

Think. Think. Think.

"Alba?" said Joaquim.

"Oh, sorry. I was spacing out."

Joaquim chuckled. "Like Ziggy Stardust?"

I smiled. Ziggy Stardust was David Bowie's alter ego.

"Exactly. Wait, that's it," I said, gripping the phone harder.

"What is it?"

"An alter ego. A look. If you're going to start a band, you can't keep on borrowing other people's characters. I mean, the guys from KISS are cool and all, but you need your own brand. Right?"

There was a pause on the other end. As if Joaquim was still trying to absorb everything I'd said.

"Sí. It is true. But how?"

"Meet me outside in an hour. I have an idea," I said.

"Okay. Gracias—"

Plonk.

Dial tone.

It was obvious he had been about to say something else, but I was so excited I hung up on him.

Manny. I *had* to find Manny.

I moved away from the kitchen, past the entryway, out of the apartment without turning back. I had better things to do than picking up the pieces of my mom's broken heart.

Twenty-Three

Joaquim was late. Maybe that's what he'd been trying to tell me when I hung up on him, that he couldn't be there in an hour.

I'd been sitting on the stoop for a long time, which, truth be told, wasn't all that bad. It was like watching TV with fresh air and sunshine. It was kind of early for Spanish time. The stores and restaurants were still officially closed, but their metal gates were rolling up one by one, just in time for the deliveries to arrive on trolleys.

"¡Hola!"

"¡Buenos días!"

"¿Qué tal?"

People greeted one another out of windows, across alleys, through open doorways. The old guy who fed the pigeons breadcrumbs was at his usual bench. He smiled and waved at me as if he knew me or something. I waved back and then waited some more.

Thwack! Thwack!

Up above on one of the balconies was a lady banging a rug with a wooden-mallet-type thingy. Dust billowed around her.

Thwack! Thwack! Thwack!

I tapped my sneaker to the beat.

Where the heck is Joaquim?

The longer I sat there, the hotter it got. I wiped my sweaty palms on my faded, holey jeans. Maybe I should have changed? I hadn't even taken a shower. I lifted my arm and snuck a whiff of my armpit, hoping that at least I smelled better than I looked.

"¡Hola, Alba!"

Oh god. Oh god. Oh god.

I was sure he saw me sniffing my armpit.

"Hey! What's up?" I said, letting my arm drop.

"I am here," said Joaquim, catching his breath as if he'd been running.

"I see that." I also noticed that he didn't have the black star around his eye. That was a good start.

"It is late."

"I know."

"Sorry. The subway . . ."

"It's fine," I said, swatting the air with my hand. I pushed myself off the step. "So."

"So what is the plan?" asked Joaquim with his signature puppy-dog look.

Hmm. This whole alter-ego thing might be more

challenging than I thought. It's not that Joaquim didn't have presence, with his towering height and shaggy dark hair. But he exuded a somewhat comical, childlike innocence that reminded me of Will Ferrell in the movie *Elf*. It was awkward but endearing.

"Well, lucky for you, my neighbor Manny has a costume room right in his apartment. And he's agreed to let you borrow whatever you like as long as you take care of it. He's even loaning us his theatrical makeup kit," I said.

"You are joking."

"I am not."

"Whoa."

"C'mon." I dragged him inside and upstairs until we were standing in front of Eduardo and Manny's apartment. I knocked lightly so the sound wouldn't echo to the other side of the hallway. The door opened.

"¡Hallo! ¡Bienvenidos!" Manny swept back with his arm outstretched.

I strolled in with Joaquim skulking behind me. "Manny, this is Joaquim. Joaquim, this is Manny, my neighbor."

"Hola." Joaquim bent down and kissed Manny on both cheeks.

When he pulled away, I noticed Manny's dark eyelashes batting a million times a minute. He leaned over to me as if to whisper, except his voice was normal volume. "Why didn't you tell me he was so cute?"

Every single nerve ending on my face and neck was on fire.

I must have looked like a human shish kebab on a hot grill. I wasn't the only one blushing, though. When I peeked at Joaquim, his cheeks were the color of sangria.

Manny chuckled. "Go ahead, Alba. You know where everything is. I'm going to go back to my telenovela," he said, smooching the air before disappearing into one of the rooms.

"This place, it is . . . very interesting," said Joaquim as he studied the room.

"Wait till you see the rest of it."

I led the way. Joaquim kept on straggling behind, ogling almost every object that crossed our path. When I opened the door to the Sala de Curiosidades, he gasped.

"Amazing!"

"Crazy, huh?" I said, walking in.

Purr. Purr. Purr.

Rita Hayworth was draped on a red chair in the shape of lips. As soon as she saw Joaquim, she leaped off and rubbed his legs.

"I am a cat magnet," he said with a sheepish grin.

"I can see that." I chuckled. "C'mon, Cat Magnet, I'll show you the costume closet."

The closet was already open. Inside, Manny had set up two stools next to a gigantic metal makeup case with legs. The case held multiple tiers and compartments with lip colors and foundations and powders and eye shadows and liners and false lashes and all sorts of other embellishments.

Joaquim began pulling costumes off racks, oohing and

ahhing at each one. Then he found a white Elvis jumpsuit with sequins and held it up to me with the most ridiculous expression I'd ever seen.

"No. Definitely no," I said, shaking my head.

Joaquim held the jumpsuit against his body. "You sure?"

"Oh god, I haven't been more sure about anything in my whole life," I said.

"Okay, boss." He hung the jumpsuit back on the rack. "So what is your idea, then?"

I plopped down on one of the stools. "We need to brainstorm."

"What is this *brainstorm*?" replied Joaquim. He carefully sat down on the other stool.

"*Brainstorming* means coming up with ideas until you find the right one," I explained.

"Ah. This makes sense. In Spanish we say *lluvia de ideas*."

"Maybe we should talk about some of your favorites—books, movies, music. We might get some inspiration from those things," I said.

Joaquim didn't even take a moment to think about it. "Easy. Favorite music, KISS and Black Sabbath. Favorite book *and* movie, *Coraline*."

"*Coraline*?"

"Si, *Coraline*."

"Okay. Hmm . . ."

It was sort of a weird choice. Not that there was anything wrong with *Coraline*. It was a great movie, but still, I found it odd for a teenage boy, especially one who liked Black Sabbath. It had been a while since I'd seen the movie. I tried to mentally picture the different characters—Coraline's electric-blue hair, the black cat, the kooky old ladies, the creepy button-eyed mom.

Hmm.

I peered at Joaquim, then at the makeup case. "I think . . . I might have an idea." I hopped off the stool and gestured for him to follow. Right outside the closet was the wall of antique buttons.

"What do you think?" I said, pointing at the thousands of buttons.

"Buttons?"

"Yes. Button eyes, like in *Coraline*. How would you say it in Spanish?"

"Ojos de botón."

"It sounds like a band name to me: Ojos de Botón. What do you think?"

"Alba, you are a genius!"

"A genius?" I said with a goofy smile.

"¡Sí!" Joaquim fist-pumped the air, his shaggy hair puffed as if he'd been electrocuted.

I laughed. "That move right there was . . . rock and roll!" I said loudly, doing the hand horns and headbanging at the same time.

Joaquim started playing an imaginary song with his air guitar.

"Okay, okay. Let's not get carried away. I'm not done with you yet." I hurried back into the costume closet. "Sit. I know what to do with your face."

I peeked into the makeup case, visually picking out the colors I would use. When I turned toward Joaquim, he stuck his tongue out. "How does this look?" he asked jokingly.

I rolled my eyes. "I need a serious face, Joaquim. Stay still so I don't mess up."

His face went blank and he stopped slouching.

"Good. Now lean down so I can reach you better."

I plucked a foundation from the makeup case that was a few shades paler than Joaquim's skin, and dabbed it on with a sponge. Once it was evened out, I took a blue crayon and carefully circled one eye. With a black crayon, I traced the border and added the details. And when that was done, I added cracks on his cheek and rivulets of blood dripping from his eye. The finishing touch was a bit of silver glitter.

I leaned back and squinted. "Almost, but not quite . . . ," I said to myself.

Joaquim fidgeted. I could tell he was getting impatient.

"I know what's missing!" I blurted out.

I found a lipstick pencil so dark red it almost looked black. Then I scooted my stool closer to Joaquim's—so close I could count his freckles. I held my breath and drew the outline of his lips first.

The smell of his breath was a strange combination of mint and coffee. Next, I started filling in the flesh and creases, making sure not to mess up the outline. The nearer I got to the corners of his lips, the more I had to lean in.

Closer. Closer. Closer.

I breathed in his minty coffee breath.

"Alba," Joaquim whispered.

I looked away from his lips into his eyes. And suddenly, he leaned in . . . and kissed me.

Just for a second. Maybe a fraction of a second. I dropped the lip pencil. It clattered on the floor. I touched my mouth with the tips of my fingers, disbelieving.

"What was that?" I muttered.

Joaquim cringed. He lifted his hands to his face as if he was going to cover himself in shame.

"No! Don't do that!" I shouted, smacking his hands.

His eyes bugged out. "I am sorry. Sorry, sorry, sorry. Please forgive me!"

"I meant, don't touch your face. You were going to ruin your makeup."

He exhaled. "You are not angry?"

"No. I mean, not really . . . I just . . . I just wasn't expecting it," I said, staring at the floor as if I was searching for the lip pencil.

When I looked back up, Joaquim had this crooked smile on his face.

"Don't move a muscle. You should see yourself," I said, pointing at the mirror on the makeup case.

Joaquim bent over and gawked. "Ojos de botón," he said

dramatically, his right eyelid closing on cue to reveal the bleeding blue button. "Genius, Alba. Genius."

And at that very moment, for some reason, I did feel like a genius.

Like I mattered.

Huh.

Twenty-Four

I dreaded going back to Abuela Lola's apartment. But there was no avoiding it. I had to shower and change. At some point I would have to confront the big elephant in the room—Mom. It didn't matter that things had changed since I'd arrived in Barcelona. I'd moved on. Well, sort of. She hadn't, though. Leaving my father was only one obstacle. I had a feeling that picking up the pieces of her broken heart, her broken life, would be much harder.

That was going to be Mom's biggest challenge.

And I wasn't sure if I had it in me to help her through it when I was still trying to figure out my own crap.

After all, I was the kid and she was the adult, right?

When I entered the apartment, I was greeted by a wall of sunlight. It was bright and warm and almost felt solid to the touch. The sun wasn't like this in New York. The skyscrapers acted like filters, creating more shadows than light. I walked into it, allowing the heat to warm me.

My thoughts jumped to Joaquim's kiss. Really, it was more like a peck. The moment when his lips touched mine, when I realized what was happening, warmth had spread from the top of my head to the tips of my toes. Standing within the wall of sunlight brought that feeling back. I basked in it, not wanting to move forward for fear of what was up ahead.

But what now? What was going to happen to Mom? To me? To both our lives?

I wasn't ready for any of those questions. Never mind the answers. I didn't want to know. I just wanted to stay in the ignorant, blissful, brand-new life I'd created for myself.

"Alba, is that you?"

All the warmth inside me evaporated the moment I heard her voice.

I stepped out of the sunlight. Mom was seated on the sofa. Her gaze drifted, eventually finding mine.

"Hi," I murmured.

"Hi," she replied, patting the space next to her with her hand. "Do you—do you want to sit?"

No. I don't.

That's what I wanted to say. What I really wanted to do was go to my room and lock the door.

"Okay." I didn't have the heart to disappoint her.

I shuffled over and sat. The springs beneath the cushion poked me, as if they were encouraging me to escape while I still could.

"I—I think we should talk," she said, adjusting her body so it was facing me.

For an instant I wasn't sure I could reply.

The cat got your tongue.

Maybe Rita Hayworth had pulled mine out when I wasn't looking. I couldn't even feel it, not my tongue or my lips or any other part of my mouth. Talking wasn't something Mom and I did. Not since I was really little. Since then, it was all telling and shouting and threatening.

I took a deep breath. Then exhaled.

My tongue—it was still there after all. "Okay," I said. "Talk, then."

Mom frowned. The bruises on her face sort of rippled, reminding me of that second when you dip a dirty paint-brush in a glass of water to clean it, the colors bleeding into the water, swirling from one pigment to another.

It was painful seeing her this way. She was almost unrecognizable without her picture-perfect makeup; her shiny, bouncy hair; her immaculate clothing. It was lunchtime, and she still had on Abuela Lola's borrowed pajamas.

"I know you must hate me, Alba."

Gulp.

Is it that obvious?

I looked down at my hands, scraping bits of dried dough off my fingernails.

"It's fine. I understand. Because I hate me, too. I hate what

I've become. I hate that for so long—too long—I did nothing to make it better for you." She let out a choked sob.

I glanced at her. The tears trickled from her eyes.

"I need to know . . . ," I started, but the words got stuck in my throat.

Mom wiped the wetness from her cheeks and nodded. "Go ahead. Say it, whatever it is."

"I need to know if—if you think you'll ever go back to him." There. I said it.

"*No.* Never. That part of my life is done now," she said with conviction.

"Are you sure?"

"I'm sure."

"Good." And I meant it. As much as I hated her for barging in and making everything upside down when I was just starting to make everything right side up again, I was glad that my father couldn't harm her anymore.

Mom reached across her lap and took my hand in hers. Her arms, her fingers were so bony. "I'm not asking for your forgiveness, Alba. Not yet, anyway. What I'm asking for is patience. I—I need to find myself again. So maybe, one day, I can be your mother again." Her voice broke. More tears. She squeezed my hand. "Mahal kita."

I love you.

That's when I lost it. The armor I'd built over the years fell off piece by piece in a matter of seconds. I squeezed her hand back. God, I so wanted to have a mother again. I wanted her to be the woman that Toni had described to me—joyful, full of laughter, the kind of woman who kicked her shoes off in the middle of a song and danced as if nobody was watching.

"All right. I'll be patient," I finally said, with tears brimming my eyes.

"Thank you, Alba. Thank you for giving me a chance."

A chance. Everyone deserved a second chance.

Right?

I stood because I could feel the telltale ache in my throat—the one that always happened right before a full-blown cry-fest. "I'm going to go to my room," I mumbled, slowly stepping away.

"Wait."

I halted. Mom pulled something out from behind her. It was a celadon-and-fuchsia-colored envelope, one of the ones from her personal stationery collection back in New York. She held it out to me with a shaky hand. "I wrote this for you the day you left for Spain . . . I meant to mail it, but, I don't know . . . I just never got to it."

I stared at the envelope, which had my name written on it in Mom's elegant handwriting. *Alba Green.* I took it, even though I was scared of what was inside.

"You can read it whenever you like," said Mom, her eyes blinking nervously.

"Okay. Thanks." I walked off without looking at her, the

envelope gripped tight in my hand. For some reason the thick paper was warm against my skin, as if it had been used as a coaster for a cup of hot coffee.

When I got to my room, I closed the door and locked it. And then I sat down by the window, under the heat of the sunlight. Part of me wanted to wait and open the letter another time, but the other part of me was too curious, too desperate for answers.

I inhaled deep.

Phew.

Then I opened the envelope, and carefully unfolded the sheet of stationery. Mom's handwriting covered the paper in evenly spaced lines, the ink a metallic silver-gray. I blinked a couple of times, then began to read.

> *Dear Alba,*
>
> *By now, you're probably somewhere over the Atlantic Ocean with your headphones on, listening to music and wondering what you did wrong. Why I sent you away with little or no explanation. It pains me to think that you're alone on that plane feeling unwanted and unloved. I only wish I'd had the courage to talk to you, to tell you the truth. You deserve it. I'm sorry to have kept you in the dark for so long.*
>
> *The truth is, I have no real excuse other than*

fear. The fear of never finding myself again. The fear of being on my own again. The fear of disappointing everyone I love. The fear of losing you forever. I'm deeply ashamed of my behavior. As a parent, I should have been braver, I should have had the fortitude to stand up for myself, and to stand up for you. But the years have weakened me, changed me into a person that I no longer know. I feel as if I've become someone I hate. In fact, I pretty much hate everything about my life. The only bright spot I have left is you—you're the only good that's come out of the mess I've made for myself. I only hope it's not too late for us. That I can, somehow, fix this.

The first step is sending you to live with Abuela Lola. My childhood years in Barcelona were the best of my life. If you give it a chance, I know you'll feel the same way, too.

Please try to be happy, Alba. I promise that from now on, things will get better. I will try my best to get better, too. To be braver, stronger, the kind of mother you should have had all along. I hope one day soon we can see each other again under better circumstances. In the meanwhile, take care of yourself—and take care of Abuela Lola.

Mahal kita,
Mom

I focused on the handwriting, her words, so I could read her letter over and over again. By then, my vision had blurred, though. A solitary tear dropped onto the paper, making the ink bleed a bit. Just like my heart, which felt as if it had been nicked by a razor, my blood slowly seeping out.

It hurt. *Really* hurt.

But as much as I wanted to keep on hating Mom, I felt my insides warming, radiating, thawing in a way I'd never felt was possible.

The only bright spot I have left is you . . .

She loved me.

I held her letter against my chest and sat there for a long while.

Thinking.

Twenty-Five

It was probably the warmest day since I'd arrived in Barcelona. The sun was relentless, flashing a yellow light so hot that the concrete sidewalks and roads were steamy. It didn't help that there wasn't a cloud in sight; the sky was an even bright blue that seemed to go on forever. The last thing I should have been doing was going to El Rincón del Pan to bake bread. If it was hot outside, it was going to be even hotter with the ovens on full blast.

But I had no choice. The conversation with Mom, plus her letter, had made me into a nervous bundle of emotions. The long shower I thought would have helped hadn't helped at all. And lying in bed listening to David Bowie with my headphones on, trying but failing to read the sourdough cookbook I'd snapped up at Els Encants, hadn't helped, either. My feet were numb. My hands were fidgety. My stomach was filled with so many butterflies, I could have called it a butterfly conservatory and sold tickets.

The uncertainty of everything—what was happening, what was going to happen—had me on edge. Baking bread would be the only thing that would truly get my mind off it.

When I entered the bakery, the little bell above the door rattled my nerves even more.

Estel the cashier waved. "Hola, Alba. Toni está en la trastienda," she said, gesturing at the back with her chin.

She knew my Spanish was terrible, just as much as I knew her English was terrible, so we just spoke to each other in our own languages and hoped for the best.

I smiled, or at least I tried to smile. "Thanks, Estel."

I hoped Toni wasn't napping or anything, because I was kind of desperate. At the back, it was empty. Nobody was around. The usual bowls and bins of dough were arranged on the counters. There was even a half-eaten sandwich, jamón and cheese by the looks of it, sitting on a plate all by its lonesome self.

But then I heard some paper shuffling and a deep sigh coming from the office. I tiptoed to the door and peeked in. Toni was sitting at his desk with a bunch of documents surrounding him, forehead so creased there was hardly any skin separating his hairline from his eyebrows.

"Toni?"

He looked up. "Oh, Alba. I didn't see you."

"I haven't been here long."

"Entra, entra," he said, waving me in with his hands.

I inched inside, unsure whether I should have been

bothering him. Something about his sighing and his frown and the ridiculous amount of paperwork on his desk told me he was in the midst of serious business. I'd never seen him like this.

"I can come back later if you're busy," I mumbled.

He stretched his back and arms. "It's okay. I need a break anyway."

I sat down on the sofa, feeling all tongue-tied. It was silent, except for some reason I could hear my heart beating in my ears.

"How is your mother, Alba?"

Ugh.

She was the last person I wanted to talk about.

"She's fine, I guess." I couldn't have sounded more unsure if I'd tried.

"You do not seem convinced," he said with a raised eyebrow.

"To be honest, I don't want to talk about her right now."

For a second, Toni looked flustered, as if he'd expected me to open my heart up and pour out all its contents in one go. His stubbly cheeks were splotched with pink, and his crystal-blue eyes had lost their sparkle.

"Um, anyway. So, like, I thought we c-could work on some bread or something," I stammered.

Toni glared at the mess on his desk. "I'm in the middle of some paperwork at the moment. Crunching numbers, you know?"

"Not really," I replied. "I'm not exactly a math wiz."

His forehead disappeared under his frown again. "Well, Alba. Running a business is complicated. The fun parts are baking the bread and mingling with the customers. The not-so-fun part is crunching the numbers. I have to make sure that after all the bills are paid, after all my employees get their checks, that I'm actually making a profit."

"And are you?" I blurted out.

The silence was back.

Not only was the sparkle in his eyes gone, but it was as if they'd clouded and were covered with a thin layer of ice. If I could, I would have literally stuck my foot in my mouth and hopped out of the room on one leg.

"I'm sorry," I said. "I shouldn't be butting in on your business."

Toni rubbed his face with his hands. "Don't be sorry. It's just that I have yet to admit it to myself."

"Admit what?"

"Admit that if the numbers don't change, I might have to close the bakery in the next couple of months," he said.

I gasped. "But—but—"

"I know," he said, flopping on the backrest with a bounce. "I know."

"You have to *do* something." I wanted to stand. I wanted to march over to his desk and shoot him with my most determined of glares. But my legs were too wobbly.

"I'm trying, Alba. I'm really trying to figure something out."

"And if you don't?"

Toni gazed at me. I gazed at him. He didn't have to reply. I knew what was going to happen by the way his lips pressed together.

El Rincón del Pan would be no more.

And I would have nowhere to go, to escape, to seek solace, to feel like I was actually worth something.

That's when I got the familiar twitch—the twitch to run.

I bolted off the sofa even though my legs still wobbled, hitting the doorframe with my shoulder as I darted past.

"Alba! Wait!" Toni shouted after me.

I ran past the oven, past the counter, past the bowls of dough, until I reached the back door. I halted and looked over my shoulder, taking in as much of the place as I could. Because maybe soon it would be gone.

"Alba!"

The door. The street. The people.

I just kept on running.

I found myself at the plaza with the fountain and the church with pockmarked walls. There was sweat on my face, on my neck, everywhere on my body, which made my T-shirt and jeans stick to my skin.

It was hard to breathe. I coughed and then collapsed on the rim of the fountain. The stone radiated heat through my pants. I glanced at the water, wishing I could hop in and cool off. But getting arrested by the Spanish police wasn't exactly on my to-do list. So I just sat there and sucked it up.

The heat.

The sadness.

The pain.

The uncertainty.

Why is this happening to me?

I thought I'd finally gotten my fresh start. My clean slate. Now this. *All* of this.

I pulled my legs up and hugged my knees, smooshing my tear-stained face against my pants. My heaving sobs were uncontrollable. I couldn't stop the chest spasms. I couldn't stop the whimpering and wailing.

I cried and cried and cried for god knows how long. It wasn't until I felt someone's presence next to me that I paused, or at least tried to. Between my leg and my arm, I managed to find a space to take a peek. It was an old lady, like *old* old, close to ninety or maybe even a hundred. But she had this youthful look about her: a flouncy floral blouse, a skirt down to her knees, chin-length silvery hair, and lipstick the same shade as peaches. On her arm was a humongous patchwork canvas purse.

She was staring at me unabashedly. When she saw me peeking, she smiled, nodded, and opened her purse. Her hand disappeared inside, and she fished around for something.

Then out came a carefully folded plaid handkerchief. She held it toward me and said, "Toma," with the kind of voice that soothed.

My reluctance to accept kindness from strangers started to kick in, but I really did need a handkerchief because my clothes were already so soaked and dirty that they couldn't possibly absorb any more tears or sweat or saliva or snot.

I reached for it, uncurling myself like a millipede. "Gracias," I said, all croaky-like.

For a couple of minutes, we sat quietly, me wiping the mess off my face, her pretending to mind her own business.

When I was all cleaned up, though, she looked straight into my eyes with her faded gray irises and said sort of dramatically, "Arból de la esperanza, mantente firme."

I scrunched my forehead and gawked at her.

She must have picked up on my cluelessness, because her shoulders popped and her brows hopped way above where they should have been. "¡Espera!"

Her hand dived into her purse again. A few seconds passed, and then out came a tiny leather notebook with a pen tucked in its spine. "Espera. Espera," she repeated, pulling the pen free and opening the notebook.

I watched her write whatever she was writing with flair. When she was done, she carefully tore the page out and handed it to me. In the most beautiful script I'd ever seen, she'd written:

"Árból de la esperanza, mantente firme."
— *Frida Kahlo*

I recognized that name. Frida Kahlo was a Mexican art-ist whose paintings were colorful, strange, *and* beautiful. I remembered studying her in art class. When my teacher held up a self-portrait of her, with a dark unibrow, thick braided hair adorned with flowers, and a scowl on her face, I was enthralled. Because this Frida Kahlo was exactly the kind of person that would have been friends with David Bowie had they lived in the same time, the same place. They were both rebels. Different. Like they were from another planet.

I squinted at the paper, trying to decipher the quote. But it was futile. Maybe the old lady could give me a clue. When I looked up, though, she was gone.

Poof!

As if she'd disappeared into thin air. But she was real. I had her handkerchief and the piece of paper to prove it.

Yet not a single soul was around. Just me, the pigeons, and the big solitary tree.

Oh, wait.

I glanced at the quote again.

Árból was "tree" in Spanish.

That much I knew.

I would need help to figure out the rest.

Twenty-Six

I found Marie at the restaurant surrounded by napkin dispensers, chopstick packets, and soy sauce bottles. As soon as she saw me walk in, her eyes shot me with this gaze that said, *Please take me away.*

"Marie, you're here!" I said, plopping down next to her.

She sighed. "Of course I'm here. I'm here till *every* single napkin and bottle and chopstick is in its place."

I leaned away, peering at her with narrowed eyes. I'd never seen Marie in such a sour mood. Her face was scrunched up as if she'd just eaten a lemon, and her eyes were rolling every time she shoved some napkins into the dispenser.

"I need your help," I mumbled, pulling the folded piece of paper out of my pocket.

"You too, huh? Seems like *everybody* needs my help today."

"Uh, well, I just need you to translate something. It'll take you a second, tops," I said, sliding the paper across the table.

Marie sighed. "Okay. Fine. Anything but this napkin drudgery."

She adjusted her glasses and then unfolded the paper. I could see her mouthing the words as she read. There was a hush. Her expression went from sour to sweet. And when she looked at me, her eyes were glossy.

"Gosh," she said. "This is beautiful."

"What does it say?"

Marie placed her hand on her heart and read the paper again—except this time, aloud and in English. "Tree of hope, stand firm."

She was right. It was beautiful.

"Who gave you this?" Marie asked.

I stared at the table for a second, because part of me wanted to avoid having to explain *everything* to Marie—the whole mess with Mom, the bakery possibly shutting down, me running away and crying like a big baby. But the other part knew that Marie was a friend—and weren't friends supposed to be there for each other?

I breathed deep, trying to fill myself with courage. Over the years, I'd built an impenetrable wall around myself. Breaking it down and letting someone through wasn't something I'd planned on doing.

"At the plaza, the one you brought me to that day we had ice cream, there was an old lady . . . She saw me crying by the fountain. And, I mean, I suppose she must have felt sorry for me or something . . . She was the one who wrote those words," I explained.

"Oh." Marie fiddled with some chopsticks. "Are you all right? Do you want to talk about it?"

It was eerily silent. There was no one else at the restaurant, since it was between lunch and dinner.

Thump-thump. Thump-thump.

I was worried that Marie could hear my heart beating in my chest. This was precisely the reason I'd kept people from getting too close. It wasn't easy admitting that my father was an alcoholic, that he beat my mother, that he'd slammed me against a wall. Who'd want to be friends once they found *that* out?

"Everything is just falling apart," I finally blurted out.

Marie placed her hand on my arm gently, as if to encourage me. I peered through her glasses into her dark brown eyes.

"The reason my mom sent me here is because—because my dad is a low-life alcoholic. A bully. Barcelona was supposed to be a fresh start for me. And now my mom is here, too. You'd think I'd be happy about that. But—but to be honest, I'm not so sure my mom can pick up the pieces, you know? Like sometimes, things are way too broken to be fixed. I—I don't know what to do. I don't know how I'm supposed to help her . . ." My voice trailed off.

"Sometimes just being there is enough," said Marie.

My face and ears and neck got all hot. I knew exactly what

she meant. I remembered so many times when I'd needed Mom there—when the kids made fun of me at school, when my father terrorized me with words like "*Get out of my face*" or "*I wish you'd never been born*" or "*No one is ever going to love you.*"

But Mom wasn't there. She hadn't stood up for me.

"I don't think I'm strong enough to be there," I mumbled.

"I have a feeling that you're stronger than you think."

I hung my head low.

Marie ducked to meet my gaze. "Look at what you've done in such a short amount of time. You moved to a new country to live with a grandmother you barely knew, you made friends—yeah, in case you didn't know it, Joaquim and I *are* your friends—and you found something you love to do, baking bread. You *are* strong. *And* brave."

"Yeah. Whatever. None of that matters now."

"What do you mean?" she said.

"El Rincón del Pan might close down—"

"Wait," Marie interrupted. "What?"

Oops.

"I just found out. Um, I don't think I'm supposed to tell anyone."

Her shoulders slumped. "Well, that sucks."

"Tell me about it. I thought for once things were going my way. But I guess the joke is on me."

Suddenly, Marie sat up super-duper straight. "Don't talk like that, Alba. You have to think positive."

201

"*Positive*," I said with a sneer. "Right."

"Maybe there's something we can do to help your mom . . . and Toni."

"We?"

"Yes, *we*." Marie pushed her glasses back. "I'm sure between you, me, and Joaquim, we can hatch some sort of plan."

"Really?"

"Why not?" she said, forcing a wad of napkins into a dispenser like she meant it.

I smiled. "Okay."

"Good. Tomorrow is my day off. We can go to the beach and put our heads together. But first, you need to rescue me from this napkin-slash-chopstick-slash-soy-sauce situation," she said with a giggle.

"On it," I said, grabbing a handful of chopsticks as if I was grabbing a bull by the horns.

By the time I got back to Abuela Lola's, it was just starting to get dark. I remembered reading somewhere that the brief period right before the sun disappears below the horizon is called "the golden hour," because the light glows in such a way that everyone is under its spell. It is a time when anything seems possible.

And that's exactly how I felt when I unlocked the front door and opened it. The golden sunlight was streaming in through the windows, casting its spell on the entire apartment—not just the inanimate objects and plants, but its inhabitants, too.

My breath halted.

Because from where I stood, I could see Abuela Lola and Mom in the kitchen basking in it. The glow almost made it seem as if they were in a dream. Abuela Lola was by the stove, stirring whatever it was she was cooking in a pot. Somehow, she managed to pay attention to what she was doing all while telling my mom some ridiculous story in Spanish and Tagalog and English. And by the table, Mom was seated in front of a chopping board full of cheery red and yellow bell peppers, chop-chop-chopping away. Instead of pajamas, she had on a turquoise tank top and white denim shorts, her hair in a loose French braid. She laughed at something Abuela Lola told her, and at that moment I tried to imagine the teenager and then the young mother she had once been.

The Isabel who was carefree.

The Isabel who was happy.

The Isabel who was filled with so many hopes and dreams.

My heart twisted and turned as if it was squeezing itself.

I wanted her back. *That* Isabel.

I stepped forward, but I could barely feel my strides past the entryway, under the doorway, into the kitchen, next to Mom. From up close, her bruises were still visible. I inched next to her. The heat from her body, from the sunlight, from the stove, making every inch of my flesh solid. Present.

I was there.

And maybe that *would* be good enough.

"Let me help," I said, taking one of the yellow peppers from the pile and grabbing another knife.

For a quick second, she looked over her shoulder. Maybe she'd forgotten where she was. Maybe she was making sure Dad wasn't there, watching her from the shadows. Maybe she just needed a glimpse of Abuela Lola's warm smile. Their eyes met and Abuela Lola *did* smile, but she also nodded as if to reassure her.

Mom smiled back, and then she turned around and gazed at me, beaming so bright her bruises seemed to fade. "Sure," she finally replied.

Chop.

Chop.

Chop.

I was tempted to open up, to tell her that I'd read her letter. But I didn't want to ruin the moment. So I didn't speak, and neither did she. Instead, we listened to Abuela Lola's stories.

I was there.

She was there.

And for the time being, that was good enough.

Twenty-Seven

I was supposed to bake with Toni that night—well, technically, the next morning. But I hadn't seen or spoken to him since I'd run off.

Is he mad at me?

Disappointed?

Does he hate me?

All those questions, those insecurities, nagged me as I loitered outside El Rincón del Pan's back entrance. I mean, so far Toni had been nice to me, nicer than nice, actually. But what if he had his limits? What if he had a dark side? First impressions could be deceiving, right?

For example, when people met my dad, he always came across as the Man of the Year—charming, successful, handsome. He could have been one of those guys on the cover of magazines like *Esquire* or *GQ*. Maybe once upon a time he *had* been all those things.

But he'd changed.

Into a monster.

And to be honest, I didn't know if all men were like that, or if I just happened to get unlucky in the father department. There was no real way to know if Toni would be different from my dad. The only thing I could do was knock on the door and hope for the best.

Knock. Knock.

I had this sudden urge to run and hide.

Toni opened the door with a sheepish grin. "Alba, I'm *so* glad you're here."

He looked relieved, just as relieved as I was.

I walked in and then halted by the entryway. "Toni, I—I just wanted to apologize. I shouldn't have gotten so upset. You have enough problems to deal with. I'm sorry."

For a second, he didn't say anything. Even though I was scared to look him straight in the face, I did. His forehead, cheeks, brow, chin, and jaw were stiff. Then, all of a sudden, his expression relaxed and his eyes crinkled at the corners. "I *do* have a lot of problems, Alba . . . But you are not one of them. I'm grateful that you care about the bread, and this place." He reached out and hugged me.

Part of me wanted to hug him back. But I didn't know how. Mom and Dad had never been the touchy-feely types. And as a result, I'd always had a hard time expressing myself physically. So I just stood there like a limp noodle in his arms, absorbing his warmth and kindness.

It felt good.

I hadn't realized how much I *needed* that hug from him.

Finally, he kissed me on the cheek, patted my back, and said, "Come, let's bake."

"Okay." I went over and grabbed an apron.

Breathe, Alba . . .

El Rincón del Pan was still around. So was Toni. And so was I.

Enjoy it and stop worrying so much.

"So what are we making?" I asked.

Toni gestured for me to follow him to one of the steel tables. "Today, we are going to experiment with a traditional Catalan pastry," he explained.

"Pastry?"

He nodded. "Yes. Well, it's more of a cross between bread, pastry, and cake, one that's popular this time of year. On June 23, we celebrate the summer solstice, and part of the festivities include what's called the Coca de Sant Joan, or St. John's Cake in English. Usually it's made with yeast, but we're going to make a sourdough version, without the commercial yeast." Toni opened a dough bin on the counter. "I started the dough earlier. *You* can help me finish."

I peeked into the bin and almost immediately I was engulfed with the most heavenly aroma, sort of sweet, citrusy, and spicy. "Wow. What's that smell?"

"Lemon zest, anise seed, cinnamon, and orange-blossom water . . . What *we're* going to be doing is forming the dough, brushing them with an egg wash, and topping them with candied cherries, orange and melon pieces, pine nuts, and crystallized sugar before baking them."

"So it's kind of like a fruity pizza?" I said.

Toni cringed and then chuckled. "Not quite." He placed the digital scale next to the bin and then handed me the pastry cutter. "I want you to dump out all the dough onto a lightly floured counter, separate it into four-hundred-gram pieces, and then gently shape the pieces into ovals."

"Got it."

"While you do that, I'm going to prepare the toppings." He went over to the other table, where there was a bowl and some eggs, a wooden chopping board, several containers of colorful candied fruit, and a jar with sugar crystals that somehow reminded me of snowflakes.

Just as Toni had instructed, I dusted the counter's surface with a bit of flour, and then pushed the fragrant dough out of the bin with a rubber scraper. The flour billowed into the air as soon as the dough plopped down.

Poof!

I wiped my floury hands together.

The mound of dough in front of me bubbled. I turned on the scale, then sliced off a hunk and weighed it: 368 grams.

I sliced off a smaller hunk, adding more dough until the reading was exactly 400.

It was mostly quiet, except for Toni's knife chopping, and the occasional footsteps and voices coming from passersby outside. Even from where I stood, the scent of the candied fruit wafted into my nose. It reminded me of Christmas and fruitcakes, even though Christmas was far off.

The scent, the thinking about Christmas, forced a memory into my mind, of the green-and-red-wrapped fruitcakes we used to get back in New York—gifts from neighbors. The cellophane would crinkle when they were opened. Back then, I would close my eyes and breathe in their boozy, sweet aroma. It used to be such a happy smell. Every year, though, the fruitcakes seemed to dwindle, as if our neighbors were dropping off the earth one by one. Until, finally, we only had one lone fruitcake left on our doorstep. That night my dad was drunk, because he drank even more during the holidays. When something Mom did or said made him angry, he grabbed the fruitcake and threw it at her, except he missed and it hit the wall.

Splat!

"*Clean up that mess,*" he commanded.

I hid behind the doorway and watched Mom get on her hands and knees. She scrubbed the wall with paper towels, and then she mopped the floor and wiped everything down again until every crumb and smear was gone.

My face had burned. I was so humiliated for her.

I blinked and blinked again, until the memory disappeared. I made the last piece of dough into an oval and exhaled. "Toni . . ."

He stopped what he was doing and turned around. "¿Sí?"

"Did you and my mom ever, um, bake together?" It was

sort of a random question, but I needed a story, something happy that would help me forget about Mom on her hands and knees, cleaning up the mess Dad made.

Toni's gaze kind of wandered, as if he was trying to find the past somewhere in front of him. After a moment, he looked at me with his sparkling eyes. "Actually, it's funny that you ask that, Alba. Because when we were children, your mom and I would always help my grandmother make the different varieties of cocas for every season. Coca de Sant Joan during the summer; Coca de Reyes during the Day of Kings, right after Christmas; and the Mona de Pascua for Easter . . . It was our job to shape the dough and arrange all the toppings, just like I'm asking you to do."

"Really?"

Toni grinned. "Yes, really. Those days with Isabel and my grandmother are my earliest memories of cooking and baking."

I tried to imagine the kid versions of Toni and my mom doing what he and I were doing. But it was impossible to visualize because the only version of my mom that I knew was the one who was married to my dad. The Isabel of before was still a fuzzy image in my mind—one I'd caught a glimpse of briefly in Abuela Lola's kitchen when I'd helped with the pepper chopping. But it wasn't palpable enough to feel real. The woman that Mom used to be was still a stranger to me.

"So let me show you how it's done," said Toni as he brought over the bowl with the egg wash, the jar with the sugar crystals, and the chopping board with the toppings. "First, we gently brush a thin layer of egg wash over the dough." He dipped a pastry brush into the bowl and spread out the golden-yellow liquid on top of one of the ovals. "Then we arrange the fruit so that it looks pretty . . ." He plucked bright red cherries, cheery orange slices, and pieces of neon-green melon from the board, making an alternating pattern from the edge of the oval toward the middle. "And finally, we finish it off with a generous amount of pine nuts and sugar crystals." He grabbed a handful of both and sprinkled them over the dough. "Voilà!"

It wasn't even baked yet, but the coca already looked like a beautiful, edible masterpiece.

"Can I do the rest?"

"Of course." Toni stepped back and let me take over.

Using the one he'd done as a sample, I assembled the rest, taking a bit of creative license on the last couple of ovals—one with a sort of abstract design of trees and flowers, and the other with a candied-fruit bird.

"What do you think?" I asked Toni when I was done.

"¡Perfecto! I think from now on, you're in charge of the coca decorating," he said with a wink. "Now let's cover these up with a damp kitchen towel, and in an hour or so, they'll be ready to bake."

And that's exactly what we did.

After an hour, the cocas were puffier, about double in size. Toni slid them one by one into the super-hot oven, and twenty minutes later they emerged—golden ovals with the candied-fruit toppings that almost resembled stained-glass windows.

Toni waited only a couple of minutes before slicing a piece for me and a piece for himself. "What do you think?" he asked.

I took a bite, making sure to get a bit of everything, and then chewed and swallowed. "It's really, really delicious. But . . ."

Toni frowned. "But what?"

"It *is* basically a fruity pizza," I said with a giggle.

He huffed and rolled his eyes, pretending to be offended. "Fine, fine. Fruity pizza it is."

From then on, I decided that fruitcakes were a thing of the past.

We were in Spain, after all, and in Spain there was a coca for *every* season.

Twenty-Eight

After baking cocas with Toni, I was more determined than ever to do *something* to help him keep El Rincón del Pan open. I kept on thinking about him and Mom as kids decorating the cocas. It was a tradition. And maybe it was time to bring that tradition back.

Marie had suggested the she, Joaquim, and me should go to the beach for our brainstorming session. I'd envisioned us taking a bus or a train to some nearby seaside town. What I did *not* expect was walking twenty minutes from the apartment and being at the water's edge. And yet that's what we did.

Barceloneta Beach was right there in the city. It was lined with palm trees and a boardwalk, curving toward a rocky point where a mirrored building in the shape of a fin jutted into the sky. Loads of people were splayed out on towels, and others were swimming.

I slipped my flip-flops off and wiggled my bare feet into

the soft beige sand. "How is this beach here? For real?" I said, staring at vibrant blue sea in front of us.

Joaquim, whose eyes seemed even bigger with his hair in a ponytail, gawked at me. "It has always been here," he explained with a shrug.

I grinned and tried not to giggle at Joaquim's literalness.

Marie grinned back and said, "C'mon, let's go find a spot."

After a couple of minutes of weaving through beach-goers, we found an open area several feet from the water's edge, not too far from the snack shack, which was clearly of utmost importance. We arranged our towels, tote bags, water bottles, and whatnot, and then I stood there for a moment, feeling a bit awkward in my cargo shorts and T-shirt. I was the only one without any swimwear on. Marie had on a lime-green one-piece with daisies on the straps, and Joaquim was wearing board shorts with a sort of graffiti pattern and a white tank top that made his gangly arms even ganglier. Not only that, but my legs were a pasty color that was almost blinding.

"Are you going to sit, or what?" said Marie, glancing up at me with one eye squinted.

I flopped down on the towel near Joaquim, adjusting my limbs awkwardly. It was the first time I'd seen him since the weirdness in the costume closet. I mean, it wasn't weird. Kissing was normal, right? What was weird was that he'd wanted to kiss *me*.

"Should we swim?" asked Joaquim.

Marie shook her head. "Nah. Let's wait till we get really

hot," she said, pulling a notebook out of her tote bag. "Why don't we brainstorm first?"

"Ah! I know what that is!" Joaquim bounced to his knees. "Ideas. We need to think of ideas," he said.

"Yup," said Marie.

"Yup, yup," I repeated.

She opened her notebook to a clean page, and then wrote a header in bold letters that said:

Operation Save El Rincón del Pan

Joaquim read what she'd written and cringed. "I understand that you want to help. But my father . . . tiene una cabeza dura." He knocked the side of his head with his fist. "He likes to do everything himself. This is why my mother left him. She says he is una isla—you know—an island."

"Well, we're going to have to change him," I said.

He shot me a good-luck-with-that gaze.

Marie tapped her notebook with her pen. "So back to the plan."

"Right." I'd been thinking about it nonstop, and the only conclusion I'd come to was that Toni needed more customers. More customers meant more money. And I was certain that his loyal following, mostly old ladies from the neighborhood, wasn't cutting it. "I think the bakery needs a makeover," I finally said.

"Ooohhh, I can make sketches! We could update the signage and the facade and the inside, too!" said Marie, excitedly.

I clapped my hands together. "Perfect. But I'm going to have to do some research. Like what other bakeries are doing, and what the bread bloggers are posting about."

"Yes!" Marie began jotting words down. "Revamping. Sketches. Research, research, research," she said to herself. Then she bolted up and held out her pen as if it was a magic wand. "You should ask your mom for help. With the research. And then when you show everything to Toni, she can back you up and help him see . . . They *were* best friends, right?"

"Like brother and sister," I said with a smile.

Joaquim just sat there between me and Marie, glancing right and left and right and left. But when I mentioned about the brother-and-sister part, he nodded. "¡Sí! It is true. My father, he showed me photos one time of him and Isabel. He told me, 'Ella es como mi hermana,' like his sister."

I could feel this tingling creeping up the back of my neck. It had nothing to do with the sun's rays blasting from above. No, the tingling was because I was picturing Mom and me going from bakery to bakery, spying on the competition, sampling their bread, popping into nearby coffee shops to jot down our notes. Helping Toni was something we could bond over. It might even help her find herself again. Find the old Isabel.

"I think this is a solid plan," I said with a grin. "Marie, in the meantime, you can play around with aesthetics while I work on my mom and gather research. And you, Joaquim, well, you can make sure all of this is kept under wraps. Keep it a secret. Don't say a word."

"Not a word. Secret. Got it," he said, pretend-zipping his mouth with the most serious look he could muster.

Marie snapped her notebook shut and placed it back into her tote bag. "Okay, I'm officially hot now." She stood. "Anyone else up for a swim?" she asked.

"Uh . . ." I glanced at the people frolicking in the sea. Everyone looked as if they belonged there—the girls with their sleek tanks and skimpy bikinis, and the guys in their board shorts and rash guards. Some of the men even had those obscenely small trunks that were like briefs. "I think I'll sit this one out," I said.

"Me too."

I turned and stared at Joaquim. Wasn't he the one who'd wanted to go swimming in the first place?

Marie shrugged and leaped across the sand on her bare feet. It was actually kind of comical, the way she hopped with this grimace from the scorching-hot sand, and as soon as she stepped into the water, she sighed, "Ahhh," so loud we could hear it all the way from where we were sitting.

Joaquim snickered.

I jabbed him with my elbow. "Don't laugh at her suffering!"

"¿Qué?"

"Don't laugh!"

By then we were both holding our breaths trying not to laugh, even though I was shouting at him not to. I could feel my face getting red, while Joaquim's was already the color of cold gazpacho soup.

Phew.

We exhaled simultaneously and then breathed deep. I hiccupped. Loud. That made the laughter explode out of the both of us so hard that we collapsed on the towel, me on my side and Joaquim on his back.

After a couple of minutes, we ran out of steam. I lay there, spent, staring at Joaquim's profile. His hair had managed to escape from its ponytail, so he looked like an odd combination of Roman statue and an '80s heavy-metal band member. The curls and frizz were like a halo around his head, sticking to his hairline where there was sweat. He must have felt my eyes on him, because he shifted and met my gaze. The sounds around us—splashing water, shrieking voices, crashing waves—seemed to disappear.

It was just the two of us.

Joaquim's arm slid across the towel. For a second, I wasn't sure what he was doing. But then I felt his hand curl around mine, one finger at a time. I flinched at the electricity crackling on my skin. Not real electricity, *obviously*. But it felt real to me.

"What are you doing?" I whispered.

"Holding your hand."

I furrowed my brow. It was confusing. For some reason I'd convinced myself that the kiss from the other day was a fluke. Like maybe breathing in the recycled air in that stuffy costume closet had forced Joaquim to do something he didn't mean to do. But he was at it again, holding my hand as if he liked me—like, *liked* me, liked me.

"But—but why me?" I asked.

Joaquim scooched closer. "Why not you?"

I pushed myself up on one elbow and gestured at the crowd with my chin. "Look at them out there . . . Look at *all* those girls who aren't me. Girls who are prettier. Girls who are smarter. Girls who are . . . girlier."

"Girlier?" he said, looking baffled.

"You know, with long hair, dresses, lipstick."

He shook his head. "I do not care about those things."

"Then why?"

"Because I like you, Alba . . . I like that you know music. Good music. I like that you are not afraid to be yourself. I like that your heart, tu corazón, is outside, where people can see it . . . You are not ashamed to show people how you feel. I like that you make me laugh, even if sometimes you are laughing at me . . ." I opened my mouth to protest, but he held his hand up. "It is okay. I am used to it. People, they laugh at me all the time, but with you, I know that you laugh because you understand. You are laughing with me."

My eyes wandered. I didn't know what to do, what to say about any of the stuff he'd said. It was all new to me. Finally, my eyes found his again. I blinked and said, "I don't know how to do any of this."

"Me either," he said.

"Okay."

"Okay."

And that was that. We just lay there on the towel with our own thoughts. Him with his. Me with mine. I supposed we would figure it out together.

Twenty-Nine

When I got home, Abuela Lola was in the living room rearranging furniture. I stood there with my throbbing, sun-burned face, hoping that she wouldn't notice the bits of sand still caked on my legs.

"What's going on?" I asked.

Abuela Lola pushed a wooden table to the center of the room. Once it was in place, she looked up at me with this gaze that oozed determination. "I've decided to host an impromptu dinner tonight, a sort of homecoming celebration for your mom."

"Oh."

I watched as she fiddled with the underside of the table. All of a sudden, she pulled both ends out so that instead of a square table, it was a long rectangular one.

"Can I help?" I said, stepping forward.

Abuela Lola clapped the dust from her hands. "I might be old, Alba, but I'm still strong as an ox," she said with a wink.

"Why don't you go get cleaned up so you can accompany your mom to the market?"

The market with Mom. *Perfect.* It was just the opportunity I needed to get her on board with the plan.

The plan.

It was going to work.

It had to.

The Mercat de Santa Caterina was one of two famous markets in the area. The other was La Boqueria, which according to Abuela Lola was teeming with too many tourists to get any shopping done.

After a short walk through a maze of narrow alleyways, we saw Santa Caterina in front of us. Mom halted. Her eyes swept the odd-looking structure, which resembled a multicolored alien spaceship that had landed on top of a nineteenth-century building.

"It's still the same," she said with a smile. "That wavy mosaic roof was added a year before I moved to New York . . ."

Her voice faltered when she said *New York.* I glanced at her from the corner of my eye. She seemed sad and wistful. I pretended not to notice.

"It *is* kind of bizarre . . . But I like it," I said with a chuckle.

Her smile returned.

Phew.

"Come. It's even better inside," she said, waving me on.

As soon as we walked past the arched entryway, there was this sound, like a swarm of insects humming. It kind of reminded me of how Grand Central Station sounded, with its chatter, footsteps, movement. Except the market was filled with stalls selling fresh produce, nuts, spices, cheeses, eggs, meat, and fish. There were also sandwich vendors, tapas bars, and a couple of coffee shops with long shiny counters and stools.

"I used to come here almost every day with Abuela Lola. When I was old enough, she gave me a list and I'd do the shopping on my own," she said with a gleam in her eye. "I even had a metal trolley to put all the groceries in."

Once again, I had a difficult time picturing everything she was telling me. When we were in New York, she ordered the little food we had in the house online from FreshDirect. She wasn't the let's-go-to-the-farmer's-market kind of gal.

She pulled a list from her shorts pocket and adjusted the tote bag on her shoulder. "Let's go, Alba."

First, we bought a dozen eggs from an old lady who had dyed her hair the same color as a brownish-red hen. She picked out "los más frescos," which I assumed were the freshest. The eggs weren't even white or brown; they were in various shades of pastel pink and green and blue that reminded me of Easter candies.

Afterward, we perused the produce section. Mom kept on gasping and shoving samples toward me, figs and peaches and plums and fruit I didn't recognize. We ended up buying a couple of cartons of strawberries, a bundle of wild asparagus, and some greens and cherry tomatoes for salad. I'd never seen fruits and vegetables so crisp and alive, as if they'd just been harvested.

Unfortunately, Mom saved the worst for last—the seafood stalls. Not that they weren't fresh or anything. In fact, they were almost too fresh. Every time I turned, there were beady fish eyes glaring at me or some sort of tentacle trying to touch my arm. And the smell? Let's just say it wasn't good—briny and fishy and seaweed-y. I pulled my T-shirt over my nose and mouth, making the vendors cackle.

Ugh.

They were probably calling me a guiri behind my back.

Pffft.

Whatever.

Mom pointed at the baby squid and at some tiny fish and shrimps, and a bearded dude scooped some up into bags and weighed them. As soon as she paid, I gestured at a coffee shop with the T-shirt still on my face.

"All right. All right. We're done with everything on Abuela Lola's list anyway," she said.

When we got to the coffee shop, I could breathe again. The fishy smell had been replaced by the aroma of coffee. It was heavenly. We climbed onto some stools, and Mom flagged one of the barista guys down.

"Un café cortado y un café con leche, por favor."

I gawked at her. "Really?"

She grinned. "I started drinking café con leche when I was

224

younger than you, Alba, except Papá used to call his 'leche con café,' because he always made it extra milky."

I sort of flinched at the word *Papá*, because in all the time I'd been in Barcelona—in all my life, in fact—not once had anyone mentioned my grandfather. It was almost like he didn't exist.

"What—what happened to him? Your dad, I mean," I asked just as the barista placed our coffees in front of us.

I peered at Mom as she dropped a scant teaspoon of brown sugar into her café cortado and stirred a little too much as if she was avoiding my question. Under the bright lights, the bruises on her face and neck reappeared; they'd turned from a purplish red to a pale green. Her eyelashes fluttered, and then she looked at me with this indescribable gaze that made me think of a trampled-on red rose I'd once seen on the subway floor.

"Papá died not long after I married your father. Abuela Lola blamed me. She said he died of a broken heart."

"A broken heart?"

Mom nodded. "I was his little girl. He thought I deserved the sun, the moon, and the stars. But I was in love. I didn't see what he saw. And when I left, he was inconsolable. I broke his heart . . . for nothing. Papá was right about your father. Of course he was . . ." Her voice cracked and then trailed off into a hush.

She might have looked more or less okay from the outside, but inside, Mom was still hurting, grieving, fragile. I reached for her hand and grazed her fingers with mine.

225

"It wasn't for nothing, Mom . . . You still have me," I whispered.

A second passed.

A long, quiet second.

I remembered Mom's words from her letter . . .

The only bright spot I have left is you.

"I read your letter . . ." I blinked, and without even realizing it, my cheeks were wet from tears.

So were Mom's. Gently, she leaned over, placing one arm around me at a time, as if she was afraid to touch me.

"I meant *every* single word, Alba . . . You *are* the brightest spot in all my life. If it weren't for you, I might not even be here. I might have given up. I might have never left him . . ."

We stayed that way, embracing and crying, until our coffees were cold. It felt like we were making up for all those times we should have been crying, hugging, forgiving each other instead of holding the tears in.

Crying *wasn't* undignified.

I knew then that it had been a lie. Mom didn't really believe it. It was something she'd made up to cope with the numbness that had hardened her heart.

When we finally pulled apart, she cupped my face with her hands and kissed my forehead on the very same spot she used to kiss when I was little.

"We should go. Abuela Lola is waiting for us," she said, fumbling with the wallet in her tote bag.

"Wait."

She stopped fumbling and listened.

"There's something you should know," I blurted out.

"What is it, Alba?"

"Toni . . ."

"Toni?" She furrowed her brow.

I scooched to the edge of the stool so that I was closer. "El Rincón del Pan, his bakery—it might have to shut down for good."

"I'm sorry to hear that," she said.

"It's just that I really like it there. I like making bread, and the place and everything, and Toni . . . he's been a good friend to me. Like he was a friend to you. He's helped me so much, Mom. Now I want to help him, too. I have a plan, but it's only going to work if you talk to him. If you convince him to give it a shot. *Please*, Mom."

She sighed, her shoulders drooping like a worn-out sofa. "I haven't seen Toni in a very long time, Alba. I'm not so sure I can do anything . . ."

"*Please*. Will you at least think about it?" I pleaded.

She didn't reply. Instead, she took some euros from her wallet and left them on the counter. Then she slid off the stool. "All right. I'll think about it," she said.

I knew she didn't want to get my hopes up.

But that was all I had left.

Hopes and dreams.

Thirty

Abuela Lola had outdone herself. Or, rather, Abuela Lola and Manny had outdone themselves. The living area had been transformed into a fancy-schmancy dining room. The table was covered with an antique brocade tablecloth. On top, on either side, was a pair of silver candelabras, and in the center a simple arrangement of roses. Manny and Eduardo were flitting around lighting the candles when the doorbell rang.

"I'll get it!" I said, rushing to the door.

When I opened it, Toni and Joaquim were standing there, Toni with a bottle of wine in one hand and a brown-bagged loaf of bread in the other, and Joaquim with a bouquet of poppies.

"Oh, wow. Are those for me?" I said in a jokey voice.

"Sí," he said, shoving them in my face.

I stared at his black-and-white T-shirt and at his gold suspenders and at his high-waisted jeans—at everything but his eyes.

"Um, uh, thanks," I said, taking the bouquet and wishing I could shrink and disappear behind them.

"May we come in?" asked Toni with a stiff upper lip that clearly meant he was trying not to laugh.

"Yeah. Of course."

For a moment we lingered in the entryway, saying and doing nothing. But then I saw Toni freeze. I turned around. Mom was behind me with tears on her cheeks. Her hands gripped her sundress at the hips. She had that same trampled-on-rose expression in her eyes.

"Toni . . . I'm . . . so sorry," she croaked.

Toni walked toward her, opening his arms even though he was still holding the bread and wine. "Mi hermanita. I've missed you."

My little sister.

They embraced.

I blinked and looked away. It felt like I was intruding.

I mouthed, "C'mon," to Joaquim and led him into the living room.

As soon as Manny saw us, he hopped off the sofa. "Ohh! Poppies! Très originale," he said, nudging Joaquim with his elbow.

I'd completely forgotten about the bouquet in my grasp. All of a sudden, they felt heavy in my arms, like two tons heavy. But I had no clue what I was supposed to do with them. Fortunately for me, Manny took them off my hands and headed to the kitchen.

Phew.

Joaquim plopped onto the sofa next to Eduardo, and I plopped onto the sofa next to Joaquim. Eduardo tilted his head and rubbed his stubble while inspecting Joaquim's outfit. Meanwhile, Joaquim was busy admiring Eduardo's green-and-pink bow tie with black polka dots, which somehow reminded me of a slice of watermelon.

"¿Tirantes, eh?" Eduardo said, pointing at Joaquim's suspenders.

"Sí, son chulos, ¿no?" replied Joaquim. Then he pointed at Eduardo's bow tie and said, "Me gusta tu pajarita."

I felt, well, kind of left out. That's when I noticed Joaquim's fingers on his lap. He'd painted his nails with nail polish that reminded me of swirling galaxies. "I like your nail polish," I said to him.

He grinned. And then he looked like he was about to return the compliment, but thankfully, Abuela Lola, Manny, Mom, and Toni came marching from the kitchen carrying platters of food.

Double phew.

Everyone was too busy arranging the platters and salivating over the various dishes to even pay me any attention. For once, I was happy to be ignored.

"¡A comer!" Abuela Lola announced.

"À table!" Manny shouted.

There was a commotion of chairs, and then at last everyone was seated. A lull spread across the table. Abuela Lola, who was at the head, gazed at each and every person, and then she cleared her throat. "My family is finally complete. Welcome home, my dearest Isabel. I am grateful to have you and Alba back in my life. Let us forgive, forget, and move forward with only love in our hearts."

Mom reached over and squeezed Abuela Lola's hand. "Thank you, Mamá."

And then Toni and Eduardo got two bottles of red wine and filled everyone's glasses, including mine and Joaquim's.

"¡Salud!"

We clinked glasses, leaning to the side, over, and across to make sure nobody was left out. I waited for a second to see if anyone would tell me not to drink the wine, well, because I was a kid, but nobody did, not even Abuela Lola or Mom.

Huh.

They really *did* do things differently in Spain.

I took a tiny sip. It was sort of awful at first. Then I gave it another chance, and it grew on me. The slightly sweet, slightly sour, kinda fruity and spicy wine wasn't bad at all.

I peeked at Joaquim. He was grinning at me through the glass, making the lower part of his face look all distorted. I giggled.

Abuela Lola clapped her hands. "¡Buen provecho!"

Platters were passed around. All the stuff we'd gotten at the market had been transformed into what Abuela Lola called "simple Spanish fare." There was a large tortilla de patata con espárragos (a potato and asparagus omelet), a mountain of frito mixto (mixed fried seafood) with lemon wedges and a garlic mayonnaise sauce, a humongous wooden salad bowl filled with organic greens and sweet cherry tomatoes, and of course a chopping board with slices of Toni's sourdough bread and all sorts of cheese and cold cuts.

It was the best meal I'd ever had. Even the baby squid and shrimp and tiny fish, which grossed me out at first, turned out to be delicious. I never knew that you could just go to the market and buy fresh food and cook it the same day. *This* was how people were meant to eat.

In between bites of food and sips of wine, I quietly observed everyone, especially Mom and Toni. And even Joaquim, because he was sort of hard to ignore.

By the time the third bottle of wine popped open, Mom's and Toni's faces were flushed and they were babbling in full-speed Spanish and Catalan. From the snippets I managed to understand, they were recounting childhood stories, most of which were pretty hilarious, judging by the amount of laughing and chortling and giggling and snorting. Every time that would happen, Joaquim would whisper something like "That is ridiculous" or "You are lucky you do not understand" or "Tu mamá, she is funny."

Mom. Funny. Those were two words I never, ever thought I would hear in the same sentence. But it seemed to be true. She had a captive audience around the table. When she spoke—in English, in Tagalog, in Spanish, in Catalan, in

Spanglish—every single person would burst into laughter, the kind of laughter that brought tears to their eyes.

I was amazed.

I could see glimpses of her now—the old Isabel that Abuela Lola and Toni would talk about. She was there, seated right in front of me, not some mythical creature I imagined in my head.

It made me happy, but it also made me sad, knowing that in all those years, I'd missed out on knowing the *real* Isabel—my mom. It was as if I was meeting her for the first time. And I liked her. I *really, really* liked her. With every smile, with every laugh, with every funny story, my insides would thaw out a bit more.

Until I was warm and cozy.

This place.

These people.

Is this what home was supposed to feel like?

After the strawberry salad with freshly whipped cream had been gobbled up and the espresso and tea had been served, Mom looked as if she'd run a marathon. Her dress was crumpled, her makeup was faded, her hair was disheveled. At some point she'd kicked off her sandals.

"Alba, why don't you help me with the dishes," she said, touching my shoulder.

"Okay." I followed her into the kitchen.

We set ourselves up in front of the porcelain sink, which

had two sides, one for washing and one for rinsing. Mom filled her side with warm sudsy water, and then she began to scrub the dishes one by one, handing them to me for rinsing. Even though her eyelids were a bit heavy from the wine, she didn't miss one bit of dirt, like she'd spent her lifetime washing dishes instead of popping a couple of plates and coffee cups into a dishwasher.

When we were done with all the plates, she halted and gazed at me with her heavy-lidded eyes. She reached out and swept aside a long strand of hair from my face. "You're growing your hair out . . . It looks nice," she said with a smile.

They were only a few seemingly harmless words. But in an instant, all the warmth and coziness I was feeling was zapped away and replaced with the ice-cold resentment that used to consume me. My body stiffened, and the back of my neck felt tingly, like it always did whenever Mom or Dad criticized the way I looked. In the past, I would have ignored her and walked off without saying anything. But that was the Alba of before. The Alba that was standing then and there was bolder, more confident. Maybe it was because of all the people that had accepted me, the real me, since arriving in Spain. Abuela Lola, Toni, Marie, Joaquim, Manny, and Eduardo—none of them judged me. And I didn't want Mom judging me anymore, either.

"Actually, I'm *not* growing it out . . . I've just been kind of busy, you know," I said, making sure to enunciate my words clearly.

Mom's eyelashes fluttered, and then she stared at the dirty glasses and cutlery in the sink. "Oh . . . of course."

Part of me wanted to say something harsh, like *Leave me alone* or *Go away* or *I'm not taking this crap anymore.* But I could tell she was embarrassed enough as it was. I'd promised to be patient with her, so that's what I was going to do.

I placed my hand on her forearm and then slid it down into her hand and squeezed.

"It's fine, Mom," I said.

She squeezed back. "It's not fine. I'm sorry, Alba. It's just going to take a while for me to think for myself again . . . I promise to do better from now on."

I could tell she meant it.

"Thanks," I said with a soft voice, afraid that if I spoke any louder, I might break down and cry. Surprisingly, though, instead of crying, I felt my insides begin to radiate warmth again. And as the warmth spread, I had this sudden burst of affection for her. "Mom?"

"Yes?" she answered.

"I'm glad you're here."

She stopped staring at the sink and looked up at me. "I am, too."

I inched closer to her. "Mom?" I said again.

I wasn't sure who moved first, but my arms and her arms wrapped around each other.

Twice in one day.

She'd held me.

And I'd held her.

I guess I did know how to hug after all.

"You know, these dishes aren't going to do themselves," she blurted into my ear.

I grinned. "I guess not."

We went back to scrubbing and rinsing. When she handed me the last glass, she held on to it, not letting go until I met her gaze. "I've been thinking about your idea . . ."

I sucked my breath in. "And?"

"You can count on me, Alba."

"I can?"

"Yes."

Thirty-One

Mom and Abuela Lola were asleep. The apartment
was quiet again. There was an aroma that lingered in the
air—a swirl of seafood and bread and strawberries and coffee
and wine. If I took a deep whiff, I could even smell a hint
of perfume and maybe aftershave or pomade or whatever
it was that Toni, Eduardo, and Manny used on themselves.

I went to my room and plopped on the bed, my laptop, a
notebook, and *Tartine Bread* beside me. I flipped the cookbook open. Research, research, research. From what I could
see, everything in the book was pretty much what El Rincón
del Pan was all about—traditional sourdough. I studied the
photos of different kinds of bread—classic loaves, some with
a variety of seeds, nuts, and herbs—and pastries like sweet
buns and croissants. If I hadn't been pressed for time, I could
have spent all night just perusing that one book. But I had a
mission. If I was going to help Toni save his bakery, I had to
come up with an irresistible plan as soon as possible.

So I put the book aside and opened my laptop. Bread-baking blogs and forums, Pinterest boards, and Instagram accounts—those were the right places to go for inspiration. All sorts of sourdough breads popped up that I hadn't seen at El Rincón del Pan: braided loaves colored with the juices of heirloom carrots and beets and turmeric root, flatbreads like pita and naan and tortillas, and even sourdough cakes.

I jotted down ideas and created my own Pinterest board.

Then I stumbled onto something *really* interesting—gluten-free and vegan sourdough bread. Toni already sold some coincidentally vegan bread, because the traditional loaves were made with only flour, salt, and water. But some kinds had butter, milk, eggs, and sugar. And for sure he didn't offer anything gluten-free. I mean, in a way, some things seemed like fads, but on the forums I was reading, there really were people with illnesses like celiac disease, which made it impossible to consume regular bread with gluten.

Hmm.

Why shouldn't a bread bakery have something for everyone?

Clearly, this was a missed business opportunity.

I jotted down more notes and added more pins to my Pinterest board. And then I sat up and gazed at the moonlight streaming in through the window. I could already picture it—a renovated bakery, old-fashioned but with modern touches, full of glass and Spanish tiles and refurbished wood and colorful murals of sunflowers next to a long bar with metal stools so customers could drink coffee or tea or hot chocolate. It would be filled with all kinds of people—families with hungry kids, talkative old ladies, health buffs in their yoga outfits, curious tourists, couples holding hands—everyone buying baguettes or croissants or whatever suited their fancy. On some days, I would help Toni in the back, making bread, and on others I would be out front with Estel and whoever else was working.

I inhaled and exhaled. Taking in the moonlight, the twinkling stars, the breeze blowing through the open window. There was this rush of emotion inside of me—hope, joy, excitement—all mixed up, radiating from my stomach to my heart to my cheeks to my forehead all the way to the tips of my fingers and toes.

It was hard to describe. But the only word that came to mind was *miraculous*. As if the universe had aligned itself and the forces were all working to my advantage.

Deep down, I *knew* this plan would work.

I just had to convince Toni of it.

But how?

Blip.

I frowned and peered at my laptop. A chat bubble materialized on screen.

Hola, Alba.

The profile photo with its shaggy hair and too-close-up eyeball was a dead giveaway. Marie, Joaquim, and me had

exchanged emails so we could keep one another updated on
our scheming.

Hey. What's up? I typed back.

I could tell by the dots that Joaquim was typing.

Blip.

The sky. The moon. The stars.

I giggled.

What are you doing outside so late?

Dot. Dot. Dot.

Blip.

I am inside my room. Uh. So the ceiling is what's up. But the
sky, the moon, the stars sounds more, you know, romántico.

I coughed, and almost choked on my saliva.

Ha. Ha. Ha. 😆 😆 😆

Maybe if I just ignored the word *romántico*, it would go
away as if he'd never typed it at all.

Blip.

  When can I see you again?

I jabbed at the keyboard.

Not sure.

Dot. Dot. Dot.

Blip.

Not sure you want to see me? 🙁

I rolled my eyes.

Of course I want to see you. What I mean is, I'm busy tomorrow with my mom. We're going to check out some bakeries.
You know, the competition.

240

Dot. Dot. Dot.

Blip.

Ah, sí. I understand. It is like watching other bands to see how they look, how they sound, what they are playing. It is what is called friendly competition, no?

Yes! Exactly, I typed back.

Blip.

Okay. So I see you soon, then?

I wanted to roll my eyes again, but his determination was, I dunno . . . Charming? Flattering? Sweet?

I grinned.

Yes. Soon. I promise.

Dot. Dot. Dot.

Blip.

😊 😊 😊 😊 😊 😊 Buenas noches, Alba.

Good night, Joaquim.

Blip.

😴 😴 😴

Blip.

The chat bubble disappeared.

I yawned, flopped on my pillow, and tried to stop thinking about everything.

Thirty-Two

I was exhausted. And Mom had a headache from all
the red wine the night before. But we had a plan. An important one. We would start our excursion by casually dropping
by El Rincón del Pan, with the emphasis on *casually*, and then
we would go on a bakery-hopping tour to check out Toni's
competition. It was going to be a crucial part of my research.

Ding. Ding. Ding.

The bell above the door announced our arrival. I made a
mental note to recommend getting rid of it. Once the bakery
was brimming with customers, it would be super annoying.

Ding! Ding! Ding! Ding! Ding! Ding!

I mean, who wanted to listen to *that* all day?

Anyway.

We lingered near the entrance. Mom was surveying everything. She breathed in the yeasty smell. And then she leaned
over and whispered, "Well, this is quite wonderful . . . But
where are all the customers?"

"Exactly," I whispered back.

That's when Estel spotted us from behind the register. "Hola, Alba. Toni está en la trastienda," she said like she always did whenever she saw me coming in through the front door.

I shook my head. "Oh. It's okay. We're just looking today," I said.

I turned around to introduce Mom to Estel, but she was already at the other side of the store, inspecting the shelves, the bare white walls, the dusty bouquets of dried flowers.

The one thing I knew for certain about my mom was that she had a knack for interior design, order, and cleanliness. Back in New York, she had stacks of design magazines. And even before we had a housekeeper coming in to do a deep clean twice a week, Mom was always meticulous about keeping the apartment spotless. As I got older, I realized it was because it was something she could control no matter how bad it got with my dad. It wasn't unusual for me to find her in the guest bathroom or in the kitchen, scrubbing the floor with red-rimmed eyes and a fresh welt on her neck.

My throat swelled up. I couldn't breathe, and my heart pushed up into my chest. I gulped, and tried to swallow the saliva, the memories, the pain.

"Isabel! Alba!" Toni appeared. He had this crumpled, just got-out-of-bed look about him. "I didn't know you were stopping by."

I glanced at Mom, hoping she would keep her cool. I

didn't want Toni to figure out what we were up to, because I was sure he was going to be all gloom and doom. But if we surprised him with the finished proposal, he would see what a great idea it was. He would give it a chance.

Fingers crossed.

I tried to chuckle, but it came out sounding like I was choking or something. "Um, uh, it's not like I ever tell you when I'm stopping by . . ."

Ha. Ha. Ha.

I fake-chuckled again.

"You have a point," said Toni.

Thankfully, Mom *did* keep her cool. She smiled and kissed Toni on both cheeks. "We're doing some errands for Mamá. But Alba wanted to show me the bakery. She loves it here, Toni."

For a second, he looked as if he'd swallowed a pine cone. Then he coughed and placed his hand on my back. "The feeling is mutual. We love having Alba here with us."

Gulp.

If the plan didn't work, there wouldn't be a *here with us* for much longer.

Toni went on. "But if you can't stay, then at least take something with you . . ." He hurried behind the counter and stuffed two swirly-looking pastries into a brown bag before handing them to Mom. "Palmeras. You used to love these when we were kids."

For a moment she seemed stunned. Her eyes blinked

rapidly and her expression was blank. It was obvious that the palmeras had stirred up something inside her. I couldn't tell if she was happy or sad or just reminiscing.

I reached for her hand and brushed it with the tips of my fingers. "Mom?"

That's when she snapped out of it. "I—I can't believe you still remember that, Toni," she finally said to him.

"How could I forget?" he asked, then turned to me. "One day after school, your mom found some money on the street, decided to buy a big bag of palmeras, and stuffed her face with them."

Mom laughed. "Oh god. Yes. I felt so sick afterward. I don't think I ate another palmera for months."

Ding. Ding. Ding.

The door opened and two old ladies walked in.

"Buenos días, Toni," they said in unison.

I tugged on Mom's shirt.

"Hasta luego, Toni. We better get going. Thank you for the palmeras," she said with a wave.

"Later, Toni," I said.

He waved and tried to say something, but the old ladies had already surrounded him, chatting him up, smiling, and pinching his arm as if he was a naughty little boy.

Toni sure had his loyal customers.

But to make the new-and-improved bakery work, he would need more.

Much, much more.

Our first stop was Pastelería Ferrer, which was a short walk away, in a nearby neighborhood called El Born. It was situated in an alley so tiny that we didn't even see it when we passed by. As soon as we *did* find it, though, I could see its charms immediately.

The facade was a delicate pink with a celery-green door. In the window display, there was this fantastical nature scene with breads as hills and chocolate roosters and cows and pigs, and cotton-candy clouds and flowers made of cookies and candies.

"This place is adorable," Mom exclaimed.

I opened the door. There was no *ding, ding, ding*ing.

Ha!

I thought so.

Inside, it was also pink and green. On one side was an old wooden farmhouse table with cakes under glass domes, and on the other a shelf with all sorts of breads and pastries and a refrigerated case with whimsical desserts, some shaped like potted cactuses and mini yogurt jars and eggs with chicks hatching out of them. There was even an area with packaged cookies and chocolates and jars of fruit jams and curds and custards. It was early, but the shop was already filled with people buying stuff. I could hear them chatting in different languages—Japanese, German, Spanish, and English. The children wouldn't stop squealing; it was almost as if they were inside a toy store or something.

"Wow," I said under my breath.

"You said it." Mom eyed the cash register. "They're really raking it in."

We joined the action, elbowing our way through the crowd so we could sample a couple of the desserts and pastries, which were out-of-this-world delicious, especially this flaky croissant filled with sweet cheese and fresh raspberry puree.

For the most part, though, everyone was ignoring the loaves of bread. It almost seemed like there was just too much eye candy, an explosion of sugar and chocolate and fruit and pastel colors sprouting everywhere. It had that Disneyland-type vibe—loads of color and fun, but not much soul.

"Let's get out of here," I said loudly so Mom could hear me.

Once we got outside, I breathed deep, and even though the air had this vague aroma of sour wine and smelly garbage, I felt immensely better. It was like walking out of the perfume section of the department store, too many different scents mingling, making my stomach all queasy.

"Why don't we go to the next place, and after that we can sit down for lunch and take some notes for your proposal, okay?" said Mom.

"Okay."

So off we went, meandering through the narrow alleyways. It was weird. There were people all around us walking in different directions. We were never alone. But at times, it felt like it. Mom's body radiated this warmth—a warmth completely different from the summer heat. It was a warmth that pulled me in. A warmth that made me hyperaware of her presence.

We were together, like any other mother and daughter, doing mother-daughter kinds of things. It was strange yet surprisingly familiar. As if all along I'd reserved a place for her beside me, and it was just now that she'd decided to finally show up.

The next spot was called Pain, which according to Mom meant "bread" in French. It seemed kind of pretentious to be naming a bakery just Bread, and in French to boot. Not to mention that *pain* was also an English word that had a completely different meaning. One that *wasn't* so complimentary. But then again, as soon as we entered, I decided that maybe the name suited it just fine. It was all black and white, metal, glass and mirrors, with a floor that was way too shiny. I was afraid if I brushed up against something I would get cut and bleed all over the immaculately displayed loaves, which were quadruple the price of Toni's.

Yeah, maybe Pain was a perfect name, actually.

The all-black-clad salespeople were giving us suspicious glances as we perused the store, as if maybe we were going to attempt to tuck a couple of baguettes into our sleeves and sneak out.

"¿Cómo puedo ayudarle, señora?" said a salesguy with a superthin black mustache.

Mom wasn't intimidated one bit. I mean, she used to shop at all these expensive boutiques and jewelry stores where they knew her by name.

She pulled her shoulders back and held her chin up high. "Solo estamos mirando," she said, sweeping her hand as if she was shooing him away.

"Muy bien," he replied with a tight lip.

I could tell he wasn't fond of being dismissed, so I stepped forward and got all into his personal space. "Actually, I was wondering if you had any gluten-free bread?" I asked in a somewhat obnoxious voice.

All the salespeople bugged out their eyes, especially Mr. Tight Lips, who even put his hand over his heart and opened his mouth into a perfect circle. "¿Sin gluten?" he exclaimed as if I had just cursed out his mother or something.

"Yes. Sin gluten," I repeated with a straight face.

"¡No! ¡No, no, no, no!"

I glanced at Mom. Her face was kind of red, neck veins sticking out like she was holding her breath and trying not to laugh.

I cleared my throat. "Well, then I guess we're done here.

Because if I eat *any* of this overpriced bread, I'm going to puke all over and maybe even *die* from a severe allergic reaction."

Mr. Tight Lips stepped back, like maybe he would catch a disease from me. *Whatever.* The whole gluten-allergy spiel was a total lie, of course, but jeez, how rude. We stomped out of the store without looking back. I kind of wanted to, because I was almost one-hundred-percent sure that they were going to whip out a broom and mop so they could rid themselves of whatever smudges we left behind. But I decided to follow Mom's lead and walk away with my dignity fully intact.

It wasn't until we were a good twenty feet outside that she finally lost it, exploding in a fit of snorts and giggles. My mother, snorting. Until recently, I had no idea that she was capable of such ridiculousness.

"Oh. My. God," she gasped. "That guy needs to take a chill pill!"

"Like a gazillion chill pills," I said.

We gazed into each other's eyes and then I started laughing, too. Not because I thought the situation was all that funny, but because Mom's snorting and giggling was contagious. I wasn't quite sure how long we were at it. But after a while, my stomach hurt and I was sweaty and thirsty, and by the looks of it, so was Mom. So we ducked into the nearest café, which was really a tapas bar with a huge wine list and a small menu of these little dishes, kind of like appetizers.

The waiter seated us outside at a table under a canopy overlooking the street. Thankfully, it was cooler under the shade. A breeze swirled by, making all the passersby's skirts and dresses and ties flutter. And even though there was some kind of Spanish music playing, I could still hear the trees swishing their leaves.

Mom ordered a bottle of sparkling water called Vichy Catalan for herself, and a lemonade for me, and a bunch of tapas. When the waiter disappeared, we just sat there catching our breaths. I was also stealing glances at her. In my mind, I could still picture the version of her I'd known my entire life. The one who was always dressed so impeccably—in fact, *impeccable* was pretty much the adjective I would use to describe everything about her: her hair, her makeup, her posture, her manners.

The Mom who was in front of me, though, was almost unrecognizable. From her flyaway hair, to her makeup-free face, to the simple blue cotton dress that was wrinkled and moist from sweat. Her bruises were almost gone; only traces of yellowish-green remained.

"This is fun," she said, breaking the silence.

I dropped my gaze to the table. For some reason I felt all awkward again. "Thanks for doing this with me, Mom," I mumbled.

"It's the least I can do, Alba. I need to make it up to you . . . to Toni. I've hurt too many people over the years."

I looked up. "But it's not your fault."

"It *is*. I let it happen. All of it." Her eyes were slick, but I could tell she was trying to hold the tears in. "My only excuse was that I was young and gullible."

I opened my mouth to ask about my father, to ask about how it all ended up spiraling out of control, to ask why she just let it happen. But something stopped me. It was too much too soon. After years of no questions, it seemed like a lot to ask of her to give me all the answers all at once. So instead, I said, "Toni told me that he saw you once at a bakery in New York but that you ran off without talking to him. Why did you run?"

She sighed for what seemed like ages. Her eyes blinked. It almost looked as if she was reliving that day in her head. Then she placed both hands on the table and leaned closer to me. "I was ashamed, Alba. I was ashamed of what I'd become, and I didn't want Toni to see me . . . Not like that. That's also why I stayed away from Barcelona for so long."

"But—but he's like your brother. He would have understood."

Mom shook her head. "I'm sure he would have tried . . . But the truth is, if you don't love yourself, it doesn't matter how much someone tries to love you. They can try and try and try, but at the end of the day, it'll be for nothing. I didn't want to put Toni through that. He means too much to me."

Suddenly, the waiter appeared. He came between us, placing our drinks in front of us. Then he dashed off again. I could hear the bubbles fizzing from Mom's glass.

"I want you to promise me something, Alba."

I flinched.

How did the topic go from her and Toni to me?

Mom took a long sip of her water and then she reached across the table and held my hand. "I want you to promise me that you won't *ever* lose yourself. If someone tries to change you in the name of love, you run the opposite direction. Because that person doesn't deserve you. Okay?"

I nodded. "Okay."

"You promise?"

"I promise."

"Good."

Thirty-Three

I was uneasy that evening. Even after Abuela Lola
and Mom had gone to bed, and the apartment was still,
there was something inside me that wouldn't settle, as if I
had a squeaky hamster wheel spinning in my stomach.

So I put on some crumpled jeans and my Ziggy Stardust
T-shirt, and I tiptoed out, holding my sneakers, until I was
in the hallway. I figured a long walk might help. Once I
finally had my shoes on and got to the street, I lingered for a
moment. I knew exactly where I was going, but for whatever
reason I was pretending that I didn't.

Anyway.

I headed toward El Rincón del Pan. I knew Toni would
be there. And even though I wasn't ready to reveal my
big plan to him yet, I felt like I wanted to be around
him. To reassure him that somehow it was going to be
all right. Because if he felt better about it, then I would
feel better about it. I'd come to depend on Toni for moral

support, and if he fell apart, well, then perhaps I would, too.

Surprisingly, the streets were pretty empty. It kind of didn't help my mood. Because the silence and the shadows and the echoes made everything seem sad and lonely.

Tree of hope, stand firm.

I had to keep reminding myself.

Finally, I reached the corner where the bakery stood. I crossed the street and hurried to the back. But I stopped abruptly when I heard music. Toni's office window was open; a melody drifted out into the alley, whirling into the breeze. The song wasn't recognizable at first. Then I went closer and listened. Closer and closer, until I was standing at the edge of the windowsill.

All you need is love . . .

The Beatles.

I knew them because Sandeep, the bodega guy in New York, used to play their music. It was his favorite band. The song always struck me as unusual, because it was sort of cheery but also sort of wistful.

Through the cracked windowpane, I spotted Toni at his desk, which was covered with papers. I was about to wave and call his name out, when all of a sudden he shuddered and covered his face with his hands. For a second, he didn't move. He shuddered again, and that's when his head wobbled in a way that I could tell he was sobbing.

I wasn't one to stereotype. Not usually. But truth be told, I'd never seen a grown man sob like that. It was the kind of sobbing that made his entire body tremble, his breath sound ragged, his tears flow nonstop.

I thought about going in there to console him. Maybe I should have, I don't know. It didn't feel right, though. Who was I to console anyone?

He needed to be alone. Not to be bothered by some pesky kid.

I backed away from the window. Toni disappeared. And then the song ended.

This sense of dread took over. My insides throbbed and twisted and knotted around themselves until it felt like I was torn. Especially my heart, which had already been ripped to shreds and patched up too many times to remember.

I was running out of time.

The plan.

I had to fast-track it.

Mach 9.

Warp speed.

Faster than the speed of light.

Thirty-Four

First thing in the morning, I called Marie with an SOS. Luckily, she was free until noon. She suggested a breakfast picnic at the park so that we could finalize the proposal. When I met her downstairs, she was holding some sort of multilayered metal container with a handle.

"What's that? Some sort of nuclear weapon?" I asked.

She smirked, and swung the container higher so I could get a good look at it. "It's a tiffin food carrier. My mom packed us a breakfast picnic."

"Huh. Cool."

"Come on. The shortcut to the park is this way," she said, dashing into a nearby alleyway.

Marie must have been hungry, or she must have taken my SOS seriously, because she marched through the streets way too quickly, even for my New York City speed-walking standards. By the time we arrived at the entrance, I was sweating so much I could smell my own armpits even without trying.

"Here we are. The Parc de la Ciutadella," she announced.

It was magnificent. I mean, I rarely used that word, because who does? But it really was. The entrance was this giant brick archway with turrets and angels and figures carved in stone. And on the other side, there was a palm-tree-lined promenade that seemed never ending, with a lush green lawn in the middle and fountains and structures that looked like antique glass greenhouses.

Squack! Squack! Squack!

I looked up. In the trees and sky were hundreds of green parakeets with ringed necks, powder-blue napes, and red beaks, as well as some other birds that looked like parrots.

"Those are all escapees," said Marie, pointing at them.

"Escapees?"

"Yeah. They're tropical birds not native to Spain. Over the years, various species have escaped from shipping crates in the port and made this park their home. Even when winter comes, they still manage to survive."

"Wow!" I exclaimed.

They were like me—outsiders who'd adapted and made this place home.

"Let's go find a spot."

I followed Marie to a square of lawn beneath a leafy tree. She took a blanket out of her tote bag and spread it on the grass. We both sat down with our legs crossed, and then she unpacked the tiffin.

"Okay, so we've got boiled quail eggs, scallion pancakes, dumplings, and some orange wedges," said Marie.

I plucked a scallion pancake and took a bite. "Hmm. I love these."

"Try a dumpling. They're my mom's specialty." Marie popped one into her mouth. She swallowed and then grabbed her sketchbook. "I've got the preliminary sketches done for the bakery makeover. It just needs a bit more color and black ink, and then I think they'll be ready."

I watched her flip through the pages. Even from upside down I was impressed. She turned the sketch so I could see it better. On one page was the exterior of El Rincón del Pan. The design wasn't too different, but the lines were cleaner, more modern, while still retaining its old-fashioned charm, with stained-glass accents and an antique door. What really popped was the larger front windows and the sidewalk tables outside. On the opposite page was the interior, which was a perfect combination of Spanish tiles, old wooden counters, a metal shelf with packaged goods, and a small, somewhat sleek coffee bar with six metal stools. My eyes scanned the page and landed on the bare white walls.

"How about a mural of sunflowers on this wall?" I asked. "I think the yellow would stand out against the black and white and wood and metal . . . What do you think?"

She bit her lip and studied the page.

Ever since Abuela Lola had given me the sunflower

key chain with the promise of going to Carmona to see the endless fields of sunflowers, they'd kind of become my favorite flower. It was *so* not me. I'd never given flowers much thought before. But in a way, the sunflowers were symbolic of my hopes and dreams. Something to look forward to in the future.

Marie fished around in her tote bag and brought out a set of colored pencils. "Sunflowers . . ." She took a yellow pencil and sketched away like she was attacking the paper. After a couple of minutes, she grabbed a black pen and added some lines. "Voilà!"

It was awesome. Like seriously, if I walked by and saw it, I would immediately want to go in.

"Marie. You're amazing."

She blushed. "Well, they were mostly your ideas. *But . . .* I do think they came out pretty nice, if I do say so myself."

I munched on another scallion pancake while examining the sketches further. "How come you left the sign blank?" I said, pointing at the empty spot on top of the front door.

Marie frowned. "*El Rincón del Pan* seems kind of outdated, don't you think? Like if the bakery is going to rebrand itself, why not name it something catchier?"

Hmm.

Maybe she was right.

I watched her do the finishing touches with a black pen. Around us, people were strolling, playing Frisbee, walking their dogs.

Squack! Squack!

The parakeets and parrots were in the tree branches up above, the sky was light blue with puffy white clouds. Even though I wasn't looking at Marie, I could hear her black pen scratching the paper.

Then silence.

"You know, Alba . . ."

I looked down from the sky right into Marie's bespectacled gaze.

"There's a chance this isn't going to work," she said with furrowed brows.

"It *has* to."

"But what if it doesn't? What if El Rincón del Pan closes down, anyway?"

Marie sat there staring at me with her head tilted. The breeze whipped her ponytail, but other than that she was still.

"That's *not* going to happen," I said adamantly.

She fiddled with the pen in her grasp. "It's not the end of the world, Alba. If the bakery closes, life will go on. You'll still see Toni. You can still bake bread."

I could feel the heat at the back of my neck and on the tips of my ears. The last thing I wanted was to think about the worst-case scenario. I shook my head. "You don't understand . . . It's all I have. You—you have parents who love you. You're good at school. You have a passion, a future. You have . . . everything," I mumbled.

261

"Everything?" Marie's face turned blotchy. "You think my life is perfect? Well, guess what? It's not. My parents work their butts off. I barely see them unless I'm helping out at the restaurant. My school? Yeah, sure, it's good and all, but I'm *that* scholarship kid, which means I have to study harder than everyone else just to stay in school. And I have to bend over backward to make friends. You know why? Because I'm also *that* Chinese girl. Even though I was born here, people still look at me like I'm some lowly immigrant. And if they don't think that, then they usually think I belong on a bus along with the other tourists from mainland China. *There*—is that perfect enough for you?"

I wanted to melt into a puddle and seep back into the earth. How could I have been so blind? So ignorant? No wonder I'd never had a best friend. Because I was horrible. I was a horrible, selfish person that didn't deserve Marie's friendship.

"I'm sorry," I said softly. "I had no idea you were going through all of that."

"You don't need to be sorry, Alba. You just need to open your eyes and realize that other people have struggles, too."

She reached out and squeezed my hand, and even though I felt like crap, I squeezed back.

"I will. Thank you."

Marie picked her pen back up and continued with her ink scratching. I'd obviously disappointed her, made her feel all sorts of emotions that she didn't want to feel. Yet she was still going to help me.

What have I done to deserve a true friend like her?

Nothing. Nada. That's what.

Maybe I could do something to help her? To repay her for her kindness?

I thought about everything she'd said to me, about her parents working too hard, about being the scholarship kid, about the discrimination she faced every single day.

Hmm . . .

Maybe Abuela Lola could hire another cook and manager so that Marie's parents could have more time off.

Hmm . . .

No, that would mean a salary cut.

Hmm . . .

Maybe I could convince Abuela Lola to give them a raise? If they had more money, then Marie might not need a schol arship anymore.

Hmm . . .

Think, Alba. Think.

Then I remembered something Abuela Lola had said. *"Our cook, Su, has been with us for fifteen years, and his wife, Ting, manages the place. I just sign the checks, that's all."*

It didn't really sound like Abuela Lola was that interested in her own business. If all she did was sign checks, why not just sell the place to Marie's parents? Then it would be *their* restaurant. They would have more money, more freedom. They'd be their own bosses. And Abuela Lola could focus on something else.

Hmm . . .

Wait. Hold on.

Something else . . .

That something else could be El Rincón del Pan! Clearly, Abuela Lola adored Toni *and* his bread. She'd even called the bakery *"one of Barcelona's best-kept secrets."* Why wouldn't she want to invest in something she loved? Especially if it would bring us all together. Like a family business or something. I mean, it was perfect. If she agreed, it would solve everything.

If she agreed.

Hmm . . .

Thirty-Five

Marie's words kept haunting me. She was right. There *was* a chance my plan wouldn't work. And if it didn't, somehow, life *would* go on. But I didn't want life to just go on—I wanted life to go on the way *I* wanted it to.

Humph.

I'm going have to convince Abuela Lola.

It's the only way.

So when I got home, I cooped myself up in my bedroom doing more research, bookmarking recipes, drafting my proposal, and studying Marie's sketches. I was at it for so long that I didn't even realize that the sun had gone down and that I was sitting on my bed in the dark, except for the light from my computer screen.

All of a sudden there was a knock.

"Come in," I said.

Mom opened the door several inches and peeked in. "It's

dinnertime. Abuela Lola made some butifarra—Catalan sausages and beans."

I scrunched my nose. "If it's okay, I'll just make myself a sandwich later. I'm kind of busy."

"You need to eat, Alba."

"Please?" I tried my best to imitate Joaquim's puppy-dog look.

She glanced at my laptop and at all the papers scattered around me. "All right. I'll leave some food out for you."

"Thanks."

She lingered for a second. "Let me know if you need any help later, okay?" she said with a smile.

"Okay." I nodded.

The door closed. I went back to the gluten-free baking forum I was on, writing notes, taking screenshots of discussions from different people with celiac disease, and how they wished they could find good-tasting gluten-free breads and pastries in the supermarkets and bakeries. I was pretty sure that this part of the plan was going to set the new-and-improved bakery apart from all the rest.

Good bread for *everybody*.

I could hear Mom and Abuela Lola gabbing away in the kitchen, their utensils scraping their plates, the water running as they did the dishes. The minutes passed. And then it was quiet.

But I was still up, tapping away at my keyboard.

I glanced at my alarm clock, shocked to see it was almost

midnight. That's when I heard something—music. It drifted in through my open window. I stopped what I was doing and listened. There were soft guitar strums and a deep voice singing something I couldn't quite recognize.

After a few seconds, though, I did. I knew what it was.

"As the World Falls Down," a song David Bowie wrote for the movie *Labyrinth*.

I scrambled off my bed and shoved my window curtains aside. Under the radiance of moonlight sat Joaquim on the bench out front. He was playing a Spanish guitar, seemingly in his own world. His eyes were cast down, hair draped over half his face like black velvet.

> *As the world falls down*
> *Falling*

Joaquim looked up, his gaze following the lines of the building until he almost reached my window.

I sucked my breath in, feeling all the heat rush to my face.

What does he think he's doing?

Oh god. Oh god. Oh god.

I pulled the curtains shut and backed away. It was like an out-of-body experience—I was there, I knew exactly what was happening, but I was stunned. In disbelief. All the sensation from my body seemed to float all around me.

Joaquim is serenading me outside my window.

It was a scene straight out of some cheesy romantic movie. Stuff like this didn't happen in real life.

Did it?

What if Abuela Lola woke up? What if Mom woke up? What if the whole neighborhood woke up and realized it was me he was singing to?

Oh god. Oh god. Oh god.

I put on a pair of slippers and snuck out into the hallway, out the door, down the stairs, and into the street, until I was standing right in front of an oblivious Joaquim.

"Joaquim!" I whisper-screamed.

He stopped playing when he saw me. "Alba?"

I put my hands on my hips and glared at him. "Why are you surprised to see me? In case you forgot, I live here."

"Yes, I know."

"It's midnight and you're playing your guitar and singing outside my window," I said, stating the obvious.

"I could not sleep."

"So?"

"So, I thought, maybe it might be nice to sing to you . . . David Bowie, yes? This song is muy romántico," he said with a stupid grin on his face.

There it was again.

Romántico.

I dropped my arms off my hips. I mean it *was* sort of sweet—in a totally intrusive sort of way.

I sighed deeply and then sat down beside him. "It's nice,

really. I love that song. But you can't be doing stuff like this, Joaquim."

A squiggly frown appeared on his forehead. "Why?"

"It's just too much—"

"Why is it too much?" he asked. "I thought that is what girls like?"

I slumped over, frustrated. How was I supposed to explain what I was feeling when I wasn't even sure exactly how I felt? Sure, I liked him. I mean, if I was going to be honest with myself, I more than liked him. But this was all new to me. In fact, *everything* was new to me. New people, new places, new experiences, new emotions.

I wasn't even standing on firm ground, yet there he was ready to sweep my off my feet.

I looked him in the eye—and noticed that for once he had no makeup on. "I'm flattered that you would even like me like that. But the thing is, I'm still trying to figure stuff out. With everything else that's going on . . ."

His lip quivered.

Oh god. Please don't cry.

He gazed down at his guitar for a second, and then he held his chin up high again. "But . . . we are still amigos—friends—right?"

"Of course!" I blurted out.

"Friends that sometimes . . . hold hands?" he said, raising an eyebrow.

I laughed. "Sure. Friends that sometimes hold hands."

My fingers found his, tucking themselves into the warmth of his palm. We stayed that way for a while. When we finally let go, he picked up his guitar and began to strum it again.

I didn't hide. I didn't feel the heat on my face.

I listened to him, knowing he was still singing to me.

And for whatever reason, that time around, I was okay with it.

Thirty-Six

"Alba. Wake up."

My eyes fluttered open. Abuela Lola was sideways. So was the kitchen table; and the half-eaten sausage sandwich; and the sketches, recipes, notes, timelines, and renovation plans. Even with my cheek resting on the wooden surface, I could see Abuela Lola's squinty gaze as she studied the clutter in front of her.

"You've been busy," she said.

I pushed myself off the table and yawned. "Uh. Yeah. Sorry about the mess."

"It's okay. You want some coffee?"

I nodded. "Yes, please."

She got up and poured me a big cup. Bigger than usual. But I wasn't complaining. I took a sip. *Ahhh*. It was heavenly. I'd never realized coffee could be so good until I moved to Spain. I mean, bodega coffee wasn't bad, but it was nothing to *ahhh* about.

"Thanks." I wiped the milk mustache off my upper lip.

Abuela Lola sat back down. "So you think Toni is going to go for all of this?"

"How can he not?" I replied.

"Well, running a business is complicated. You can have the best business plan in the world, but if you don't have the finances to back it up, then it's useless."

I shrugged. "There are banks. I'm sure he could get a bank loan with a plan like this. Or even an investor."

"I'm sorry, Alba. But it might be a little too late for all that. Getting a bank loan is a long and complicated process. And finding an investor is like finding a needle in a haystack. Especially for a business that's already struggling to make ends meet," explained Abuela Lola.

I stared at her and held my breath.

Go ahead. Ask her!

I sat up straighter and stuck my chest out in an effort to drum up some courage. "Well, how about—" I stopped midsentence.

What if she laughs at me?

What if she says, no?

Abuela Lola raised her eyebrows. "How about what?"

"How about you? What if *you* were the investor?" I looked down at the table, afraid of her reaction.

"Me?" She sounded surprised. "I don't have that kind of money, other than my retirement savings."

"But—but the restaurant . . . I was thinking, you could sell it to Marie's parents. I'm sure they'd buy it from you. Didn't you say that all you did was write checks, anyway?" I said, shifting my eyes so I could look directly into hers.

Abuela Lola sighed. "I did. And, yes, that's mostly true. But the restaurant was my mother and father's. Now it's mine . . . And one day, it'll be yours and your mother's."

"I don't—" My voice got caught in my throat.

What I wanted to say was *I don't want the restaurant, Abuela Lola.*

But I knew it would hurt her feelings.

So I went back to staring at the table.

It was silent.

Finally, after what seemed like ages, Abuela Lola lifted my chin with her hand. "Why is this so important to you, Alba?"

I fiddled with a piece of paper, curling it and uncurling it while I thought of the exact words I wanted to say. It wasn't that complicated of a question, but for whatever reason, the weight of it felt heavy on my chest, as if a giant loaf of bread had been jammed into my rib cage.

I coughed.

Then the words just came to me.

"For so long, I've felt like I was nothing, you know? Like it wouldn't matter if I just disappeared into thin air. Nobody would care. Nobody would miss me. Especially my dad. I was always such a disappointment to him . . . because I didn't turn out to be the picture-perfect daughter he'd wanted for his picture-perfect life. But when I came here with you, I started feeling like I was *there* again, like maybe one day I could be a person that mattered, a person that made a difference." I paused and caught my breath. "Toni . . . He's been like the father I never had. I know it sounds corny, but he was there for me when I needed it most. When I was feeling completely alone, abandoned by the people who were supposed to take care of me. He picked me up and made me feel like somebody. I've never felt that in my life. And . . . and I don't want it to end, when it's only just begun. Do you know what I mean?"

Abuela Lola bent over and kissed me on the forehead. "I do, Alba. I do. And I think you're doing a wonderful thing by trying to help Toni. I promise that I'll do whatever I can to help."

It wasn't the exact response I'd wished for, but I tried my best to smile. At least she hadn't said no.

She placed her hand on Marie's sketch. "These drawings are amazing. But how come the sign is missing?"

Funny that she asked me the *same* question I had asked Marie.

"Marie thinks we should come up with a new-and-improved name for the bakery. Something catchier and more modern," I replied.

She raised an eyebrow. "Well?"

"Dunno. I haven't thought of one yet."

"Hmm." Abuela Lola clasped her hands together and

gazed into the air. "Take a minute. Close your eyes. Think. And then toss out the first thing that comes to mind."

I felt kind of weirded out sitting there and closing my eyes. Like, what was I supposed to think about? But I didn't have anything to lose. So I did.

I could see the entrance of El Rincón del Pan. I could see myself in the back with mounds of dough, stretching, folding, kneading. I could see Toni through the window in his office, his tears, the notes, the melody, the song "All You Need Is Love" playing, the words swirling around him like musical fireflies.

I opened my eyes. "All You Knead Is Love," I said in a hushed voice.

Silence.

Then I made a motion as if I was kneading some dough there on the table.

Abuela Lola's lips curled into the beginnings of a smile. "Knead, huh? . . . A bread pun! I love it!"

"Really? You think so?"

"Yes. Yes. But I think it needs something else . . . something in Spanish. Hand me that black pen," she said, gesturing at the Sharpie in front of me.

I gave it to her and watched her fill in the blank space on the sign with elegant letters.

All You Knead Is Love
Pan Para Todos

She put the pen down and beamed at her handiwork. "All You Knead Is Love . . . Bread for Everyone," she said out loud.

It was perfect. I mean, more perfect it couldn't have been. The bread pun, the inclusivity of it—exactly what I was going for.

Bread for everyone.

Yes!

"Thanks, Abuela Lola," I said.

"Good. I'm glad this old brain of mine still works," she said, bonking her head with her fist. "So how about some breakfast, then? I think you're going to need Abuela Lola's huevos a la flamenca! Guaranteed to give you a full day's energy."

I had absolutely no clue what huevos a la flamenca was, but just the name of it sounded delicious.

"Yes, please."

Abuela Lola grabbed the basket of eggs; some tomatoes, onions, and chorizo; a chopping board; and a bunch of bowls and a baking dish. Whatever she was cooking up, I hoped it had all the energy, magic, and good luck I would need.

Because today was the day I was going to present my brilliant plan to Toni.

Thirty-Seven

I had on my Ziggy Stardust T-shirt even though it hadn't been washed in, like, a week. It was my good-luck shirt. Not that I'd had much good luck wearing it in the past or anything. But something about that shirt made me feel, I don't know, invincible.

I'm going to do it.

I'm going to kick some butt.

I'm going to save the bakery.

We're all going to live happily ever after.

The end.

"You ready, Alba?"

"I'm ready," I said to Mom.

We were standing side by side at the entrance of El Rincón del Pan. Me with my somewhat stinky T-shirt, hole-on-the-knee jeans, and scuffed-up sneakers, and Mom fresh as a daisy in her crisp white pants, yellow tank top, and sandals. She had her hair pulled back in ponytail, not a wisp out of place, as if she was celebrating the fact that her bruises were finally gone.

Ding. Ding. Ding.

That dang bell rattled my nerves.

Inside, the bakery was empty, except for Estel, who was busy writing in a green ledger. She pointed at the back room with her pen and continued her scribbling. As we marched down the hallway, I couldn't help thinking about how quiet the bakery was—too quiet, even for crickets.

I held the proposal tight against my chest. Mom had helped me bind it with this folder thingy with a slip-on plastic spine that held all the pages together. On the cover, in printed-out letters, it said:

All You Knead Is Love: Pan Para Todos
A Business Plan

It looked so official and businesslike. Just what I needed to convince Toni to take it seriously.

Gulp.

Stay calm.

Stay calm.

Stay calm.

We entered la trastienda. Toni had his back to us. He, too, had a ledger-type notebook in his hands. In front of him on the counter were piles and piles of stuff: metal bowls, bins, baskets, spatulas, rolling pins, sheet pans, and pots.

Mom cleared her throat. "¡Hola, Toni!" she said in a cheerful voice.

He spun around, almost dropping the notebook. For a second, his face fell. I almost missed it because of his thick beard. But it most definitely fell. And then he smiled so wide his eyes crinkled at the corners. "Isabel! Alba! What a surprise!" He pulled out a couple of stools. "How about some tarragon tea?"

"Sure, that sounds lovely," said Mom, taking a seat.

"Um. Yeah. Okay." I plopped down on the other stool and glanced nervously at Mom.

We watched Toni turn on the electric water kettle, snip fresh tarragon leaves from a nearby jar, and drop them into a teapot. He was awfully fidgety, which made me even more nervous because Toni was usually as calm as a lump of resting bread dough.

"So, Toni, we're actually here for a reason. Alba has something she wants to show you," Mom said casually.

Toni placed some cups on the counter and glanced at me before pouring some tea into them. "Oh, really?"

I stumbled off the stool and pulled the proposal away from my chest. "I—I thought I could help you . . . do something to improve this place."

Toni furrowed his brow like he was confused. "I don't understand."

"I have a plan . . ." I went over to him and placed the proposal on the counter.

Toni stared at the cover for too long, his eyes scanning the words over and over. But he didn't say anything. He didn't react. I reached for it with shaky hands and flipped it open.

"See, I've got a marketing plan so, you know, you can drum up more business. It's got research and recipes, and some suggestions on how to renovate the space . . . Marie even made some renderings of what it could look like." I showed him the exterior and interior sketches.

Still he didn't say anything. All I could hear was his shallow breathing.

"What do you think, Toni? Isn't it wonderful?" said Mom from behind.

"It is . . . It is wonderful," he said with a croaky voice.

I searched his face for any clues but found none. "Well?"

Toni traced the sketches with his fingers, and then slowly— really, really slowly—he closed the proposal. "The thing is . . ."

His eyes found mine, and that's when I saw the clues—the frown, the clenched jaw, the pale face.

"The thing is, I've already decided to cut my losses, Alba. I'm closing up shop next week."

I heard Mom gasp. Or maybe it was me who gasped. Because all of a sudden the air was burning my throat. My hands and feet went numb. My legs were so wobbly, I started to sway. Toni dragged the stool so that it was behind me, and then he gently guided me until I was seated.

"I'm sorry, Alba," he said softly.

Mom got up and touched his back. "¿Estás seguro, Toni?"

"I have no choice, Isabel."

They stared at each other as if they were speaking some silent language with their faces. But whatever they were saying, I knew it was too late.

I'd failed.

Soon, El Rincón del Pan would be gone. Forever.

The old Alba would have bolted off the stool and run away, because she'd never loved a place well enough to stick around. But the new Alba—all I wanted was to chain myself to the pillar in the middle of the room, pour concrete over my feet until I was stuck to the floor, and superglue every inch of my skin to the walls so that there was no way anyone could make me leave.

Toni leaned into me. "Just because the bakery is closing doesn't mean we can't see each other anymore, Alba. We're family. We can continue baking together. I have so much more I want to teach you."

"Okay," I whispered.

My voice sounded like someone else's. Like that of a robot or some humanoid or zombie.

Toni handed me a cup. "Come on, cheer up. Have some tea."

I took a sip of the hot liquid. The tarragon was bitter on my tongue, on my palate, in my throat. The bitterness spread and spread and spread. Until I was one big lump of bitterness.

It wasn't just the tarragon.

I *was* bitter.

Because life was so frigging unfair.

Thirty-Eight

After we got back from El Rincón del Pan, I holed myself up in my bedroom. I needed to be alone. I peeled off my Ziggy Stardust T-shirt.

So much for good luck.

I slumped on my bed wearing my sports bra and jeans. Pathetic. If I were a vegetable, I would have definitely been that long-forgotten cucumber at the bottom of the produce drawer—limp, mushy, weepy.

I grabbed my headphones and jammed them on my head. My body collapsed, and I curled up against the wall. The world had to go away so I could grieve in peace. I searched my playlist and found the most depressing David Bowie song I could find—"Quicksand." Its melody was filled with sadness. And Bowie's voice wailed, as if he was on the verge of crying. The lyrics were razor-sharp, cutting me every time he screamed about losing power, sinking, failing to believe in himself.

It really did feel like I'd stepped into a giant pool of quicksand; no matter how many hands reached out to save me, no matter how many branches I grabbed, I was stuck. And I didn't know if I would ever get out.

Because life had beat me down one too many times.

I shifted, searching for something to wipe the tears from my face.

Then I saw her. Mom. She was standing by the door, looking like that broken porcelain doll again.

"I knocked . . ."

The music blaring in my ears muffled her words. I slipped my headphones off and stared at her through my tears.

"I'm sorry, Alba." She came closer and sat on the edge of the bed.

"I— I really thought . . . it would work," I croaked.

Her hand touched my leg and stayed there. "I know . . ."

"I'm so stupid."

"No, you're not. What you did was *amazing.*" Mom sniffled and then she dabbed her eye with the tip of her finger.

I sat up. "Then why? Why didn't Toni even think about it?"

"It's way more complicated than just one person, Alba. Toni has to think about his employees, his suppliers, his landlord. He made the decision that he thought was right."

Complicated. I hated that word. To me, it sounded like an excuse. Whenever people, more specifically grown-ups, didn't want to explain something, they would always say, "It's complicated."

Whatever.

Why couldn't they just be straight up? All my life, I'd had to deal with adults glossing over the truth.

Mom: "*Oh, I slipped and hit my face on the bathtub.*"

Dad: "*Your mother has a headache.*"

Mom: "*He didn't mean it, Alba. He still loves you.*"

Dad: "*I'd love you if you were normal.*"

Lies. All lies.

It wasn't just about Toni and me and the bakery anymore. The anger inside me was welling up, about to burst. I glared at Mom. She'd run away. She'd cried her tears. She'd started to heal. And now it was all hunky-dory again. But me, my *entire* life was ruined because of her bad choices.

It just wasn't fair.

"Why didn't you ever think of *me*, Mom? Why? Why did we have to stay with Dad for *so* long?" I spat the words out hard and fast

Mom flinched. "Nothing I say will take away the pain and suffering you've had to endure, Alba. *Nothing.* All I can say is that it's the biggest mistake I've ever made. And I will regret it for the rest of my life . . . I'm so, so sorry."

I watched her skin turn from a pale shade of golden to a deep, shocking pink. Her lip quivered. Her cheeks and forehead crumpled. For a second, I felt ashamed of myself for dragging the sadness out of her again. But the second passed. And I realized that the sadness had always been there. She just got really good at hiding it.

"What made you finally leave him?" I asked.

She made a strangled sound, and then tears leaked from her eyes in thin streams. "I realized that if I didn't get away, one day he'd go too far . . . and kill me . . ."

My bones, my muscles, my blood went cold. It had never even occurred to me that my father could have killed my mother. But of course he could. He was tall and strong and angry. And Mom was like a little bird with a broken wing. All he had to do was lose his temper, lose whatever bit of self-control he had left, and stomp on her until she was dead.

I was trembling. And even though I wasn't certain I could move, I tried anyway, inching across the bed toward her, slowly. When I was finally close enough, I got on my knees and wrapped my arms around her neck. "Mahal kita, Mom," I whispered.

I love you.

She took me and held me on her lap like I was a little girl again. Both of us crying and trembling against each other, until eventually it felt like we were one.

We'd survived. The two of us.

After a while, we couldn't cry anymore. The emotions had drained us of whatever strength we had left. Mom kissed me on the forehead. "We should get some rest," she said.

I slid off her lap. "Okay."

She gathered herself, smoothing her clothes and hair, and then taking a deep breath before getting off the bed. When she got to the door, she paused and looked back at me. There was a light from the window illuminating her neck and collarbone, so open, so smooth, so bare, as if something was missing.

"Wait!" I called, and lunged for my nightstand. I opened the drawer and pulled out a paper bag. "Here . . ." I handed it to her.

Mom opened the bag and pulled out the fiery red scarf I'd gotten her at Els Encants. "It's beautiful."

"It's not like you really need it now . . . But I thought of you when I saw it," I said.

She held it against her heart. "I love it, Alba. Thank you."

It may have sounded stupid, corny and mushy and all, but seeing her holding that silk scarf—one that she could put on just because she wanted to, not because she had something to hide, made my insides warm and gooey.

All along I'd convinced myself that I hated her.

But really I was just desperate to love and be loved.

Thirty-Nine

The next couple of days blended together like one of those fancy superfood smoothies that Mom used to buy at Whole Foods. It was impossible to tell what the individual ingredients were, just like it was impossible for me to tell what day I did what.

I was in a haze.

At some point Marie had come over with sweet-and-crispy peanut dumplings that her mom had made in an effort to cheer me up. I was usually a sucker for sugar, but as I munched on them, all I could think about was the soft crumb of sourdough bread, and how its crunchy crust would shatter as you sliced into it.

One night, Joaquim appeared to serenade me again. He'd chosen a medley of happy songs. Too happy and too loud, because a lady from the neighboring building opened her window and told him to shut up or she was going to call the police.

Most of the time I just hid in my room with my headphones

on. And when Mom or Abuela Lola nagged me to get some fresh air, I would go outside and sit on a bench and do nothing.

That was exactly what I was doing when the old guy who fed the pigeons appeared out of nowhere. He sat down on the other end of the bench and tipped his straw hat at me. I smiled, or at least I tried to. Something about his expression told me he hadn't bought it. Because he held out his brown baggie of breadcrumbs toward me. "¡Toma!" he said in a gravelly voice.

I looked right and left, hoping someone would come save me from having to talk to this old dude. But nobody was around.

"¡Toma!" he repeated, dangling the bag closer.

I peeked at his thick, dark-rimmed glasses; at his watery gray eyes; at his bulbous nose; at his smile, hidden behind sagging cheeks; at his clothes, clean but rumpled. It was then that I realized he was harmless. Just a lonely old man with nothing to do but feed the pigeons.

I stuck my hand into the bag. "Gracias," I said with a nod.

He smiled even wider, and then he patted his chest and said, "Jorge." The way he pronounced it, with a super-thick Spanish accent, made it sound as if he was clearing phlegm from his throat.

"Alba," I replied.

He kind of did this pseudo-sign-language thingy, swinging his arms and pretending to scatter crumbs at the pigeons around us, while glancing at me. I guess he'd figured out from my obviously American accent that my Spanish was atrocious.

I sprinkled some of the crumbs at the nearest pigeons. They began pecking the ground.

"¡Muy bien!" he exclaimed.

Then he scattered his own crumbs, calling the different pigeons by name and chatting with them as if they were his dearest friends. For whatever reason, watching him made me all emotional. This lonely old man and his pigeon friends.

We continued feeding the birds in silence. With every passing minute, more and more pigeons materialized. Every once in a while, Jorge would glance my way, as if he was checking on me. He seemed comforted by my presence, despite our lack of conversation.

It was nice.

There was something calming about tossing those bread-crumbs, watching the pigeons peck at the ground, and hearing them coo when they wanted more. In fact, I was feeling much better. I mean, not completely better. But at least good enough to smile and enjoy the sunlight on my face.

"Alba!"

I whipped my head around and saw Manny walking down the street. He looked like he was off to sail in a yacht or something, with his navy-and-white boatneck shirt, crisp white shorts, and espadrilles. When he got to me, he kissed me on both cheeks.

I grinned. "Hey, Manny."

"Well, hello there," he said cheerily. Then he leaned closer to Jorge and said, "Hola, Señor García. ¿Qué tal?"

"Muy bien. Muy bien." Jorge's eyes lit up at the sight of him. "Tengo un asistente hoy," he said, gesturing to me.

"Sí, Alba es una chica *muy* simpática."

I didn't have much of a clue as to what they were chitchatting about, except for *chica*—I knew that was Spanish for "girl."

The pigeons pecked at Jorge's shoes, so he continued scattering the breadcrumbs while telling them some animated story.

Manny held his hand out to me. "Vámonos, chica. Why don't I bring you for a haircut and then we can have some halo-halo afterward?"

"A haircut?" I said.

He chuckled. "Yes, dear. It looks like you're growing weeds on your head."

"Uh. Okay. But let me go tell Mom and Abuela Lola." I stood and then went over to the other side of the bench. "Adíos, Jorge."

He reached out and cupped my hand. "Adíos, Alba . . . ¿Mañana otra vez?"

I glanced at Manny.

"He's asking if you'll join him again tomorrow."

I smiled. "Sí. Mañana," I replied.

For an instant, Jorge's gray eyes sparkled. And then he went back to his beloved pigeons.

Coo. Coo. Coo.

I sprinted up the stairs, because I was suddenly too excited by the prospect of a haircut to wait for the slow-as-molasses elevator to take me. My keys jingled, then *snap*, the lock opened and the door slammed open.

Thwack!

The doorknob hit the wall.

Oops.

"Alba?" Mom came out of the kitchen with a frown and a steaming cup of coffee.

"Uh. Sorry about the door," I said, biting my lip.

Mom placed her finger to her lips and shushed me. "Abuela Lola is taking a nap."

"Oh." My feet fidgeted in place, not only because I was eager to go but also because I wasn't sure how Mom was going to react to me getting a haircut. "So, um, Manny is downstairs. He invited me to get a trim at his friend's barbershop and then go for a snack . . ."

For a moment she didn't react. Or at least she tried not to. But I saw the crease between her brows deepen just a bit. Her gaze wandered above my forehead, as if she was searching for someone behind me. I knew what she was doing, though. Mom was taking one last look at my overgrown hair. After a couple of seconds, her gaze lowered and she smiled—the kind of smile I would describe as resigned. She wasn't going to fight it. She would make the best of the situation. Go with the flow.

"Do you mind if I tag along?" she said with a cheery voice. "I wouldn't mind getting out of the house."

My chest tightened. For *so* long, my short hair had been the cause of argument between Mom and me, Dad and me, Mom and Dad. And all of a sudden, here she was, smiling and asking if she could come along. I wasn't sure I wanted her there.

What if she objected at the last minute?

What if she tried to bully the barber into leaving my hair longer than I wanted it?

What if she was really asking to tag along because she wanted to intimidate me into changing my mind?

Hmm . . .

I gazed right into Mom's eyes. They glimmered, and her smile—well, her smile *did* seem somewhat genuine.

Maybe she *was* trying to make it up to me?

I guess it could be a sort of bonding moment. A way for us to move forward and leave the past behind for good.

"Okay," I finally replied. "Sure."

Mom practically hopped up in excitement, almost spilling her coffee. "Great! Let me go get my purse."

I watched her go back into the kitchen.

Gulp.

Thump-thump. Thump-thump.

I was nervous and tense and panicked, but all I could do was cross my fingers and hope I wouldn't regret it.

Forty

I was sitting on a barber's chair, cringing at the mirror in front of me. Manny was right. My hair was an overgrown mess.

The shop was a teensy-tiny place in El Raval; there was only room for four chairs. But the way it was decorated made it seem ginormous. A painted mural of glamorous Hollywood icons covered one wall, the floor was an explosion of tiles that reminded me of a kaleidoscope pattern, and odd-looking knickknacks were scattered all around. Manny was on one side of me with his head tilted, and his barber friend Ruby, a lanky Filipino guy with a bleach-blond pixie cut, was behind me, running his hands through my locks.

"Anong iniisip mo?" asked Ruby in Tagalog.

Of course he wasn't talking to me. Manny had taken it upon himself to become my personal stylist.

Maybe it was his way of pitying me?

Or maybe he was just sick at looking at the rat's nest on my head.

Whatever.

After a few seconds, Manny clapped his hands and said, "Young Audrey Hepburn meets David Beckham . . . O, diba?"

They shrieked in unison.

I glared at them, wondering what *that* would look like. And then I peeked over to where Mom was seated, perusing some Spanish magazine called ¡*Hola!* It was kind of obvious that she was pretending to read while eavesdropping.

Manny squeezed my shoulder. "Trust me, Alba . . . Ruby is *the* best barber in Barcelona.

"Mom?" I wasn't sure why I was calling for her. I mean, I hadn't even wanted her to come in the first place. But maybe that was it. Maybe I needed to test her. To see if she'd really, truly accepted that I would never be like her.

She looked up with raised eyebrows. "Oh, well, it's your decision, Alba . . . But I'm sure whatever Manny and Ruby have planned will come out lovely."

Hmm. At least she *was* trying to be supportive.

I shrugged. "Okay," I said to Manny and Ruby.

It was game-on after that. Ruby moved like a flamenco dancer, twisting and stomping, twirling the scissors, the comb, the spray bottle, the razor, and the blow dryer. I was so caught up in the chaos of it all that I wasn't even paying attention to my reflection in the mirror. Not until Ruby grabbed a tub of some sort of pomade and massaged a bit of it into my hair.

Suddenly, everything was still.

I barely recognized myself. The person staring back at me was a person who knew exactly who she was. Strong. Confident. One side of my head was nearly shaved. On top, though, a long wave fell toward my forehead, turning wispy at the edge of my face.

"Well? What do you think?" said Manny.

I blinked. Then I searched for Mom's reflection in the bottom corner of the mirror. She was staring at me, eyes round and glossy, mouth parted, the magazine forgotten on her lap.

Ruby clutched his face, beaming. "Ay. Ang gwapo naman."

I frowned. "Gwapo?"

"Handsome," said Manny with a wink.

"Handsome? Can girls be handsome?" I asked.

Manny shoved my arm playfully. "Of course! Just like boys can be beautiful . . . I mean, hello?" he said, fluttering his eyelashes.

He had a point. Manny *was* beautiful, with his high cheekbones, amber eyes, long thick lashes, and smooth skin that glistened in the sunlight.

"You *are* beautiful, Manny," I said, and then stared at myself again and grinned. "And I suppose I *do* look rather handsome."

"Alba . . ." All of a sudden, Mom was beside me.

Manny and Ruby went off to the side, busying themselves

295

with sweeping the floor and gossiping in high-speed Tagalog. I fidgeted in the barber chair, because Mom was gaping. But then she reached out and swept my temple with her hand, touching the wispy strands of my hair with the tips of her fingers.

"You look . . ." Mom paused, as if she was thinking of the exact way to say what she wanted to say. "You look like you . . . like the best, most beautiful version of you."

I gazed into her tear-filled eyes.

She meant it. She really, truly meant it.

I held out my hand. She placed hers on mine, our palms cupped together, fingers intertwined. "Thanks, Mom."

I could have said more. I could have explained my feelings, my emotions, my everything. But it wasn't necessary. Her eyes, my eyes, her smile, my smile. Our hands. Our tears. It was *all* there in the moment.

After my makeover, we walked to a nearby café. It was called Miss Matamis, which according to Manny meant "Miss Sweet" in Tagalog. The place was what I would describe as adorable, with its candy-colored walls, heart-shaped chairs, and decorative displays.

"Hoy! Manny, kumusta?" said the lady behind the counter when she spotted us. She had a round face with apple cheeks, glossy black shoulder-length hair, and a smile that could have easily been featured in a toothpaste commercial.

"Ate Darla, my darling," replied Manny, tiptoeing past the counter so he could kiss her. Then he gestured to me and Mom and said, "Ito si Isabel at Alba, anak at apo ni Tita Mags."

Darla squealed and speed-walked around to where we were standing. She kissed Mom on both cheeks, and then she leaned over and cupped my face with her frosting-scented hands. "Sus! Ang payat mo, naman!" she exclaimed.

I shot Mom and Manny a look that asked, *What the heck did she just say to me?*

Mom furrowed her brows and waved at me in a manner that made it seem like she was saying, *Just go with the flow, Alba.*

Manny, on the other hand, giggled and swatted Darla on the arm. "Ikaw talaga, ha! Mag English ka, nalang . . . Si Alba, hindi siya marunong mag Tagalog."

She gasped and let go of my face. "You need to come visit your Tita Darla *every* week. I will fatten you up and teach you some Tagalog, okay?"

I nodded and smiled. Ordinarily, I would have been super offended by some random person calling me skinny and squeezing me like a squishy toy. But Darla had some serious fairy-godmother vibes; I couldn't resist her charms. And neither could Mom.

Even after Manny got us a table, Mom lingered by the counter, chitchatting and laughing with her as if they were long-lost BFFs. Mom was joking around in English, Tagalog, and Spanish. The way she was—cheery, friendly, and carefree—made me happy. But it was also too much, too soon—*everything* was suddenly overwhelming.

Breathe, Alba.

I looked out the storefront window toward a small plaza with trees, benches, sidewalk cafés, and a statue right smack in the middle. People were sunbathing and schmoozing, and teenagers were doing tricks on their skateboards. Back in New York, people didn't care about what other people were doing, except for the rare gems, like my subway guardian angel, Ramona. But in Barcelona, everyone seemed to be aware of everyone else. They smiled and greeted one another on the streets—even total strangers.

Like the old lady who gave me the Frida Kahlo quote.

And like Jorge—the pigeon man.

There was something comforting about him.

Something familiar. Something that calmed me.

"So what's the story with the old guy, Señor Garcia?" I asked Manny.

He touched his heart and made a sad face. "He's a widower . . . His wife died last year, and he's been all alone since then."

"Doesn't he have any children?"

"Yes, a son and a daughter, but they're grown. One lives in

Valencia, and the other in Madrid. They tried to convince him to sell his apartment and move in with them, but he refused. He says there are too many memories of his wife there . . . Eduardo and I help him clean his place once a week, and we cook extra food and bring it to him. That man, he's a good soul. In a way, he's become a sort of uncle to us."

I was kind of sorry I'd asked, because my eyes began to sting, and I could feel the back of my throat swell.

That poor, lonely old man.

I gazed out the window again, trying to make the stinging go away. I knew what it was like to be lonely, to feel like there was nobody in the world that cared one bit about you. All those times I'd run away, I had no idea where I was going or to whom I was running, because there wasn't anyone.

Not until now.

"Halo-halo time!" Darla announced as she made her way across the room with Mom by her side. On the tray she held was a humongous glass bowl with a mountain of shaved ice mixed in with a bunch of other stuff. She placed it down on the middle of the table, along with three spoons and a bunch of napkins. Then she proceeded to pour a small pitcher of creamy liquid on top. "Enjoy!" she said before sashaying back to the counter.

Mom plopped into the chair beside me. "Ohhh . . . I haven't had halo-halo in ages!" she said.

"Um. So what is this exactly?" I asked.

Manny gawked at me. "Summertime isn't complete

without halo-halo, my dear. Under this refreshing pile of shaved ice, you'll find ripe jackfruit, coconut shreds, sweet beans, and all sorts of jellies. On top are a couple pieces of flan, slices of sweet plantain, ube ice cream, ube halaya, and some sprinkles of pinipig. That liquid she poured on top is evaporated milk."

"Weird," I said.

"Not weird. Delicious!" he replied. "Come on. Dig in."

I watched Manny and Mom mix the ice with their spoons so that it absorbed the milk and stirred up all the bits. I was hesitant. But what the heck! I stuck my spoon in and tried to get a bit of everything. Then I put it into my mouth. The cold numbed my tongue and gums for a second. When the numbness passed, there was an explosion of textures and flavors.

"What do you think?" said Mom.

My mouth was still full, but I managed a crooked, closed-lip smile. "Good!" I mumbled. After I swallowed, I pointed at the purple ice cream and at the bits of purple mashed stuff. "What's that stuff?" I asked.

"That's the ube ice cream and the ube halaya . . . It's from a kind of purple yam that's used in Filipino cakes and pastries," said Manny.

Mom nodded. "Gosh, when I was little, Abuela Lola used to have jars and jars of it that her family would send her all the way from the Philippines. I remember she used to make these delicious buns filled with it."

I took my spoon, scooped some of the ube halaya onto it and tasted it. It was sweet and earthy and had an indescribable aftertaste, like vanilla or pistachio or something.

My heart started palpitating.

Delicious buns.

Bread.

All I could think about was what I could make with this ube stuff—a traditional sourdough loaf with a soft purple crumb, a knotted or braided bread with violet stripes, a pillowy milk bun with a creamy ube filling. I wanted to run to El Rincón del Pan and tell Toni.

But then I remembered.

Tomorrow was the last day.

After that, it would be vacated and boarded up, and eventually become something else.

I sighed.

Oh well . . .

All good things must come to an end.

I guess it was really time to suck it up and move on.

Forty-One

That night, Toni invited us over to bid El Rincón del Pan farewell—a last hurrah of sorts. As we approached the front of the store, I nervously gripped the jar of ube halaya I bought at Miss Matamis. It was a thank-you gift for Toni. My hands were sweaty. Hopefully, I wouldn't drop it and make a huge neon-purple catastrophe all over the floor tiles.

Thank god Abuela Lola and Mom were too busy carrying all the other food to notice that I was dragging my sneakers. Like, literally dragging them.

Squeak. Squeak. Squeak.

I halted at the entrance. The bell above the door, the most annoying bell in the world, hadn't *ding, ding, ding*ed. It was gone. And so was everything else. The only thing that remained was the built-in counter. That was it. My eyes scanned the room. On the walls, there were holes and grooves where the shelves had lived. The counter was discolored where the cash register used to be. By the storefront display were sun spots shaped like bread baskets. All those marks were traces of what used to be.

"Vámonos, Alba," said Abuela Lola.

I followed her and Mom to the back. I could hear guitar playing, and I smelled something like pizza.

"¡Hola!"

"Hello!"

"¿Qué tal?"

"Bien. Bien."

"Great."

There was an explosion of greetings. But I hung back and let them kiss one another's cheeks while I took the room in. Every line and corner. Every slat of wood and tile. Every smudge and scrape. Every dust bunny and cobweb. It was the last time I'd see it all.

"Alba. Thanks for coming." Toni embraced me. He smelled like sourdough, tomatoes, and basil. I closed my eyes and tried to remember that moment, that smell, so I could store it in a hidden compartment in my brain for another time.

We pulled apart. "I'm glad to be here," I said, trying to smile. It was true. I was glad.

Closure was something I desperately needed.

But why did it have to be so hard? So painful? So heart-breaking?

Ugh.

Toni grinned, but behind the veneer of cheer, I could tell

he was feeling emotional, too. "Tonight, let's bake something together. In this place. One last time."

I nodded, and then handed him the jar of ube halaya. "It's purple yam paste . . . I thought you might like to experiment with a sweet bread or pastry or something."

"Ahhh!" He held the jar up as if it was a trophy or something. "Thank you. I already have an idea for later," he said with a wink.

"Toni, where's the wine opener?" asked Mom.

He went off to the other side of the room. Abuela Lola was fussing with the food and plates and cutlery. Mom was swinging a bottle of Spanish wine. And Toni was ducking in and out of boxes trying to find the missing wine opener.

I turned aimlessly.

Yeah, I'm fine. Totally fine.

That's when I spotted Joaquim on a stool in the corner playing his guitar. He smiled at me with the goobiest smile I'd ever seen. And even though I wanted to cringe, I didn't. Because at that moment, I needed all the smiles I could get. Even gooby ones.

I went over to him. "I hope you're not planning on playing anything depressing."

Joaquim winked. "Do not worry, Alba. Tonight, I will only play cheerful songs."

I plopped down on the stool beside him. Joaquim

continued with his guitar strumming. For a second, I didn't recognize the song he was playing because the tempo was slower than the recorded version. But then he sang a couple of the words softly, and I knew.

It was Bowie, of course.

I grinned.

"'Modern Love,' huh?"

"Yes, I am practicing," said Joaquim.

"For a gig?"

"No. Just practicing. Because that is what musicians do. Practice."

I watched him play and sing. He was in his own little world. It was him, his guitar, and his music. His hair covered half his face, but every time he moved his head it swished aside, revealing his clenched jaw and furrowed brow. It was the same look Toni had when he was concentrating on something.

Joaquim finished the song. He looked at me and relaxed, his own little world opening up again. The gooby smile was back. "Your hair. It is beautiful, Alba," he said with sparkling eyes.

I touched a wisp near my temple.

He'd noticed my haircut.

I met his gaze. "Not handsome?"

"Not handsome. Beautiful."

At that moment, I kind of wished my hair was long so

I could hide behind it, because I was quite sure that my cheeks were a humiliating shade of radioactive red.

"¡A comer!" said Abuela Lola with her too-loud voice.

Phew.

Everyone gathered around the food and helped themselves to Toni's sourdough pizza and Abuela Lola's fideuà, which was like a seafood paella but with noodles instead of rice. We sat wherever and ate with plates on our laps. In between the chatter and laughter, there was more wine. And then finally, dessert—leche flan, a recipe that had been passed down from Abuela Lola and generations before.

I didn't even know we *had* family recipes.

The hours went by. All the food was gone. So was the wine. Mom was kind of tipsy, but she was making her best attempt at cleaning up. Joaquim had just fallen asleep with his head on the counter. I gathered all the dishes and glasses and brought them to the big washbasin.

"Thanks," said Mom.

"No prob," I replied.

Her eyes drifted from my face to my hair. She tucked a wisp behind my ear and said, "Today was fun . . . Maybe we can go back to Ruby's barbershop sometime? I was contemplating a summer cut, something chin-length and layered. What do you think?"

What do I think?

Mom had never asked me for beauty advice, ever. I gawked at her with my mouth slightly open. Her face was flushed.

Her long hair was escaping from its French braid. Her mascara was a bit smudged. But she was beautiful. She could shave her head bald, and she'd still be beautiful.

"Yeah, I'd like that," I said.

"It's a date, then." She grinned wide, then reached for the faucet and turned the water on. "Why don't you go tell Abuela Lola that it's time to leave soon."

I turned from side to side, scanning the room.

Where was Abuela Lola, anyway?

And Toni . . . he was MIA, too.

I wandered to the back, where Toni's office was. The sound of talking was muffled by the closed door. I knocked, and for a moment the talking stopped.

"Come in," said Toni.

I went inside. The office was pretty barren, except for the big desk and a couple of chairs.

"Um, s-sorry to interrupt," I stammered.

Abuela Lola got up. "It's okay. We were just reminiscing about old times," she said.

Toni chuckled. Even though he'd had as much wine as Mom, his eyes were somehow bright and awake. "So, you ready to bake something, Alba?" he asked.

"Yes," I said.

Abuela Lola glanced at Toni and then at me with this knowing kind of look. "I suppose the two of you are going to be at it all night . . . I'll have coffee and breakfast ready when you get home, Alba."

"Thanks, Abuela Lola."

"Anytime, Alba. Anytime." She kissed me on the forehead, and I was reminded of that day at the airport when she'd first held me; she smelled like caramel, just as she did now.

If only I'd known then what an amazing grandmother she'd turn out to be.

Forty-Two

This was it. Our last bake at El Rincón del Pan.

It was just Toni, me, and a conked-out Joaquim.

"Should we wake him up?" I asked.

"No. Leave him. He's like a sack of potatoes when he's asleep."

I giggled.

Toni pulled out some aprons from one of the boxes and handed me one. "So, I propose we make something special *and* fun tonight."

"Special. Fun. Okay, I'm in," I said.

He plucked the jar of ube halaya from the counter. "I was thinking we should create a knotted swirl bread with this. I've still got butter, milk, eggs, and coconut cream in the fridge. Normally, the bulk fermentation would take eight to ten hours, but it's so hot that I think we can make it in four to five. What do you think?"

"Yes!" I exclaimed. "That sounds amazing."

In fact, swirl bread was precisely the kind of pastry I'd included in my proposal. I could just imagine little kids begging their parents to buy them one or two or three pieces.

I mean, who didn't like swirl bread, right?

"Okay. Let's get started," said Toni.

He measured some milk and butter into a small pot, and then simmered the mixture on the stove until the butter was all melted. While that cooled, we weighed some sourdough starter and sugar and dumped it into a mixer along with some eggs.

Whir. Whir. Whir.

The mixer did its magic rather noisily. I glanced at Joaquim.

Yup. Still a sack of potatoes.

Then we slowly poured the milk and butter into the mixer bowl, letting it incorporate into a frothy liquid. Next in was the all-purpose flour and salt.

Whir. Whir. Whir.

The paddle went around and around until the dough was soft, pulling away from the sides. Toni transferred the billowy mass into a medium-sized bin. "Go ahead and do some stretch-and-folds while I gather the ingredients for the filling," he instructed.

Stretch-and-folds were my favorite. There was something so calming and soothing about pulling clumps of tacky dough from one side to the other. Resting. Then doing it all over again until the dough turned stretchy and supple. It was seriously the most relaxing thing ever.

Toni placed a food processor beside me, along with the ube halaya, coconut cream, and sugar. "Alba, why don't you take a break from that, and make the filling?"

"Uh, okay," I said, wiping my hands. "What do I do?"

"Just dump the yam into the food processor and pulse it with some coconut cream and a bit of sugar until it looks right. Use your baker's intuition," he said with a wink.

Well, easier said than done. I mean, I wasn't even technically a baker yet, so how was I supposed to trust my own intuition?

Whatever.

Intuition it is.

I scooped the purple paste into the processor and then added a couple of tablespoons of sugar and a quarter cup of coconut cream.

Pulse. Pulse. Pulse.

It was still kind of gloopy, so I added a touch more cream.

Pulse. Pulse.

A touch more.

Pulse.

Voilà! The gloopyness was gone, replaced by a silky-smooth purple paste.

"What do you think?" I asked Toni.

He peeked into the food processor bowl, then scooped a bit out with a teaspoon and tasted it. "¡Perfecto! See, I told you—baker's intuition!" he exclaimed. "Now do two more sets of stretch-and-folds, and then it's ready for the bulk ferment."

Stretch. Fold. Stretch. Fold. Stretch. Fold. Stretch. Fold. Stretch. Fold.

Rest.

Stretch. Fold. Stretch. Fold. Stretch. Fold. Stretch. Fold. Stretch. Fold.

"Done."

Toni clapped his hands and took his apron off. "Well, we've got four or five hours to kill . . . Why don't you take a nap in the office?" he suggested.

"¿Qué?" Joaquim lifted his head off the counter and rubbed his face.

I cracked up; my laughter must have been contagious because Toni started guffawing while clutching his belly.

"What is so funny?" said Joaquim, glaring at us with half-asleep eyes.

"Nothing. Just a sack of potatoes," I replied.

"Huh?"

"Never mind . . ."

Joaquim threw his hands up.

"Okay, then . . . Does anyone have some playing cards?" I asked.

So that's what we did for the next four hours. Because the last thing I wanted to do was to take a nap. I was going to stay awake for every hour, every minute, every second until sunrise.

And then I would say my goodbyes to El Rincón del Pan. We had freshly brewed coffee—lots of it. Joaquim, Toni, and I played endless rounds of poker, and a Spanish game called chinchón, which was sort of like gin rummy. When we got tired of playing, Toni told me more stories about Joaquim as a kid, embarrassing the crap out of him. One time when he was two, he'd tried to take a bath in the toilet and then used the bathtub as a toilet. Another time, when he was seven, he took his guitar and a hat, and stood on the street in front of their apartment building trying to sing for money, except all he got was the old ladies pinching his cheeks and the police dragging him back home like some criminal or something. And then, when he was nine, he'd fallen madly in love with his math teacher, so much so that he filled every single homework assignment with hearts where the numbers were supposed to be.

I'd never laughed so hard in my life.

"¡Basta!" said a pink-faced Joaquim.

I covered my mouth with my hand and sputtered. "Sorry . . . It's just, hearts . . . I'm trying to picture all those math equations ending with cute little red hearts."

He rolled his eyes.

Toni chuckled. "Okay, mi hijo. You're off the hook. We've got a swirl bread to finish."

By then, the dough was puffed up to twice its size. Toni dumped it onto a floured counter and flattened it gently into a rectangular shape with a rolling pin.

"Go ahead and spread the filling evenly. Just make sure you leave about a half-inch border. Okay?" he said, handing me the bowl with the filling.

"Okay."

I spooned it on and then, with a spatula, smoothed it from side to side. It wasn't until then that I realized Joaquim had his guitar out again.

Dun. Dun. Dun. Dun-dun-dun-dum.

Dun. Dun. Dun. Dun-dun-dun-dum.

I glared at him. He laughed so hard I could almost see the back of his throat. "Under Pressure" wasn't exactly the song I wanted to hear when I was using every last ounce of concentration not to mess up.

I swirled the spatula several more times. Then I straightened my back to get a good look.

"Good, Alba. It's just right," said Toni. "Now you have to roll it tightly. No need to rush. Just do it slowly. And when you're done, pinch the seams and ends."

Roll. Slowly. Tightly. Pinch the seams and ends.

The first roll was the hardest. But once I tucked in the edge, it wasn't so hard.

Dun. Dun. Dun. Dun-dun-dun-dum.

Dun. Dun. Dun. Dun-dun-dun-dum.

I was so in the zone that even Joaquim's sarcastic guitar playing didn't bother me. I rolled and rolled and rolled and rolled. At the final roll, I made sure the dough log was seam-side down before crimping the two ends.

314

Perfect.

I didn't even need Toni's approval. I knew it was just right.

"Lovely." Toni grabbed a small knife. "I'm going to do the rest. Just pay attention so you can do it on your own next time."

In one fluid movement, he sliced the log lengthwise, leaving an inch at the top uncut. Then he twisted the two halves, braiding them together, before twirling the whole thing into a circle.

"There it is! Our purple-yam swirl bread," said Toni.

"*Ube swirl bread* sounds better," I said.

"Okay. Ube swirl bread it is."

I studied the twists and knots and the lines of purple, bleeding like veins. "Actually, it kind of looks like a human heart, don't you think?" I said.

Toni squinted. "Sí. There is most definitely a resemblance."

It was sort of ironic when you thought of it. Because my heart was broken into tiny pieces, and there we were, creating an entirely new one.

If only it were that easy.

Forty-Three

I held the finished ube swirl bread against my chest. It was in a brown bag, or else I would have gotten crumbs and purple smudges on my T-shirt. But then again, why did it even matter? I was already a sweaty, dirty mess.

We were in the empty store, Toni, Joaquim, and I, watching the outside through the window go from dark to not-so-dark to light. The sun was just rising, so it was that pale, bluish haze that hadn't turned golden yet. It was beautiful. But it was also sad and kind of lonely.

Nobody spoke.

Not even Joaquim, who was the king of awkward blabbering.

I'd already said my goodbyes to la trastienda, touching its cool metal counters and stone walls with the tips of my fingers.

Gulp.

I still couldn't believe it.

For some reason, though, it was the front of the store that had me all emotional. Under the warm heart-shaped swirl bread, my heart, my *actual* heart, ached, its beating was slower, as if it was trying to delay the inevitable. That room was where I'd first heard the *ding, ding, ding*ing of the bell above the door, where I first smelled the most heavenly scent imaginable, where Toni and I first officially met.

As I swept my hand across the smooth wooden counter and the hard glass case, I could feel the tears pushing, shoving, clawing their way out.

No, Alba.

You're not going to cry.

I'd cried the first time I'd set foot in El Rincón del Pan.

I wasn't about to cry on my last.

Goodbye.

I looked around one more time. Joaquim was leaning against a wall, staring at his boots, and Toni was near the entrance, gazing at the empty storefront display. I shuffled toward the door. With each step, the back of my throat hurt more and more. My hand touched the metal handle, and then I paused and looked at Toni.

"I'll see you around." I'd meant it to sound casual, but for whatever reason it ended up sounding so final, like I was bidding a dying relative farewell.

I opened the door.

Ding. Ding. Ding.

I wanted so badly to think that I'd hear those stupid bells again.

"Alba." Toni's hand was on my back. I turned around and we just stared at each other. "Here. For you." He handed me a glass jar with a handwritten label. I squinted and read the words JABBA THE HUTT JUNIOR. "It's your own starter. So you can experiment at home . . ."

"Oh." I studied the white blob inside the jar. It was my very own piece of El Rincón del Pan. A remembrance. "Thanks, Toni."

I sniffled in an effort to delay the onslaught of tears.

"It's going to be okay," he said with a smile. "You'll see."

But I couldn't see.

And I wasn't sure I ever would.

So instead, I fake-smiled, clutched the swirl bread and the jar, and walked out.

Don't look back.

Don't look back.

Don't look back.

Of course I did. I looked back for a split second, and that's when the tears finally gushed out.

And I ran.

I ran as fast as I could, telling myself I would never, ever go back to that street, that building, that place.

When I got home, Abuela Lola had the freshly brewed coffee ready, as promised. She still had on her white pajama dress and her slippers, as if she'd only just woken up.

"Good morning," she said.

I didn't reply, because I feared the tears would start up again.

Before entering the apartment, I'd done my best to wipe away all the evidence. But I was sure my eyes were still red-rimmed and puffy. I handed Abuela Lola the paper bag with the ube swirl bread in it, placed Jabba the Hutt Junior on the counter, and then sat down and glared at the kitchen table. From the corner of my eye, I could see her getting two cups from the shelf, pouring coffee, and, finally, placing the swirl bread on a plate in front of me.

"This is lovely, Alba. It reminds me of my childhood in the Philippines. Twice a week, my lola used to make something called pan de ube, a soft bun with a sweet ube filling."

I looked up at her. "Yeah, Mom mentioned it."

"We can make it together sometime."

I nodded. "Sure. That would be nice."

Abuela Lola smiled. "So should we have some of this? I bet it goes great with coffee."

I glanced at the purple swirls on the bread, the way it was braided and knotted into the distinctive heart shape. It smelled heavenly—sweet, coconutty, and yeasty. My mouth watered.

"Okay," I replied.

She tore off a large hunk with her hand—it was that soft—and put it on a small plate for me. The inside was fluffy, with gooey stripes of filling.

It had come out just as I'd imagined it would.

I took a bite. It was delicious. Of course it was.

I swallowed. "It's good," I said.

"Everything Toni makes is good. Better than good." Abuela Lola helped herself to a piece, *mmm-mmm-mmm*ing as she ate it.

For a while, all we did was drink our coffee and eat. It wasn't awkward or anything. Abuela Lola and I had gotten to the point in our relationship where we could just sit around each other and not have to say anything. Being together was all that mattered. The rhythm of our breathing, the heat of our bodies, the scent of our shampoos swirling together.

I supposed it was like that in other families. But for me, silence had always been uncomfortable, full of pain. It was something I avoided by simply not being there, shutting myself in my room, or running away.

When Abuela Lola finished her coffee and bread, she brought her dirty dishes to the sink. Then she touched my arm and said, "I have something for you," before disappearing into the hallway.

My reaction was to frown, because her words were so cryptic. What did she mean, exactly? Some new clothes? Books? A one-way ticket for two back to New York City?

Thump-thump. Thump-thump.

My heart was beating against my chest.

Why was I so nervous?

Abuela Lola came back with her purse and sat down. I watched her open the side pocket and pull out an envelope. She handed it to me with a glimmer in her eyes. "It's an early birthday gift."

Birthday?

My god.

With everything that had happened, I'd completely forgotten that my thirteenth birthday was next week. "Uh, um, thanks," I muttered.

I opened the envelope and peeked in. There were some rectangular pieces of paper that *did* look like tickets.

Plane tickets?

My eyeballs must have bulged out of their sockets, because Abuela Lola took the envelope from my hand and pulled out the slips of paper. "They're train tickets. I promised I would take you to see the sunflower fields, remember?"

Phew.

Right.

"Oh yeah," I said, relieved.

"It's only an overnight trip. I have a lot going on at the restaurant. But I thought it would be nice to do something, just the two of us, before your actual birthday," she explained. "It's June, nearly the end of the season. In a few weeks, all the sunflowers will be gone."

I relaxed. My heartbeat slowed down.

I wasn't used to promises being kept, so whenever someone promised me something, I'd usually dismiss it and forget. It was the most foolproof way to avoid disappointment.

"But what about Mom?" I asked.

Abuela Lola took my empty plate and cup. "She has a lot of loose ends to tie up. And Toni asked her to help him with all the bakery stuff—inventory and storage, what to sell, what not to sell."

"I see." I stood and yawned. "Thanks for the coffee, Abuela Lola. And the tickets. And everything."

Abuela Lola's face lit up, like a full moon against a dark sky. "Anytime, Alba. I love you. Now, go get some rest."

"I—I love you, too," I said.

I love you.

Those three little words felt weird coming out of my mouth. Like they didn't belong there.

Yet they did.

Because I loved Abuela Lola, more than I cared to admit. It was scary. But it also felt right.

I glanced at her before leaving the kitchen. She was smiling, but I could see the beginnings of tears in her eyes—happy ones.

Forty-Four

I was so exhausted that I slept all day. By the time I dragged myself out of bed it was late at night—almost eleven.

How had I slept for sixteen hours?

It seemed impossible.

But I had.

I opened my door and peeked outside. It was quiet. Most of the lights were off. But not the kitchen light. Even from the other end of the hallway, I could tell it was still bright in there. I tiptoed quietly. For whatever reason, I was always tiptoeing when I could have probably been walking like normal. It had become second nature to me. All those years I'd snuck around our apartment in New York, hoping my father wouldn't catch me, hoping that if I was quiet enough, maybe he would forget I even existed.

Maybe now that I was on another part of the planet he *would* forget.

And I was glad.

Because I never wanted to see him again.

When I got to the kitchen, nobody was there. On the table, there was an aluminum-foil-covered plate with a sticky note that said, *Alba*, with a big heart next to it. I lifted the foil. Underneath was a gigantic sandwich. My stomach groaned. So I sat and scarfed it down in thirty seconds flat.

Burp.

I cleaned all the crumbs off myself and the table, and washed and dried my plate.

Now what?

The kitchen appliances hummed. I sat there in a daze, staring at the basket of fragrant Spanish oranges, at the bowl of perfectly ripe tomatoes by the windowsill, at the braid of garlic hanging near the pot rack, at the fresh herbs in glasses of water. And then I saw it, the jar I'd left on the counter—Jabba the Hutt Junior.

I grinned.

I guess I should have been sad or something, because it almost felt like I was staring at a jar of a loved one's cremated ashes. But I wasn't. I was happy. Relieved. Having a piece of El Rincón del Pan made me feel better somehow. I went to the jar and hugged it against my chest. It was warm. The starter was nice and bubbly.

Suddenly, I had this urge to bake.

But could I make something on my own?

Without Toni to guide me?

I scanned Abuela Lola's kitchen and spotted the ceramic container of flour, the bottle of rosemary honey, the jar of sea salt by the stove, the stainless-steel bowls stacked up on a shelf, the loaf pan Abuela Lola used to make banana bread.

Why not give it a shot?

I brought Jabba the Hutt Junior to the kitchen table and then gathered the rest of the baking stuff. In no time, the table was crowded with bowls, measuring cups, spoons, and the ingredients I would need to make a sandwich-style loaf of bread. But not just any sandwich loaf. The rosemary honey had given me an idea—honey, fresh rosemary, walnuts, and dried figs. I didn't have a recipe, though. So I winged it. After all, Toni had told me to use my baker's intuition. Since Abuela Lola didn't have a kitchen scale, I measured out three and a half cups of flour into a large bowl and then whisked in one teaspoon of salt. Then, in another bowl, I measured about a cup and a half of water, half a cup of starter, a generous drizzle of the rosemary honey, and some olive oil, whisking it all together before pouring it into the bowl of flour. At that point I mixed it with a fork until it was a shaggy pile of dough. I covered the bowl with a kitchen towel so it could autolyse for about thirty minutes.

While that was happening, I plucked a couple of sprigs of rosemary, gathered a handful of walnuts, and took several dried figs from the pantry. I arranged them on a wooden cutting board and chopped away.

Dun. Dun. Dun. Dun-dun-dun-dum.

Dun. Dun. Dun. Dun-dun-dun-dum.

I found myself humming "Under Pressure." I'd been kind of annoyed when Joaquim had played it on his guitar last night at El Rincón del Pan, but somehow, in Abuela Lola's kitchen, the song encouraged me.

After I was done with the chopping, I wet my hands with some water and kneaded the shaggy dough, stretching and pulling it over itself a couple of times until it was pretty smooth. Then I folded in the rosemary, walnuts, and figs, stretching and folding some more, so they'd spread out evenly. Surprisingly, the dough felt good—supple, not too wet, not too dry. Perfect, actually.

Maybe I *did* know what I was doing after all.

Huh.

I covered the bowl again with the kitchen towel.

Now what?

The bulk ferment would need about five hours. Maybe less. Even at night, the kitchen was hotter than hot. I wiped the sweat off my forehead and drank a tall glass of cold water.

Hmm . . .

I guess I could go outside for some fresh air. Mom and Abuela Lola *were* always nagging me to explore the neighborhood more. And even though I was pretty sure they expected me to do it in the daytime, what did it matter? Fresh air was fresh air.

Right?

So I stuffed my feet into some sneakers, not even bothering to change out of my ratty sweatpants and T-shirt. Then I left and went down by the stairs instead of the elevator, because the elevator made such I racket I was sure the entire building would wake up and scream at me.

When I got to the entrance, I lingered by the front steps, breathing deep.

Fresh air.

Hmm . . .

Who was I kidding?

I couldn't care less about fresh air.

For a second, I wished that Joaquim was seated on the bench with his guitar, serenading me like the cheeseball he was. At least I would have something to do, someone to talk to. But the bench was empty.

So I strolled. That's what people did in Europe—stroll. Like I didn't have a care in the world. I wandered through the alleyways. It was late, but the streetlamps were casting a golden glow on everything, the bars and restaurants were full of life, and people on the sidewalks were laughing and having a good old time. Every once in a while, I would stop and gaze at street signs and at the buildings up above. The way they were lit, they kind of reminded me of old tombstones with fancy carvings.

Then something strange happened. I turned a corner, one I'd never turned before.

And there it was.

El Rincón del Pan. Except I was seeing it from a totally different angle.

I'd strolled the opposite direction, down unfamiliar streets, yet still I ended up at the one place I didn't want to end up. Like a moth mindlessly fluttering around bright light, a whale beaching itself on the same beach over and over again, a spooked deer running toward an oncoming vehicle instead of away from it.

It was hopeless.

So I just stood there and accepted my fate. I gazed at it longingly. Even though it had been less than twenty-four hours since I'd been there, half of the place was already boarded up and the sign was gone. It was as if the landlord couldn't wait to wipe out every remnant of El Rincón del Pan. Not even one tiny breadcrumb left.

That moment was when it finally sank in.

El Rincón del Pan was gone.

Really, truly gone.

I spotted a nearby bench, sat on it, and thought. About *everything*.

Before I knew it, hours and hours had passed.

The night sky was no longer pitch black; streaks of blue-gray appeared on the horizon. I stood. I took one last look at the building across the street, then went back home.

It was time to finish what I'd started.

By the time I shaped the dough into the loaf pan, let it rise on the counter until it had puffed an inch over the rim, and baked it in Abuela Lola's ancient oven, it was just past six in the morning.

Ta-da!

I pulled the loaf out of the oven. It was a tad lopsided, but other than that, it was glorious—golden brown, with a sheen from the egg wash I'd brushed on top.

I did it. I really, really did it.

On my own.

I nudged the hot loaf out of the pan and placed it on a cooling rack. And then, for a good five, maybe even ten minutes, I stared at it and stared at it and stared at it some more.

I'd never been so proud of myself.

"Mmm . . . Good morning, Alba. What smells so divine?"

Abuela Lola waltzed through the doorway, sniffing the air like a squirrel in search of nuts.

I quickly reached for the oven mitts and held up my finished bread. "Breakfast," I replied with the smiley-est smile I'd ever smiled.

Forty-Five

Six days had gone by.

Even though I tried to stay busy, baking loaf after loaf of bread, I couldn't help still feeling heartbroken. I wasn't done grieving the loss of El Rincón del Pan.

Those six days were torturous.

Six days of pretending to be fine.

Six days of small talk and fake smiles.

Six days of giving myself pep talks.

You're doing good, Alba.

Just take it easy.

After a while, you're going to forget all about it.

You'll see.

Finally, it was the day Abuela Lola and I were going to see the sunflowers. I was ready for a change of scenery, even if it was just for two days and one night.

We were on the train platform, waiting to board. It was morning, so there were a bunch of tourists and commuters with breakfast sandwiches and cups of steaming coffee. Supposedly, it would take us around five hours to get there, and that was on the high-speed Renfe train. Obviously, a plane would have been much faster, but Abuela Lola said train travel was much more civilized. Whatever that meant.

Mom was there to send us off. She kept on shoving snacks into my backpack and checking her watch and asking me a billion and one times if I needed to use the bathroom.

"Mom. I'm sure they have snacks and a bathroom on the train," I said matter-of-factly.

"That they do," said Abuela Lola.

Mom sighed. "Okay. Okay . . . I was just trying to be a mom, you know."

"I know." I rolled my eyes.

All of a sudden, the loudspeaker dude started making a bunch of garbled announcements.

"It's boarding time," said Abuela Lola.

Everyone around us moved toward the train.

"Well, have a safe trip, then!" said Mom.

They hugged, and as they pulled apart, Mom glanced at Abuela Lola all suspicious-like. In response, Abuela Lola widened her eyes a bit and puckered her lips to the side as if she was trying to say something without saying it. I frowned.

What's that all about?

"Call me when you get there," Mom added. She kissed me on both cheeks. "Have fun!"

"I will . . . Bye, Mom."

"Bye!" Mom waved and sent us flying kisses even though we were still only two feet away. I laughed at her. Or, rather, I laughed *with* her. It was cute, actually. I never knew Mom could be so corny.

"Come on, Alba." Abuela Lola gestured for me to follow, except she seemed to be going the opposite direction from everyone else.

"Um. Aren't we supposed to be going that way?" I said, pointing to the crowd.

"No. I booked us first class."

"Ooohhh. Schmancy!" I exclaimed.

Abuela Lola winked. "At my age, I get to splurge a little."

"Well, I'm happy to reap the benefits of your splurging," I said with a chuckle.

We marched past a couple more cars. The train was ultrasleek, with a slanted front that reminded me of a shark. Along the sides it had a set of thin stripes, orange and purple.

"Here we are." Abuela Lola led us through the doorway closest to the front.

Inside there were purple velvet seats in configurations of two and four, with white tables in between that had modern nightlight-type lamps. It was clean and roomy. I could totally chill there for five hours without having much to complain about. There were only a handful of people, mostly older folks. Abuela Lola picked out a pair of seats facing each other by the window.

"You should take the one facing front," she said.

"Why? What difference does it make?" I asked.

"Some people get motion sickness facing back. Besides, don't you want to see what's up ahead?"

I squinted through the window, imagining the dizzying blur of landscape coming straight at me. For some reason my heart thumped. "Not necessarily," I said, plopping on the back-facing seat.

"Up to you. Let me know if you want to switch." Abuela Lola placed her duffel bag into the overhead compartment and settled in.

I did the same. As I sank into my seat, the train moved forward slowly. The conductor greeted everyone on the loudspeaker, and then we were off. The glass-domed train station disappeared in a flash. For a while, the train zoomed past cityscapes and then suburbs and more suburbs and what looked like industrial areas with factories. It was kind of weird seeing everything from reverse, not knowing what was out there until it was almost too late for me to see it.

When the scenery began shifting to stone farmhouses with pastures, grazing cows and horses, and orchards and forests in between, a lady appeared with a breakfast cart. She was blond and perky despite her drab gray apron.

"Buenos dias, señora," she said to Abuela Lola. "¿Le gustaría alguna cosa?"

Abuela Lola smiled politely. "Sí, un café con leche y un cruasán, por favor."

The breakfast lady poured her some coffee with milk and

333

then gave her a croissant on a plate with butter and jam, all the while chatting politely. At one point she glanced at me and said, "¿Y a dónde vas con tu nieto?"

Abuela Lola's eyes widened. "Mi *nieta* y yo, vamos a los girasoles de Carmona," she replied.

I scowled, because I suspected they were talking about me and I had no idea what was being said. I *really* needed to start learning Spanish.

"Would you like a croissant and some coffee or juice?" Abuela Lola asked me.

"Yeah, sure."

The breakfast lady placed the croissant and coffee and juice in front of me before smiling and moving on. There was something about her smile that seemed, well, less perky than when she first appeared.

"What was her deal?" I asked.

Abuela Lola cut her croissant in half, spreading butter on one half and jam on the other. Then she looked up at me with a sly grin. "She thought you were my grandson."

I should have been shocked, but I wasn't. That kind of thing had been happening to me since that first time I cut my hair short. I was so used to it, sometimes I didn't even bother correcting people. It was just easier not having to explain myself to complete strangers.

"What's new?" I said, rolling my eyes.

Abuela Lola chuckled in relief. I guess she wasn't as used

to it as I was. "So, Alba. I've been meaning to discuss some-thing with you," she blurted out.

"What?" I said, with my coffee cup midair.

"School."

"Oh."

Truth be told, I'd forgotten about school. I mean, it kind of felt like I'd moved to a new country and become an adult. I had aspirations now. Who needed school?

"Your mom and I were thinking of enrolling you at the Colegio Americano with Marie. You'd be a year below her, but we think it will be a good fit, and convenient, too, since you'll already have a friend there . . . What do you think?"

I put my coffee down so I wouldn't spill it all over myself. Was that why Mom and Abuela Lola were eyeing each other at the train station? Figures. Mom knew I hated school. I guess they'd decided that Abuela Lola would be the one to break the news.

"Um, well, I haven't really thought about it," I admitted.

"I know it's been difficult, Alba. But we think this is an opportunity for you to make some changes. Your mom and I are going to be there with you every step of the way. And Marie will be there, too. You won't be alone. Not anymore."

For a second, I just stared at my plate. At the mediocre, half eaten croissant; at the cup of lukewarm coffee; at my chewed-on fingernails. I thought about what she'd said, about not being alone anymore. She was right—I hadn't felt this loved in a long, long time. Not since I was a toddler, before everything changed. And I thought about what Marie had confessed to me, about being the scholarship kid and being *that* Chinese girl, and how she had to fight tooth and nail to fit in.

Was it going to be like that for me, too?

Would I get made fun of?

Bullied?

Ignored?

"But isn't the school, like, expensive?" Those were the only words that managed to come out of my mouth. I found Abuela Lola's brown eyes, flecked with the same shade of amber as the jar of rosemary honey in her kitchen. Her gaze soothed me.

"Don't you worry about any of that," she said, patting her hand on mine.

"Okay," I said.

"Good. It's settled, then."

After that, we continued with breakfast; Abuela Lola ate hers with gusto, and I, well, I sort of just picked at my croissant and barely sipped my coffee. It wasn't that I'd lost my appetite or anything. But the thoughts whirling in my head, going as fast as the train we were on, made me kind of dizzy. I didn't want to think about the crap that had happened to me in New York. All the schools I'd gone to, all the teachers and classmates I'd hated, all the tests I'd failed, all the assignments I'd ignored. All that was in the past.

The future—*that* was what mattered. I still had a chance to make changes. Good ones. I sat up. My fingers tingled. My insides fluttered, as if all the croissant flakes in my stomach had turned into tiny butterflies.

"Abuela Lola?"

"Yes, Alba?"

"Is it okay if we switch seats?" I said.

Her eyes crinkled at the corners. "Of course. Just wait till you see what's up ahead."

Forty-Six

It was around two in the afternoon when we arrived at the train station in Sevilla. Abuela Lola's cousin Paquita was supposed to meet us. Apparently, she lived in Carmona, the town that was surrounded by the world-famous sunflower fields.

We wandered around for a while, because there were, like, a billion and one people in the station. The place was pretty huge, kind of like a modern glass airport hangar with multiple train tracks.

Finally, after going back and forth between one entrance and another, we heard someone shouting Abuela Lola's name.

"Oye! Ate Mags!"

Abuela Lola waved. At first, I couldn't tell who she was waving to because of the crowd, but after a couple of seconds, a petite lady emerged, waving and hollering like she'd just won the lottery. Something about her reminded me of a cross between a poodle and Miss Piggy. I guess it might have been her curly dyed-blond hair, her frilly blouse in a shocking shade of violet, and her fitted jeans and platform shoes.

"¡Magda! ¡Estás guapísima! Ang ganda mo naman!" she shouted in Spanish and Tagalog before grabbing Abuela Lola into a tight hug.

I could tell by the slickness in her eyes that Abuela Lola was feeling emotional. She hugged Paquita back tightly. When they pulled apart, she took my hand and brought me closer.

"Paquita, this is Alba. Alba, this is Paquita," she said.

Paquita cupped my cheeks with her bejeweled hands and said, "Dios mío, you look just like Isabel."

I couldn't help but smile. She was the kind of person who exuded rainbows and hearts and glitter from her pores. "Thanks."

"We better get going. We're on a schedule," said Abuela Lola.

Paquita frowned. "I haven't seen you in two years, and you're going to throw your schedule in my face?"

"Well, if you would just come and visit me, then we wouldn't have to worry about schedules. I'm still a working woman, you know."

I tried not to laugh at their bickering as I followed them to a parking lot jam packed with cars. And out of all the cars, we ended up stopping next to a bright orange SUV that was way too big and tall for someone like Paquita. I mean, I was pretty sure she would need a small ladder just to get in it.

"This is my new car, Naranjita," she said as she unlocked it with one of those automatic clickers.

"*Little* orange?" said Abuela Lola with a raised eyebrow.

Paquita waved the air as if to dismiss Abuela Lola's sarcasm. "¡Adelante!" she exclaimed, hopping into the driver's seat.

I was impressed.

I climbed into the truck with about as much grace as a sloth, and fastened my seat belt. Naranjita *vroom-vrooom*ed, and then we jolted forward. I looked out the window while Paquita and Abuela Lola clucked up front like a couple of hens. From what I could see, Sevilla was pretty similar to Barcelona. It was a mixture of classic and modern architecture, with palm trees and little parks tucked in between. But some of the old buildings and monuments looked different, almost Arabic, with their ornately carved arches and pillars and mosaics. It was also much hotter; the sun was so strong that it cast a glow over the horizon that made everything kind of yellowish. I guess everyone must have been used to it, because Paquita had the air conditioner on Antarctic-blast level. I pulled out my hoodie from my backpack and put it on just as the truck merged onto the highway.

"Since *someone* insists on being on a schedule, I bought some bocadillos to eat in the car so we don't have to stop for lunch," Paquita announced. She pointed at a shopping bag next to me that said FILO SANDWICHERÍA PIJA. "Help yourselves."

I grabbed a random sandwich and handed one to Abuela Lola. It was delicious, whatever it was. Every bite I took had something different in it, grilled chicken, eggplant, pepper, feta cheese, and even hummus.

"Hold on to your bocadillos!" said Paquita. She changed lanes, and then we were cruising fast. The stereo came on, blasting the song "Dancing Queen" by ABBA, which was pretty much the cheesiest song ever. But I was obviously the only one who thought so, because Paquita and Abuela Lola were singing along at the top of their lungs.

Whatever they were on must have been contagious, because after a couple of minutes of eye-rolling, I found myself bopping along to the music and screeching, "Ooh, see that girl!" as the city disappeared and the countryside appeared.

Paquita exited the highway, onto a smaller road, and then an even smaller road, and then onto a dirt road. At first, dust was flying everywhere, but as soon as Naranjita got into cruising mode again, the dust settled and the landscape outside my window was bright green with dots of yellow as far as the eye could see.

I gasped.

Abuela Lola looked over her shoulder at me. "It's all sun-flowers from here on, Alba."

I sat up straight and leaned closer to the window so that my nose was almost smooshed flat. ABBA was still playing, some song I didn't recognize about someone called

Chiquitita. The melody was kind of dreamy and sad and hopeful, all at the same time.

Sorrow.

Heartache.

Pain.

Those words were like pins poking into my pin cushion of a heart.

But then the words were about dancing once again and the sun in the sky and singing a new song. The pins disappeared, and my heart welled up with hope.

It felt as if they were singing about me.

To me.

The sunflowers went on and on and on. In the distance, though, a lone tree appeared. It was huge, with a bright green canopy of leaves and branches. When we got close to it, I poked my head between the two front seats and said, "Can we stop for a while? Please?"

"But the really nice fields are farther ahead," said Paquita.

"It's okay. I like these ones just fine," I insisted.

She pulled off to the side of the road. "All right. I could use a break, anyway."

I opened the door and slid off the leather seat. My sneakers crunched on dirt and gravel. Almost immediately, the hot sun baked my skin. It was especially intense since the white puffy clouds were so spread out.

Paquita settled on a big rock to eat her sandwich, and Abuela Lola popped open a cold fizzy drink.

"I'm going to walk over there," I said, pointing at the tree.

"Don't lose your way!" said Abuela Lola.

"I won't."

I waded through the sunflowers. They were so big that they grew past my head. The bright yellow flowers were tilted down as if they were gazing at me, their heart-shaped leaves brushing my arms. It was a strange feeling, being completely surrounded, not being able to see where I was going. But as I walked, the terrain sloped upward into a small hill, and it was then that I was high enough to see the miles and miles of yellow around me.

It really was like a dream.

A beautiful dream I didn't want to wake up from.

And then I reached the tree. Its branches swayed softly in the breeze. I went up to the trunk and placed my hand on the rough, knotty bark.

Tree of hope, stand firm.

It was a sign. I wasn't normally a believer in signs, but at that moment, I believed. That tree was there to remind me.

Stay hopeful.

Stay strong.

It was only the beginning of brighter skies and sunnier days ahead.

Everything was going to turn out fine.

I just had to give it a chance.

I turned around, leaned on it, and gazed as far as I could

gaze—so far, the sunflowers blended into one another, creating a solid carpet of golden yellow.

Somewhere out there was my future.

I couldn't see it.

But I knew it was there.

And for the first time ever, I was excited to go out and find it.

Forty-Seven

The sunflowers disappeared in the blink of an eye.

Before I knew it, we were back in Barcelona at Abuela Lola's apartment. Not only that, but it was my birthday, too. My thirteenth birthday.

I pulled my key chain out of my backpack and traced the gold sunflower before unlocking the door.

"Hurry up," said Abuela Lola, breathing down my neck.

I scowled. "What's the deal?"

"We're meeting everyone for your birthday dinner, that's what."

I glanced at the wall clock by the kitchen. "It's not even five yet."

Abuela Lola darted back and forth like a nervous grasshopper. "You have ten minutes to change."

"Ten minutes?" I whined.

"Ten minutes."

Ugh.

I hurried to my room. What the heck was going on? Abuela Lola was always yammering on about Spanish people and their traditions, but as far as I knew eating dinner before nine o'clock definitely wasn't one of them. And here she was rushing me to get ready for my own birthday dinner and the sun wasn't even down yet.

Not only that, but I kind of wanted to throw myself on my bed for a while and take a nap.

But whatever.

She wanted ten minutes, she was going to get ten minutes.

I threw my backpack on my bed, unzipped it, and fished around for my deodorant. If I didn't have time for a shower, a fresh layer of deodorant would have to do. I yanked my shirt off and rolled some Spring Rain onto my armpits. I fished around in my backpack again and pulled out a clean black T-shirt. Perfect. Black was dressy, right? Then I ran my fingers through my hair. I was as ready as I was ever going to be.

Pfft.

Who needed ten minutes? Not me.

I marched back to the front door. Abuela Lola was already there with her purse, a fresh coat of lipstick, and one of her colorfully embroidered skirt/blouse combos.

"Festive," I said, eyeing her outfit.

She eyed mine back. "*Humph.* Come on," she said, grabbing my arm.

"Okay. Okay."

As soon as we got outside, Abuela Lola started speed-walking, which was also most definitely not a Spanish tradition.

"Wait!" I said, trying to catch up.

She glared at me from the corner of her eye. "Everyone's waiting."

"So what? They're not going kill us if we're a few minutes late. It is my birthday, you know."

Still, she didn't slow down. In fact, she seemed to be going even faster. I was trying so hard to keep up that I wasn't even paying attention to where we were headed. Not until Abuela Lola stopped abruptly.

"Where are we going, anyway?" I asked.

"A Cuban restaurant. Don't worry, you're going to love it," she said, pulling her cell phone out and jabbing at the screen.

I frowned. "What are you doing?"

"Telling your mom that we're near."

I frowned even deeper. "Well, if we're near, then what do you need to text her for?"

She swatted the air before putting her phone away. "Mind your own business."

For whatever reason, we loitered on the corner for another minute. Abuela Lola's lips were moving as if she was silently reciting something. I squinted and looked around. There were passersby strolling in every direction, and the usual restaurants and shops and benches. It was just a neighborhood spot where several alleyways met. Nothing special. Yet something about it seemed familiar.

"Let's go," Abuela Lola finally said.

She led the way around a corner and then, several feet after that, she stopped again. I was about to shoot her with my what-the-heck-is-going-on-here glare, when I realized where we were.

I gasped.

It was the intersection where El Rincón del Pan was. The exact same way I'd come that one night when I unintentionally brought myself there. Except this time, Mom and Toni and Estel and Manny and Eduardo and Marie and Su and Ting and Joaquim and a bunch of random dudes were standing there with looks on their faces like they were about to explode. Behind them was a gray piece of fabric, like a construction tarp, covering the entrance.

"What—what's going on?" I stammered.

Abuela Lola didn't say anything. Instead, she smiled and lifted her hand into a thumbs-up. Toni gave her a thumbs-up back, and then he pulled a rope and the gray fabric fell away.

"Happy Birthday, Alba!" Everyone cheered and jumped up and down and clapped.

El Rincón del Pan wasn't there anymore. But something else was. It was Marie's drawing—except it was real. There was a sculpture of a heart-shaped loaf of bread over the door, and on top of it a sign that said:

All You Knead Is Love
Pan Para Todos

"I—I don't understand," I said to Abuela Lola. *"How?"*

She squeezed my shoulders. "It was *you*, Alba. You're the one who planted the idea in my head. About investing, about doing something new with my life, with the family. *Our* family. It wasn't until you mentioned it that I realized for the longest time I've wanted to do something else. I was just too scared to admit it to myself . . . So I made Ting and Su an offer they couldn't refuse. And then I made Toni an offer *he* couldn't refuse. We're partners now. All You Knead Is Love is yours, too, Alba. Yours and your mom's. Happy birthday, my sweet girl."

By then, I had tears in my eyes. I stared across the street. Everything looked blobby and wet, but it was the most beautiful sight I'd ever seen. Even more beautiful than the endless fields of sunflowers.

I was speechless.

My throat was all tight.

My lips were numb.

My ears were hot.

My toes and fingers were tingly.

My heart . . . Oh, my poor broken heart had swelled up inside my chest and miraculously patched itself back up again.

"Come on. Everyone's waiting," Abuela Lola whispered in my ear.

She took my hand in hers, and we crossed the street really, really slowly. When we were almost on the other side, I heard music.

Not just any old music.

"Modern Love" by David Bowie.

It was Joaquim and his band—Ojos de Botón. I stepped onto the curb and stood there, motionless. I hadn't even realized that Joaquim was in full costume, his signature shaggy hair even shaggier, with a velvet top hat and a matching vest, bell-bottom pants, silver platform boots, and the same button eye makeup I'd drawn on him that day at Manny's. He was singing his heart out and playing his guitar, and the dudes had their instruments—a full drum set, a bass guitar, even a saxophone.

They were good. God. They were *so* good.

More tears gushed from my eyes, down my cheeks, all over my black T-shirt. For a second, Joaquim's gaze met mine. There were tears in his eyes, too. He smiled his goobiest, totally un-rock-and-roll-iest smile, and I melted. *Totally* melted into a puddle of tears and emotions and whatever else.

Everyone was dancing. I mean, *everyone*. Not just Toni and Mom and Manny and Eduardo and Abuela Lola, but all these strangers—tourists and neighborhood regulars and kids and the old folks. It was a big ol' block party.

I was the only one not moving.

Because there was just so much to look at.

Mom in her billowy white dress, the red silk scarf I'd given her in her hair, flowing like flames in the wind. She was dancing just like teenage Isabel used to. Toni was beside her, doing all these outdated dorky moves that made me laugh despite the tears in my eyes.

Marie was twirling in a lavender skirt, with her parents, Su and Ting, shimmying nearby.

Manny and Eduardo were slow-dancing against the upbeat tempo.

And Abuela Lola, well, she was in front of Joaquim and his band, cheering and dancing like some sort of groupie.

I laughed and cried and tried my best to dance along. But my limbs were a jiggly, jellylike mess, and I probably looked more like a drunk octopus than anything else.

When the song was finally over, I managed to find the strength to walk over to Joaquim. He grinned and grabbed me into a bear hug, and then he whispered, "Feliz cumpleaños, Alba."

"Thank you, Joaquim." I pulled away from him and gawked at his makeup. "You look so good! You *sound* so good!" I exclaimed.

He chuckled. "Manny helped me. And almost every day, I practiced with my band. You like?"

I nodded. "I like."

And then I was accosted from behind. "I knew you'd be surprised!" said Mom.

I raised an eyebrow. "*Surprised* is kind of an understatement."

"Come. You have to see the inside. Toni, Marie, Manny, Eduardo, Estel, and I worked on it all week, with a little help of course." She tugged my hand toward the entrance. And at the door, she stepped aside. "Go ahead," she said.

I turned the handle, pushed the door, and held my breath.

Ding. Ding. Ding.

I grinned. The super-obnoxious bell was back. I stepped inside. The smell. It was the same heavenly smell, except it was better somehow—sweeter, spicier, with the added note of freshly brewed espresso.

The interior still had the same bones—the black-and-white Spanish tiles, the old wooden counter, the high ceilings, the large storefront windows. But it was so much fresher, more modern with the additions that Marie and I had come up with—industrial metal shelving, a refrigerated case for desserts and sandwiches, an espresso bar with a sleek counter and high metal stools. And last but not least, a massive sunflower mural.

"Wow," I said under my breath.

"So what do you think, partner?" Toni appeared from behind the counter with a brand-new apron on, black with the All You Knead Is Love logo right over his heart.

The shock had finally worn off, replaced with a burst of uncontrollable excitement. I jumped up and embraced him with my cheek resting on his chest. "Thank you. Thank you. Thank you," I kept repeating.

"No. Thank *you*, Alba. None of this would have been possible without your proposal. I'd forgotten what it was like to ask for help. To listen to new ideas, to evolve, to dream of something bigger and better. For the first time in a long time, I'm excited and hopeful."

I gazed up at his sparkly blue eyes and smiled. "Me too, Toni. Me too."

"Come, I want to show you something," he said.

I followed him to the display of breads and pastries and sandwiches. He pointed to the variety of crusty sourdough loaves. "On that side, we have our classic sourdough breads, labeled as 'Pan Tradicional,' and on this side"—he pointed to a bunch of breads I'd never seen before—"we've got our brand-new selection of 'Pan Sin Gluten.'" Then he gestured to the pastries and sandwiches. "We now also have all sorts of pastries and sandwiches. You'll notice the ones labeled as 'Sin Gluten' and 'Vegano.' And on the top shelf there, you'll see something that we're *sure* the kids will love."

I scanned the top shelf, my eyes bouncing from a chocolate croissant to a cinnamon Danish to an apple fritter to . . .

Oh my.

There was a dozen or so perfect little ube swirl breads, with a label that said CORAZÓN DE ALBA.

"Alba's Heart," said Toni.

I gazed at him, feeling the tears stinging my eyes again. "Really?"

"Really. What else would we call them?"

For a good long while, I just stared at every loaf of bread and every single pastry and every sandwich and all the details of the new-and-improved bakery.

All the people in it.

My friends.

My family.

These people. This place.

They were my future.

I could see it now—bright and clear as the endless blue sky over the endless fields of sunflowers.

Forty-Eight

Two months later.

Now I was always running from one place to another, unlike in the past, when I was always running away.

I had people to see.

I had things to do.

And despite the chaos of it all, I was happy.

For the first time in my life, I was really, truly happy.

Contented. That was the right word for it.

"Bye, Alba!" said Marie, like she did every time we emerged from the subway station after school.

"See you at five!" I replied with a wave.

We'd developed a sort of ritual. At five on the dot, I'd go over to her parents' restaurant and help her refill all the bottles of soy sauce and chili sauce, set up the chopstick canisters, fold napkins, and make sure the place was spick-and-span. Afterward, we would do our homework together at my place.

But before any of that, I had a bunch of other stuff to do. Busy. Busy. Busy.

That was me.

I zipped up my hoodie, adjusted my backpack, and placed my headphones over my ears.

"Rebel Rebel" by none other than David Bowie, of course.

And then I ran down the streets and alleyways, expertly dodging cars and people and dogs and trees and benches and water fountains and statues, until I reached *the* intersection. My most favorite place in all of Barcelona.

All You Knead Is Love.

Even as I ran across the street, I could already tell it was bustling. The outdoor tables were occupied with people sipping coffee and munching on whatever pastry they'd ordered. Señor Grey, the neighborhood greyhound, was there, enjoying the organic dog treats that I'd recently convinced Toni to start making. I mean, you couldn't advertise yourself as Pan Para Todos unless you included dogs and cats, right?

"Hola, Señor Grey," I said, giving him a pat on the head before zooming through the entrance.

Ding. Ding. Ding.

I took my headphones off and halted for a second, scanning the store like I always did.

The old ladies were there in full force, chatting with Toni and Abuela Lola. Then there were the yoga peeps buying their daily supply of gluten-free and vegan goodies, and the tourists browsing the shelves of packaged cookies while waiting for their coffee, and the moms and dads with their kids, who were ogling the sweet treats.

Toni was right—Corazón de Alba was a *total* bestseller.

I ran to the counter and ducked under it. "¡Hola!" I greeted Estel, who was behind the register punching in sale after sale after sale.

"¿Qué tal, Alba?" she replied.

I ran over to the espresso bar and kissed Mom on the cheek. "Hey, Mom."

She kissed me back, then continued pulling levers and pressing buttons and steaming milk. "Have a snack before you run off again, okay?" she said.

"Yeah. Yeah."

I ran toward the back—la trastienda—passing Toni and Abuela Lola along the way. "Hey, Toni. Hey, Abuela Lola."

"Hola, Alba," they said in unison.

Before I disappeared, Toni looked over his shoulder at me. "Don't forget your pain de mie. It's on the rack by the oven," he said.

"Okay! Thanks!"

I ran down the hallway, my sneakers *squeak, squeak, squeak*ing on the tile floor.

Phew.

I took a breather.

Everything in the back was in order. All the glass jars of yeast water and sourdough starter were in their respective places; all the bins and bowls were clean and ready for dough mixing; all the counters were spotless; all the cooling racks were positioned just right, ready for sheet pans of hot bread and pastries.

Good.

I didn't have to do anything until after dinner, when I helped prepare all the dough with Toni and Agnès, the new assistant baker. Since business had picked up, I'd convinced Toni to hire someone from the nearby culinary school to help out. The minute Agnès marched in with her tattoos and her nose ring and her Smurf-blue hair, I knew she was the one. She worked hard and took risks and was totally game for experimenting with me on recipes.

I glanced at the wall clock; it was a quarter past four.

Late again, Alba.

I zigzagged to the racks and grabbed the two brown bags waiting for me, and a cheese Danish, which I clutched with my teeth. Then I left through the back door—the VIP entrance.

I ran past the garbage cans and down the cobblestone streets, trying my best to chew and swallow the Danish without dropping the bags or choking. Every once in a while, one of the shopkeepers would shout out, "¡Hola, Alba!" or "¿Qué tal, nena?" and I would shout back, "Hola, señor so-and-so" or "Hola, señora so-and-so" or "¡Muy bien, gracias!"

I ran and ran and ran some more. And when I was almost out of breath and ready to collapse from so much running, I finally reached my destination.

"Alba!" Jorge was at his usual bench. His cloudy gray eyes lit up when he saw me.

I tried to croak out an "Hola" as I plopped down beside him, but my hyperventilating wouldn't allow it.

"Respira," he said, patting my shoulder. *Breathe.*

I was doing so much running around these days that sometimes I forgot to breathe. But Jorge always reminded me.

"Respira. Ve más despacio, Alba." *Breathe. Slow down, Alba.* And I did.

Every afternoon, Jorge and I would feed his beloved pigeons with fresh breadcrumbs that I brought from the bakery. And twice a week, I would also bring him a loaf of pain de mie, a pillowy soft sandwich bread that he could easily chew with his dentures.

When I'd finally caught my breath, I placed the bag of breadcrumbs between us and opened it. Jorge scooped out a handful, and so did I.

Coo. Coo. Coo.

The pigeons crowded around our feet. I scattered some crumbs and watched them peck at the ground. By then, I could identify some of Jorge's favorites. There was Guapa, a plump female with a brilliant throat of iridescent green-and-purple feathers; Pirata, who was missing one foot, so he would hop and peck, hop and peck; and Cary Grant, the debonair one, with smooth feathers and striped markings that made him look as if he was wearing a suit.

We kept on scattering the breadcrumbs until there were none. And then, one by one, the pigeons flew away, disappearing behind the tops of buildings around us.

"Adiós, mis palomas," Jorge called out to them.

I gazed up at the sky and at the mellowing sun and at the breeze ruffling the leaves of the trees.

My neighborhood.

My home.

I stood and kissed Jorge on both cheeks. "Hasta mañana, Jorge."

Until tomorrow. And the next day and the next day after that.

Acknowledgments

After successfully birthing and nurturing my first book baby, all sorts of doubts began to pop up in my mind.

Was it a fluke?

Could I do it again?

Would my next book baby be welcomed with open arms?

Thankfully, I have a phenomenal support system that allayed all my anxieties and fears. And I did it. Again. This second time around has been such an awesome experience, and I have so, so many people to thank.

First, to my wonderful agent, Wendy Schmalz, thank you for being such an amazing advocate of my work, thank you for always knowing when I need some encouraging words, and thank you for all the invaluable advice. I look forward to more books together!

To my editor, Trisha de Guzman, thank you for championing my quirky, multicultural stories. I sincerely appreciate your sharp editor's eye, your thoughtful feedback, and your use of smiley emojis whenever I write something humorous. I couldn't have a better editor in my corner.

I shall always be grateful to Joy Peskin for picking me out of the submissions pile and for being the one to say yes. Thank you for continuing to believe in me and my books.

The entire team at FSG BFYR/Macmillan has been an absolute delight to work with. They run a tight ship, and it shows. I'm most especially indebted to my book designer, Cassie Gonzales, for creating a swoon-worthy cover that I cannot stop looking at.

To my cover artist, Zhen Liu, thank you for bringing Alba to life in the best way imaginable. There aren't enough heart-eye emojis to express how much I love her and everything else about my cover.

To my mom, Helena—thank you for all your *bravos* and for always being the first one to shout about my books.

To my dad, Wahoo—I'm grateful for your continued support and encouragement.

To my big sister, Katya—thank you for always having great feedback and advice, and for always referring me to the right people who can help me get stuff done.

Thank you to my husband, Daemon, for bearing with all my writing deadlines and for bringing our daughter to the beach when I need some solo time to work.

To my daughter, Violet—you keep doing you. Never let anyone change that. Thank you for being one of my biggest fans, thank you for telling everyone about my books, and

362

thank you for inspiring me to write authentically. I love you, infinity fins.

To my writing squad—Janae Marks, Lorien Lawrence, and Shannon Doleski—thank you for all the encouragement, advice, and laughs. I couldn't have chosen a better group to hang with.

I'm grateful to my imprint sister, Adrianna Cuevas, for her friendship and for her Spanish grammatical skills.

To my college buddy Debra Ochoa, thank you for your Spanish/Catalan language input with the early draft of my story.

Kaela Noel, I'm so thankful to you for sharing the most beautiful Ursula K. Le Guin quote with me. I couldn't think of a better way to start this story.

I'm fortunate to have a great writer friend, Melly Sutjitro, in the same time zone so that we can talk craft, talk books, and talk trash. Thank you for always being there over the years.

To my middle school crew—Michelle, Apple, Guada, and Irene—thank you for your lasting friendship and loyalty. Never underestimate the bond of childhood friendships.

Thank you to all the wonderfully supportive and generous Waldorf moms in my day-to-day life. Thanks especially to Alma Hiatt for encouraging me to take walks and exercise during a particularly rough time with anxiety, and to Olive Desamero for kicking my butt into shape.

A huge thanks to all the book bloggers, teachers, and librarians who have recommended my books since debut year. You are invaluable members of the kidlit community! And last but not least, to my readers—thank you for continuing to love my stories. You make me feel like I have the best job ever.

Spanish/Catalan/
Tagalog Glossary

5 ♥ **Mahal kita:** I love you (Tagalog)

19 ♥ **Oye, ¿qué tal, Magda?:** Hey, how are you, Magda?

19 ♥ **Muy bien, Nuria. Tengo mi nieta, Alba, conmigo . . . ¡desde los Estados Unidos!:** Very good, Nuria. I have my granddaughter, Alba, with me . . . from the United States!

19 ♥ **Así, te daré los mejores, entonces:** So, I'll give you the best ones, then

20 ♥ **Buen provecho:** Enjoy your meal

38 ♥ **Hola . . . ¿Estás bien?:** Hi . . . Are you okay?

40 ♥ **Aquí, tomaló:** Here, take it

41 ♥ **Te sentirás major despues de comer algo. ¿Bien?:** You'll feel better after eating something. Okay?

45 ♥ **Buenos días:** Good morning

49 ♥ **Hola, nena. ¿Qué tal?:** Hello, young girl. How are you?

49 ♥ **quiero:** want

49 ♥ **pan:** bread

51 ♥ **Estel, voy un ratito a la trastienda:** Estel, I'm going to the back room for a little while

52 ♥ **De nada:** Think nothing of it (This can also be translated as "You are welcome.")

66 ♥ **¡Fantástico!:** Fantastic!

69 ♥ **¡Perfecto!:** Perfect!

76 ♥ **¡A comer!:** Let's eat!

79 ♥ **turrón:** nougat

79 ♥ **arroz con leche:** rice pudding

79 ♥ **higo y vainilla:** fig and vanilla

79 ♥ **Dos helados de fresa, por favor:** Two strawberry ice creams, please

94 ♥ **mi papá:** my father

96 ♥ **Sí, comprendo:** Yes, I understand

97 ♥ **Lo siento:** I'm sorry

100 ♥ **¡Ya voy!:** I'm coming!

100 ♥ **¡Un beso!:** A kiss!

101 ♥ **¡Vámonos!:** Let's go!

103 ♥ **Susmaryosep!:** A contraction of "Jesus, Mary, and Joseph!" used in moments of surprise, disbelief, anger, or frustration (Tagalog)

103 ♥ **¡Dáte prisa!:** Hurry up!

104 ♥ **Ate Mags! Musta na po?:** Sister Mags! How are you? (Tagalog)

104 ♥ **Uy, Manny! Ang ganda naman ng kilay mo!:** Hey, Manny! Your eyebrows are looking beautiful! (Tagalog)

104 ♥ **Tita! Matagal din tayo hindi nagkita!**: Auntie! Long time no see! (Tagalog)

104 ♥ **Huy . . . Parang tumataba ka, ata!**: Hey . . . it looks like you've gotten fatter! (Tagalog)

104 ♥ **chismisan:** gossiping (Tagalog)

105 ♥ **Hay naku!**: Oh my! (Tagalog)

105 ♥ **Diba?**: Right? (Tagalog)

105 ♥ **Grabe!**: A word sort of like the equivalent of "Holy cow!" (Tagalog)

105 ♥ **balikbayan:** Literally translates as "return country," used when referring to a Filipino returning to the Philippines after living abroad. When used with *box*, it refers to a package sent by a Filipino living abroad to their relatives back home. (Tagalog)

105 ♥ **¡Gigantisimos!**: Gigantic!

105 ♥ **Por fin:** Finally

109 ♥ **¡Por supuesto!**: Of course!

118 ♥ **Claro que sí:** Yes, of course

118 ♥ ¡Allí!: There!

119 ♥ **Discúlpame:** Excuse me

127 ♥ **¿Qué quieres tomar?:** What would you like to drink?

127 ♥ **¡Espera!:** Wait!

127 ♥ **¡Un momento, por favor!:** One moment, please!

128 ♥ **¿Límon o naranja?:** Lemon or orange?

128 ♥ **guiri:** A pejorative term for foreigners in Spain (slang)

128 ♥ **Oye, tío:** Hey, man

129 ♥ **Vale:** Okay

133 ♥ **¡Genial!:** Brilliant!

136 ♥ **Gracias:** Thanks

136 ♥ **Buenas noches:** Good evening

136 ♥ **Hasta luego, señora:** See you later, ma'am

136 ♥ **Gracias, mi hijo:** Thanks, my son

137 ♥ **Adios:** Goodbye

137 ♥ **Adéu:** Goodbye (Catalan)

143 ♥ **un pajarito:** The literal translation is "a little bird," but it's also playful slang for "a penis."

144 ♥ **sukis:** regular customers (Tagalog, slang)

145 ♥ **Hola, nena. ¿Te interesan los libros de cocinar?:** Hello, little girl. Do those cookbooks interest you?

146 ♥ **rebajas:** discounted/on sale

148 ♥ **¿Te gusta algo?:** Do you like anything?

148 ♥ **Ah. Sí, es precioso:** Ah. Yes, it's beautiful

148 ♥ **Para tí, diez euros:** For you, ten euros

151 ♥ **Os veo en el restaurant:** I'll see you at the restaurant

152 ♥ **La Casa de Tesoros:** The House of Treasures

154 ♥ **Sala de Curiosidades:** Room of Curiosities

168 ♥ **Come, Isabel . . . Es tu favorito:** Eat, Isabel . . . It's your favorite

170 ♥ **¿Puedo hablar con Alba, por favor?:** Can I speak to Alba, please?

175 ♥ **¡Hallo! ¡Bienvenidos!:** Hello! Welcome!

191 ♥ **Toni está en la trastienda:** Toni is in the back room

191 ♥ **Entra, entra:** Come in, come in

196 ♥ **Toma:** Take

196 ♥ **Arból de la esperanza, mantente firme:** Tree of hope, stand firm

215 ♥ **tiene una cabeza dura:** has a hard head

215 ♥ **una isla:** an island

216 ♥ **Ella es como mi hermana:** She is like a sister

217 ♥ **¿Qué?:** What?

219 ♥ **tu corazón:** your heart

223 ♥ **los más frescos:** the freshest

224 ♥ **Un café cortado y un café con leche, por favor:** A macchiato and a coffee with milk, please

229 ♥ **mi hermanita:** my little sister

230 ♥ **tirantes:** suspenders

230 ♥ **Sí, son chulos, ¿no?:** Yes, they're cool, aren't they?

230 ♥ **Me gusta tu pajarita:** I like your bow tie

231 ♥ **¡Salud!:** Cheers! (The literal translation is "Health!")

240 ♥ **romántico:** romantic

249 ♥ **¿Cómo puedo ayudarle, señora?:** How can we help you, ma'am?

249 ♥ **Solo estamos mirando:** We're just looking

249 ♥ **Muy bien:** Very good

249 ♥ **¿Sin gluten?:** Without gluten?

269 ♥ **amigos:** friends

280 ♥ **¿Estás seguro, Toni?:** Are you sure, Toni?

290 ♥ **Tengo un asistente hoy:** I have an assistant today

290 ♥ **Sí, Alba es una chica *muy* simpática:** Yes, Alba is a *very* nice girl

290 ♥ **¿Mañana otra vez?:** Tomorrow again?

293 ♥ **Anong iniisip mo?:** What do you think? (Tagalog)

294 ♥ **O, diba?:** Right? (Tagalog)

295 ♥ **Ay. Ang gwapo naman:** Oh. How handsome (Tagalog)

296 ♥ **Hoy! Manny, kumusta?:** Hey! Manny, how are you? (Tagalog)

297 ♥ **Ito si Isabel at Alba, anak at apo ni Tita Mags:** This is Isabel and Alba, daughter and granddaughter of Auntie Mags (Tagalog)

297 ♥ **Sus! Ang payat mo, naman!:** Jesus! (slang) You're so skinny! (Tagalog)

297 ♥ **Ikaw talaga, ha! Mag English ka, nalang . . . Si Alba, hindi siya marunong mag Tagalog:** You, ha! Speak English, instead . . . Alba doesn't know any Tagalog (Tagalog)

313 ♥ **¡Basta!:** Enough!

333 ♥ **¿Le gustaría alguna cosa?:** Would you like something?

333 ♥ **Sí, un café con leche y un cruasán, por favor:** Yes, a coffee with milk and a croissant, please

334 ♥ **¿Y a dónde vas con tu nieto?:** And where are you off to with your grandson?

334 ♥ **Mi *nieta* y yo, vamos a los girasoles de Carmona:** My *granddaughter* and I are going to the sunflowers of Carmona

339 ♥ **¡Estás guapísima!:** You're gorgeous!

339 ♥ **Ang ganda mo naman!:** You're so pretty! (Tagalog)

339 ♥ **Dios mío:** My god

340 ♥ **¡Adelante!:** Onward!

351 ♥ **Feliz cumpleaños:** Happy birthday